VALIDATION

Infiltration Series (Book 3)

SUSANNA ROGERS

Bucher & Reid

Bucher & Reid

Cover by Amygdala Book Design

978-0-6481868-5-4

DEDICATION

To my buddy, James,
because you're the best
.

ALSO BY SUSANNA ROGERS

Infiltration (Book 1)
Regeneration (Book 2)

Parallax Error – coming soon

ACKNOWLEDGMENTS

I have too many people to thank and can't possibly do this in any particular order. I'm also very nervous I may have left someone out. A big thanks to James Rogers, Louis Rogers, Chris Kunz, Michael Cain, Lotte Plumb, Josie Kelly, Sacha Pulsford, Sophia Robbins, Annie Sommer, Stephanie Swain and a special mention to Taya Lunn because I made you cry and that made me very happy.

The list goes on – thanks to Claire Boston, Lorraine Mauvais, Juanita Kees, Teena Raffa-Mulligan and Anna Jacobs. Also to my technical and medical experts Tessa Plumb, Nick Stott, Tony Rogers, Andrew Tran, Jo Taylor and Brendan Murphy.

CHAPTER ONE

"Two more days until ultimate freedom!" Lauren threw her arms around my shoulders.

I hugged her back even though we were a long way from ultimate anything, then heard her ribs crack and eased off.

The 'ultimate freedom' she couldn't wait for was a week in a cabin in the woods where we were getting away from it all – our reward for surviving school and finishing exams, kind of like spring break in Cancun, only with trees and mountains.

Lauren prattled away as we ambled down the front path of Hamilton High, then asked, "You're not upset at leaving, are you?"

It was less than a year since I first met Lauren at our old school where she insisted she'd met me before. *As if.* Still, I'd grown up so much since I got here that it made me feel I was leaving a piece of myself behind.

"Earth to Nicola." Lauren waved her arms wildly, doing an excellent impersonation of a crazy person. "Ben'll be here any minute."

Our exams finished at the same time and we'd agreed to meet Ben at the front of the school.

"Why so serious?" She whacked me on the shoulder and I pretended to be hurt, then turned to see Ben approaching.

He shook his finger at Lauren. "Watch it. Beat up my girlfriend and you'll have to answer to me."

She rolled her eyes. "Yeah, like that's ever going to happen."

"I suppose you've already packed?" he asked her.

"Of course. It's only two more days until–"

Ben held a hand out. "Yeah, I know."

Lauren's phone buzzed, so she looked down, scowling. "My mother again…" Her expression changed, her face clouding over.

"What is it?" I asked.

"My mom wants me to come home right now." Her hand shook as she passed me her phone.

I read out the message. "Honey, George Withers has been arrested because of your article and the magazine is being shut down. You need to come home immediately. Love Mom."

"Who's George Withers?" Ben asked.

"The editor," Lauren said in a small voice.

The *Altabena Times* had recently published an opinion piece Lauren had written about the new *Security Act* which had attracted lots of attention, most of it from college students who were rallying against it.

Lauren felt she had every right to state her outrage at the legislation and how it was an infringement of our civil liberties, not to mention the fact it was downright un-American. Where I came from, she would've been shot for saying things like that.

Ben searched his phone. "That's not everything. George Withers is in jail, all right. Detained indefinitely."

That was the beauty of the *Security Act*. If the authorities suspected you of anti-government activity, you could be imprisoned for life and there was nothing anyone could do about it, no trial, no legal recourse, nothing. Soon, human rights would go out the door along with freedom of speech and any other rights we thought we had.

My heart was hammering. If the editor had been thrown into jail, who knew what they could do to Lauren. *No, not her.* I couldn't let this happen. Damn it, this was New Nation all over again.

I grabbed her arm. "You won't be safe at home."

Lauren opened her mouth but no words came out.

"It's okay." I had to think straight. "We'll go to your place first, grab your bag, then head to the cabin early and lie low until things calm down. It'll work out…"

It was on the tip of my tongue to say "I promise" but I didn't make promises I couldn't keep.

I asked Ben to call Dominique to see if we could go to her parents' cabin early. She'd wanted to surprise us, which was why she'd only told us about the place a couple of days ago. Just as well not many people knew we'd be there. Maybe the police wouldn't even make the connection.

I gave Ben a quick kiss on the lips, then drove Lauren's car to her place because she was too nervous to drive. My stomach was clenched in nervous fear too, but I didn't let on. Refused to let myself fall apart.

Her mom greeted us at the door, gave Lauren a big hug and led us into the kitchen where we explained our plan.

"You're overreacting." Marion Wilson poured coffee into three mugs. "Your place is at home with me and Dad."

Lauren turned to me. "I've got all my gear down to one backpack. Just a couple more things to put in there and I'll be ready."

Ignoring her mom, she left for her bedroom.

Marion put the coffee mugs and some cookies on the table where I was sitting. "The only reason I'm letting her go is because you had this cabin trip planned anyway."

"She's not safe here." I knew where society was headed and this was only the beginning.

"This is her home, Nicola."

"You can't protect her," I said. "Don't tell anyone about the cabin or where we're going. I'll take care of Lauren."

Marion tossed her head back as she sat down. "Honestly, Nicola, sometimes you should hear yourself."

A huge smashing noise made her jump. My heart leapt in my chest. A pause, then another huge blast crashed through the air. Sounded like a battering ram.

Lauren… They'd get to her in a matter of minutes, maybe seconds.

I picked up my phone. "Get out now. Through the window. Close it behind you, then jump the fence to the Hendersons' place and hide in their yard."

A small voice from the other end. "Nicola…"

"*Now*, Lauren."

She hung up. I had to hope she was quick.

I got to my feet. "Marion, I'm pretty sure that's the police."

Confusion contorted her face. "The police wouldn't…"

"We'll go together."

I took her hand and helped her up but only made it as far as the doorway where two officers in black uniforms blocked our way.

"Where's Lauren Wilson?" demanded the bigger of the two.

"She's not here," I said.

Louder, this time. "Where is she?"

Marion's lower lip trembled. "Not here."

The smaller officer barged in and started surveying the kitchen, not that there was much to find.

"Who are you?" the big guy asked me.

"Nicola Gray," I said.

This guy was zero body fat and a hundred percent muscle. Reminded me a lot of Arnold Schwarzenegger. He kept staring at me, his eyes so hard I wished he had The Terminator's sunglasses.

"What are you doing here?" he asked.

"Waiting for Lauren."

"There's no other vehicle outside. Where's your car, young lady?"

If there was one thing I was not, it was a lady. "I walked. I like the exercise."

"Watch that smart tongue of yours." He turned to Marion. "We're searching the house. If you know your daughter's whereabouts, you'd better tell us now."

Marion shook her head, said in a small voice. "She's just a child."

"Not according to the law," Officer Schwarzenegger said. "*The Security Act* covers anyone over the age of twelve."

As if Lauren was a threat. As if national security was in danger because she voiced her opinions.

It wasn't that long ago I'd been a lot like this guy, loyal and obedient, only I hadn't been a soldier for a long time. Now I hoped desperately that Lauren had gotten away.

Marion and I were frisked though the closest thing I had to a weapon was the box of cookies on the table. I offered her sympathetic looks because that was all I had to give under the circumstances.

Officer Schwarzenegger barked out orders to the other police and asked us the occasional question. Footsteps thundered through the house and eventually I saw men carrying Lauren's laptop and some of her belongings through the house.

Worried, Marion reached for my arm. I covered her hand and gave it a rub. Maybe she hadn't worked it out. If they were taking Lauren's things, it was because they hadn't found *her*. Yet.

"Schwartz!" the officer yelled. "You're staying here. Get everyone else cleared out."

Schwarzenegger calling out to Schwartz. I would've laughed if I wasn't so terrified for Lauren.

Staring at me, he lifted one eyebrow. "What are you still doing here? Don't you have a home to go to?"

I gave Marion a hug, nuzzling into her hair. "I'll take care of Lauren."

"Don't come back until it's safe," she whispered.

Holding me at arm's length, she didn't say anything more. She didn't need to. The fear in her eyes said it all.

Weaving my way past the other officers, I walked out the front door and along the sidewalk until I'd turned the corner. Then I ran, driven by fear.

No one was following me, not as far as I could tell, but I couldn't risk leading the authorities to Lauren. Better to wait.

When I reached Ben's place, he took me up to his room. He was worried about my frenzied state, but I assured him my state was merely sweaty, told him about the police at Lauren's house and that I had to talk to her first. He kept his arm around me the whole time as I sat on the bed with the phone in my hand.

"Where are you?" I asked. "Are you okay?"

"Hiding in the Henderson's cubby house," she said.

"Perfect."

I explained how she'd have to stay there until dark when we'd come and get her.

"I'm scared." Her voice wavered. "Everyone knows I wrote that article and all the things I said about the government."

She was right. And her article had hit the spot with the college population who were rallying and organizing protests.

"One step at a time, Lauren. You're not on your own." I knew how devastating it was to be alone at a time like this. "Have you talked to Will yet?"

A sniffle at the other end of the phone. "He's worried. He wanted to come and get me right away but I told him to sit tight."

"You did the right thing. There's something else. You need to disable the GPS function on your phone so no one can trace your location."

"I did that ages ago," she said.

"Really?"

"My mom was checking up on me so I made sure she couldn't."

I squeezed my eyes shut. "You're a star, Lauren. You can do this. *We* can do this. It won't be long now."

I told her we'd see her soon, wrapped my arms around Ben in a huge hug as soon as I hung up the phone, then gave him the full story about the police at Lauren's house.

"Dominique was cool with the change in plans." Ben took my hands into his. "She said we might as well all leave tonight. Reece was there when I called."

The two of them had become inseparable except for when Dominique was training in judo which was, in fact, a lot of the time since she hoped to make the Olympic team. Such a strange couple.

"Now we definitely need to get away," Ben said. "Even if this isn't how we planned it."

Nowhere near it, in fact.

Ben held my gaze. "I want to spend time with you before I leave."

I stiffened. We were going to UCLA together. Fine. In the meantime, Ben wanted to take a two-week internship outside San Francisco – on his own – and that was not so fine.

Nothing about Ben and me was normal. I was a soldier who'd been sent back in time from the future and since I'd known Ben, he'd been in almost constant danger from forces from the future that wanted to get rid of him. I was the only one who could protect him. I had to be there wherever he went.

"It's not that I want to hold you back, Ben," I said. "But you can't go on your own."

The green eyes that could be so loving narrowed. "I

don't need a babysitter."

"What about a bodyguard?"

"You know what the problem is? You don't trust me to take care of myself."

"It's my job to look after you."

"I don't need a bodyguard," he said. "I need a girlfriend."

I love you, Ben. The words I couldn't say.

In truth, I had said the words once but that had been under extreme circumstances and Ben couldn't remember any of it. I'd made sure he couldn't. Besides, this wasn't the right time to tell him. I didn't want to blurt it out or beg.

And I wanted him to love me back. Wanted it with all my heart.

"The problem is not that I don't trust you," I said.

"Look," he said. "I'm not being complacent. Not any more."

It was true. He wasn't. He'd been through a lot too, but he still didn't get it. I'd lost him once and couldn't bear to lose him again.

"This is a world-class research center we're talking about," he said. "With Max Alonzo, one of the biggest names in medical investigations today. The man is a living legend and I'm getting the chance to work at his facility. I can't turn this down. I'm not going to get stabbed by some research nerd. That's not going to happen. There aren't going to be any more drones or assassins from the future."

"It's still the future that's the problem."

I'd tried to explain it to Ben before but it wasn't the same for him. He hadn't seen what was to come, the way we would live, the lives that would be lost.

In 2041, a virus was going to kill off most of the population. Billions of lives gone. The timing would be perfect for the Bartley government to consolidate the police state and create a new nation with a brainwashed population who offered complete loyalty. Because nothing less would be tolerated.

We might be able to fight the new *Security Act* for now. Who knows? Maybe if the college student protest was strong enough, the government might be forced to repeal the legislation. But after the virus there would be complete control.

And Ben was going to create the virus – that's what was in our history. I believed in Ben. He wasn't going to be a mass murderer. There was some mistake with the history. There had to be.

One thing was for sure. In coming years, Lauren could wave goodbye to her idea of 'ultimate freedom'. It would be ultimate annihilation followed by ultimate oppression. We were headed for ultimate death for most of the population. Ben, Lauren, my friends, Mom and Dad who I loved so much…

I had no idea who would live and who would die.

CHAPTER TWO

Even though we were in a hurry, Ben came inside the house with the express purpose of talking to my parents. He shook Dad's hand and tossed his arms around Mom for a hug, which would normally have been overkill.

"I'll take good care of Nicola," Ben said.

Dad wrapped his arms around me and held me close. He smelled faintly of the chicken cacciatore he'd cooked for dinner, his signature dish and also Mom's favorite.

It killed me how much the two of them loved each other. How much they loved me. And I loved them right back.

Mom was next as we hugged each other and I pressed a kiss to her cheek. She felt so slight, not frail exactly, but not sturdy either.

It brought back memories of the previous time I'd said goodbye when I hadn't known if I'd be coming back and had risked my life for Ben. This was different. Still, it made me anxious.

Mom held me at arms' length. "I know you're worried about Lauren, honey, but you're doing the right thing."

The parental pride was a killer too, so I added, "Except for the fact we'll be harboring a criminal."

Dad shook it off. "A minor detail."

They didn't truly believe Lauren would be punished or the rest of us thrown in jail. That wasn't the world they'd grown up in but it was where we were headed.

"You might as well enjoy yourselves up at the cabin," Mom said.

Ben nodded, rather too vigorously. "For sure, we'll be taking hikes through the woods and toasting marshmallows over an open fire."

And drinking. He didn't mention that.

"I'll call and text whenever we're in town," I said. "Probably every few days."

I'd already been through the drill with them. We wouldn't have cell phone reception on the mountain, only in town. Will was taking Lauren. Meanwhile Dominique and Reece were going together. Ben was driving the two us, supposedly because his car was bigger but I knew the real reason. He thought I was a lousy driver.

Mom leaned over for a kiss. "Love you, honey. You should get going. We'll have to say goodbye when you go to college so this'll be good practice for us."

She smiled, beaming with pride, and it tugged at my heartstrings. Maybe I was the one who was frail, who still had trouble with emotions, who didn't quite fit in.

Time to pull myself together. I'd had my allocated time for vulnerability.

I turned to look at them before I walked out the door. "Love you both."

Ben practically dragged me out of there. "Come on, I can't take any more of this domestic bliss."

"Aren't you expecting any domestic bliss at the cabin?"

His hand on my lower back, he ushered me into the

car, his face close to mine. "Plenty of it."

Despite our disagreement about his internship, Ben and I had been getting closer. Very close indeed. In more ways than one.

He started the engine and took off. "Remember, Nicola. This works two ways. You have to let me look after you as well."

Easier said than done. I'd been a one-woman fighting machine for so long I wasn't sure I could do that.

*   *   *

This was our vacation, our way, though not exactly the way we'd planned it.

Maybe it was the mountain air or maybe it was the fact we'd spent two hours driving under duress to get to the cabin after dark but the next day we all agreed we'd slept like logs.

Ben and I were making pancakes for breakfast while the others sat on benches surrounding the huge trestle table in the dining area. The place wasn't fancy and didn't need to be. It was a log cabin and that meant instant atmosphere.

Both hands on the frying pan handle, I flipped a pancake that made a perfect landing back on the pan. "I'm getting the hang of this."

Ben grinned. "Only because it involves throwing things around."

After another minute, we slid the pancakes from our pans onto a plate, called out for someone to get them, then started on the next batch. Since I'd come to Altabena, I'd learnt the basics about cooking and now I was learning about teamwork.

It had been truly a team effort. Dominique had had the

foresight to buy some basics like butter and milk on the way here, and her family kept the pantry well stocked so we could eat in style, then replenish the food later in the day. Meanwhile the boys' efforts extended to stocks of booze and sporting equipment. If it was down to them, we might not be able to eat but there'd definitely be plenty of games of drunken football. In my current mood, that didn't sound so bad.

Ben and I cooked up the last of the pancakes and joined the others at the table.

"This is like summer camp," Lauren quipped.

The others agreed while Reece and I just looked at each other. The only kind of camp we knew was military camp and that had never included anything as frivolous as pancakes.

Lauren's face clouded over. I should've seen it right away. She was trying to put on a brave front.

Nudging her, I said in a low voice, "You're safe here and you're with friends."

She looked down at her plate. "I'm a fugitive from justice."

Silence.

"I wonder if I've done the right thing," she said. "And at the same time, I can't sit back and do nothing when I see our human rights being trodden on."

"We're all really proud of you," I said, "for doing what you believe in."

Her shoulders slumped. "I can't believe the uproar. Can't believe how strongly people have reacted to what I wrote. It was only a newspaper article, and I didn't think it was revolutionary or anything. Most of all, I can't believe the police are after me."

Will put his arm around her. "You've got to be true to yourself."

"We need more people like you, Lauren," Ben said.

"We're all behind you," Reece added.

A smile crept to her lips. "Thanks, guys. I'm definitely feeling the love in the room."

"Anyway, Lauren," Reece said. "This is bigger than you. There's no telling what'll happen tomorrow. You can never tell what happens when people band together. Could be history in the making."

Lauren screwed up her nose. "I don't think so."

What had started off as a lot of talk by college students from neighboring towns was turning into a mammoth demonstration, and they weren't wasting any time.

"Yep, that's enough from you, soldier," Dominique said to Reece.

That shut him up. He hated the nickname, and Dominique had no idea how close to the bone it was.

"Right now, you guys are the only ones I want to be banded with." Lauren smiled wanly. "I'd rather not think about everything else. It's only going to scare me more."

Will reached for her hand. "Hey, this is meant to be a vacation. We've got a cool cabin in the woods, great company, no one to disturb us. What more could we want?"

"Meat for tonight's barbecue," Ben said.

Will nodded. "Now you're talking."

"More beer," Ben added.

More nodding. "You can't have too much beer."

I'd seen the results of too much beer many times and could have argued the point but didn't want to destroy the mood, especially since we were all trying so hard to be upbeat.

"Anyone interested in going for a hike later on?" I asked.

Lauren frowned. "Sounds way too much like hard work."

"I was thinking of a run," Dominique said. Reece shot her a dirty look, so she added, "I can't take a vacation from training. You can always join me...if you think you can keep up."

She had no idea of the training Reece had been through or what he might be capable of, and maybe it was better it stayed that way. To look at him now with his crazy bleached hair with dark roots, you'd never guess there was a soldier underneath.

We hung out at the cabin for the rest of the morning and it was another couple of hours until Ben and I headed off for our hike up the mountain. I found all of this relaxing quite stressful, but told myself we didn't need to be on a schedule.

Dominique cut a striking figure as she shot up the mountain ahead of us. So fit and strong. I was too, only I didn't need to be a fighting machine any more, or not in the same way as before. Besides, it suited me that she was hardcore. Took the attention away from me.

Ben and I headed up the trail, setting a steady pace. Though I wasn't exactly a nature lover, there was something about being among the trees that got to me, invigorated me, made me feel anything was possible. And maybe it was.

Suddenly steeper, the path narrowed, and rocks formed natural steps leading up the hill. Ben went ahead, then turned to help me up. My hand warm in his, I let him.

I didn't have to be a hard ass all the time, especially when it was more fun being a girlfriend.

We paused at the top of the rocks in a small patch of mottled light. Tree branches towered overhead while squirrels scampered through the undergrowth off the track.

I hadn't grown up with this sort of scenery. In New Nation, much of the countryside had been devastated by flood or storms or other natural disasters, though I'd been told there were still patches of forest like this.

Taking a deep breath, I gazed around. "I want to enjoy the moment."

Ben nuzzled up beside me, pressing little kisses against my neck. "I want to enjoy *you*."

I slid my arms up over his shoulders, pulled him close and kissed him. Being with Ben felt good in every way. Maybe he was right. Maybe it was time. Maybe even tonight.

We continued up the hill, only to be passed by Dominique who was on her way down. She was breathing deeply through her mouth and had a look in her eye I recognized. She was in the zone.

"There's a viewpoint at the top," she said. "Spectacular."

And she was off.

Ben and I might have got into a zone of our own too as we made our way to the top of the mountain. The track opened up into a clearing that looked south across the hills and towns that dotted the countryside.

Altabena lay to our right, hidden by the hills. It made me feel further from home, a feeling I liked because I was with Ben, with my friends waiting for us at the cabin.

We sat on a couple of boulders and Ben produced lunch from his backpack, two peanut butter sandwiches that were hardly stale at all and a couple of bottles of water.

"There was a time when you'd have been racing Dominique up the hill," Ben said.

I laughed. "Why race when we can sit in the sun together?"

"You tired yet?"

"A little." Nowhere near it would've been a more accurate answer, but I'd learnt to tone things down.

"We can always relax when we get back." He held my gaze. Looked kind of sheepish. Or maybe he was aiming for sexy. "I know what'll help you relax. A long slow massage."

Peanut butter stuck to the roof of my mouth as I tried to swallow. He could see I was having difficulty and chuckled. That slightly lopsided, extremely charming grin got to me every time. He wasn't trying to look sexy any more. He just was.

I took a drink of water, then crouched on a rock behind him, my hands on his shoulders as I gave them a gentle rub. "Maybe you'll need a massage too."

Tilting his head, he seemed to be enjoying the sun on his chest and my hands on his back.

"You know what would be really good about now?" he asked. "Chocolate."

I moaned. "Stop taunting me."

Reaching into his backpack, Ben produced two Mars Bars and handed one to me. A miracle. He was truly the perfect guy for me.

I nudged his bottom with mine so I could sit on the

rock beside him, our shoulders and thighs touching as we ate.

"It's so nice, just the two of us," I said, looking out across the horizon.

It felt as if the rest of the world was hundreds of miles away. This must be what people meant when they talked about 'getting away from it all'. The moment was different from the exhilaration I so often felt when Ben and I were together. For one thing, there was a sexual rush I was finding harder to ignore whereas this was a sense of contentment, satisfaction, perhaps even freedom.

Ben put his arm around me. Drew me closer. I felt safe. He pushed some stray tendrils of hair behind my ear and kissed the sensitive spot on my neck. Hell, when I was around Ben, all of me was a sensitive spot. His other hand was on my thigh, sending a sizzle up my spine and I didn't feel safe any more. I felt something else.

I kissed him gently on the lips, once, twice. Looking at him through lowered lids, a strange thought hit me. Not a thought so much as a feeling, a sensation of knowing and certainty. If the world was to end tomorrow, I'd want to be with Ben tonight. In every way that mattered.

A familiar sound cut through the silence, a low buzzing part way between the flapping of wings and the deep hum of machinery. Ben and I turned to look. Helicopters. Plural. Military helicopters to be more precise.

"Any idea what's going on?" Ben asked.

"Nope."

We waited for what might've been a few minutes or may have been much longer as the giant roar of air force planes flying in formation ripped through the air.

Ben motioned to his right where our hometown lay

hidden in the distance. "Do you think they're headed for Altabena?"

"But why...?" I got up and reached for Ben's hand. "We need to get back to the others."

The student demonstration was being held today. If those military aircraft were headed for Altabena, it was no coincidence.

I thought about the police response to our anti-curfew party last year, the authorities looking for Lauren, the newspaper being shut down. I thought about the place I'd come from and where we were headed.

Ben zipped up his backpack and stood. "I know what you're thinking, Nicola, but it doesn't make sense. There's no way they'd send in the military, not for something as small as a bunch of students demonstrating. It's not like we're at war or anything."

His voice tapered off at the end. A fighter jet roared through the air. This wasn't about war. It was about obedience and subservience and a government who would do anything to maintain loyalty. Anything.

Wars had their own rules, treaties, declarations and armistices. Where I came from, there was only one way, the Bartley government way.

And they would obliterate anyone and anything that stood in their way.

CHAPTER THREE

Suddenly this whole cabin-in-the-woods idea sucked. No phone reception, no wifi, no nothing. What a time to be out of touch. How on earth were we supposed to work out what was happening in the world?

By the time Ben and I reached the cabin, in true Lauren style she'd already written a grocery list of items to buy in town because a trip for supplies was on the agenda anyway. The boys had added booze to the list, not that Lauren minded.

We told the others about the helicopters and planes headed for Altabena but it was taking a while for the information to sink in, with the exception of Lauren. The look on her face told me she understood exactly what we were saying. Unlike the others, she'd been at the receiving end of the government crackdown.

Ben and Will stayed at the cabin to console Lauren while Reece drove Dominique and me into town along the winding road down the mountain.

"Can you go faster?" I said from the back seat.

"And crash?" Reece said. "That's a great idea."

I gritted my teeth. Didn't care that he was right. Though the whole point of coming to the cabin was that it was remote, now all I wanted was phone reception. I felt like I'd gone back a hundred years in communications and maybe I had. I wanted to know what was going on in Altabena and I didn't want to know. Damn it, I wanted to go back to a time when my home was safe.

The first messages that came through were from Mom. My stomach dropped as I stared at the phone in my hand. Wished it wasn't true.

"My mom is using the word 'massacre'," I said, hunched into the back seat of the car while I flicked through other messages from friends. Dominique was riding shotgun, her head down as she checked her own phone.

Horror in her voice. "My god, you're right."

Reece kept driving while Dominique and I searched social media and the web and gave a running commentary. It was the same story on every news feed, on PeoplePlace and in other messages.

College students from neighboring towns had gathered in Altabena Square to demonstrate against the *Security Act* and the associated government crackdown. It had been huge, much bigger than anyone anticipated, with the possible exception of the authorities.

At first police had been sent in, but the students linked arms and refused to budge. More young people arrived. Many more students than police.

So they called in the military. The police had fired shots into the air whereas the military fired at the students. Hundreds were dead. Maybe thousands. No one could confirm the death toll yet.

I despaired…for the lives that had been lost, for the families devastated, for humanity.

"I can't believe it, I can't believe it," Dominique said over again, her face fixed on the small screen in her hand. "They had no right."

Tightlipped in the driver's seat, Reece must be thinking that rights had very little to do with it. He didn't say much.

Pulling into a parking spot outside a newsstand, he made a beeline for an evening edition of the local paper. Not the *Altabena Times*, of course, because that had been closed down.

Dominique looked over her boyfriend's shoulder, tears in her eyes as she stared at the giant color photo. Girls screaming. Two young men crouched by the dead body of a friend. Other bodies on the ground. Blood. Gunshot wounds.

"All those people…" Dominique said. "They're not much older than us."

I'd been hardened once. Not any more. My stomach was churning, my nerves on edge.

Then Reece opened the newspaper to another page that had a photo of a woman carrying a girl of about ten, blood streaming from the child's head. Her daughter perhaps. It captured a moment, the woman's horror, a mother's love.

My eyes welled up. Anger surged in my stomach. How dare they? We couldn't let them get away with this. If we did, it'd be the beginning of the end.

Reece put his arm around Dominique but his eyes were on me. "What do you want to do?"

Scream, yell, cry. I did none of the above. Deep breaths. I had to think.

"We should get the groceries," I said. "We've still got to eat. We need to talk about this with the others. We can't stay here. *I* can't stay here, not while our community is being killed."

Dominique's lips parted in surprise not judgment. "How can you be so calm?"

"Only on the outside," I said.

"You're like Reece."

A surprising insight from Dominique. Also accurate. As much as I hated being a soldier, that discipline took over at times like this.

"Come on." Reece pointed toward the store down the street. "We gotta get food."

I was thankful for the list Lauren had prepared because it meant we didn't have to think too much. Also, with the three of us constantly on our phones, it was one of the all time slowest trips to the grocery store.

Ahead of me, Reece and Dominique picked some items off the shelf while I spoke to my mom, assuring her I was okay, that we were all okay.

"Do you know what State Ruler Bartley has been saying?" she asked. "That the dissident activity had to be dealt with. That this sort of behavior has been tolerated for too long."

So anyone who disagreed with the government was a troublemaker? And it didn't matter that they were young and staging a peaceful demonstration.

"Bartley also insists he'll be here tomorrow to reassure the people," Mom said. "There's going to be another protest, only this one will be bigger. Not just students but everyone from the young to the very old, whole families, people from all around. Dad and I'll be there too, of course. This is causing an uproar, not just in Altabena or California, but across the country."

Maybe a national uproar was exactly what was needed.

"Do you know Charlotte who lives one block back from us?" Mom asked.

"Y-yeah." Charlotte was a college student only a couple of years older than me. I had a horrible feeling I knew what was coming next.

"She's dead," Mom said. "They shot her. Her parents are beside themselves but they're determined to come to the demonstration. They don't want her life to be a waste."

Despite the fact I barely knew her, my stomach sank. Such a waste. A tragedy. What was worse, there'd be lots of tragedies like hers.

My mind ticked over. Ben's older brother was back home from college and Will had an older sister too. I had to find out if they were okay. For Ben. For Will. There was too much to think about and it was hitting me all at once.

Still, I knew what I had to do. If there was another protest I had to be part of it. And if something went wrong, I could help protect the people I loved. I'd done it before and I could do it again.

"I'm coming back, Mom," I said.

"But you're safe where you are, honey."

"I want to be part of this."

"I know but…" She couldn't hide the tremor from her voice. "Oh, honey…"

"We'll go to the demonstration together," I said. "As a family. It's the right thing to do."

"There's no point arguing, is there?" Her voice trailed off.

"I'll be fine, Mom. "We'll get a good night's sleep and

drive home in the morning."

Not all of us, though. Not Lauren. There was no way she could go back, not with the authorities still after her. They wouldn't bother with jail. They'd simply get rid of her.

I pressed a hand to my temple. This wasn't the world I wanted to live in.

"Love you, Mom," I said. "Tell Dad I love him too and that I'll see him tomorrow."

Meanwhile at the supermarket we'd moved on to the next aisle.

Reece was glaring at Dominique. "You won't be able to live with yourself if you don't come with us."

"I need time for this to sink in," she said. "That's all I'm saying."

"Something big is happening and I want to be part of it," he added.

I stared at him. This was from the young man who didn't normally say much, who was from a different place altogether.

He loaded some steaks into the trolley. "The man needs meat."

"The man needs more fiber in his diet," Dominique muttered under her breath.

To think, there'd been a time I thought she had no sense of humor.

"Enough arguing," I said, then explained what we had to do next.

Reece was PeoplePlace friends with Will's older sister so he checked on her only to find out she was still on the other side of the country completing some extra studies. Just as well.

I called Ben's dad to assure him we were all okay and ask about his brother who was in town but luckily hadn't bothered with the protest. Ben would probably say that was typical of his brother. At least he was in one piece.

PeoplePlace was overloaded with multiple messages from people who were devastated and in shock. I think we were too, even though we were miles away from the event.

I whacked my hand on my forehead in realization. "Lauren's mom."

I'd nearly forgotten about her. I phoned but she didn't pick up so I left a long message so she knew her daughter was safe.

Dominique paid at the checkout while Reece and I loaded the groceries back into the trolley to take to the car.

He leaned close to me. "You must've learned the same history as me at military school. Did you ever hear about anything like this?"

I shook my head. In New Nation we were all told that people welcomed State Ruler Bartley's policies. We'd known nothing of protests or demonstrations or anger against the government, let alone about massacres of innocent people.

Reece's lips were thin. "We can't let this happen."

Maybe if we banded together, we could achieve more than any of us could on our own. I felt a sense of hope and a sense of despair. All those lives lost. All those people we'd never get back.

The three of us were silent in the car as we headed back up the mountain. It felt a bit like a funeral and perhaps in a sense, it was.

Back at the cabin, we gathered in the living room. Ben, Lauren and Will pored over the newspaper and listened to our reports.

Beside me, Ben reached for my hand. "We can't stay here. We'll go back first thing in the morning, like you said."

Lauren was kneeling in front of the coffee table, staring at the paper. Behind her, Will placed his hands on her shoulders. "Lauren, you can't go. It's too dangerous."

"He's right," Dominique said. "You should stay here."

"With me," Will added. "I'm not going anywhere."

Lauren kept her gaze lowered. "I feel like such a coward."

"No way," I said. "You were brave enough to write your true opinion and you nailed it in your article."

And we absolutely couldn't let the authorities get their hands on her.

"It's the only way, Lauren." Will moved around so he was facing her. "It won't be easy, though. You'll have to learn to survive without your phone and without wifi."

She smiled grimly. "Sounds tough."

"You're a warrior," I said. "A warrior with words. And that's much harder than using your fists."

"It's not as though we'll starve out here." Her gaze wandered to a tequila bottle on the coffee table. "Or die of thirst."

Ben stood. "There's only one thing for it."

Dominique joined him in the kitchen and they came back with glasses and a bottle of 7UP.

Slammers? At a time like this? I didn't say anything, tried not to ruin the mood, then looked around and noticed there was no mood to ruin. This felt more like a wake than a party.

Ben poured a generous amount of tequila into a glass

and placed it in front of Lauren. "You're first."

He topped it up with a less generous amount of 7UP. Lauren covered the glass with her hand, slammed it on the table so it fizzed up and knocked it back.

Though I wasn't a big drinker, I slammed one down anyway and enjoyed the relaxing feeling that settled in my stomach afterwards. The others had a second round, then started discussing dinner.

After a while, Dominique fired up the barbecue, insisting she'd do a better job of the steaks than any of the boys.

"Reece," she said when she came back into the room briefly. "You're in charge of salads."

He raised his eyebrows. "Salad?"

"Time you learned about the wonderful world of vegetables."

"I'll give you a hand," Will said. "Some of those little suckers can be pretty scary."

Dinner had an otherworldly feel about it, as if we were going though the motions, as if the severity of the situation hadn't sunk in, and perhaps it hadn't. We talked about the massacre and the demonstration that was to come. We talked about a lot of things.

After we finished eating, Ben and I carried the dishes into the kitchen.

"I don't mind if you want to have another drink," I said. He'd stopped after the second slammer.

He pulled me close. "I'd rather have *you*."

I kissed him gently on the lips. "I'm here, Ben."

"All of this makes me realize what's important," he said. "What I want and don't want, how important our time together is. All those people dead... It could've been us. It makes me feel as if life is hanging by a thread." He rubbed my cheek with the back of his hand. "And I don't want to think about what I'd do without you."

This was why I loved him. He thought about things. There was always something going on underneath.

Lauren dumped some glasses on the kitchen table.

"We'll take over in here."

Will followed close behind. "Then you guys can do the cleaning up in the morning."

We didn't need to be asked twice to get out of there.

Ben's hand lingered on the doorknob outside the bedroom door. "I've got a surprise for you."

He pushed open the door to reveal a fire in the hearth that had the whole room glowing. Suddenly, I didn't care what was going on around us. I only cared about Ben. I didn't even care that it wasn't cold enough for a fire.

Up on tiptoes, I cupped his cheeks in my hands and pressed a kiss to his lips. He took my hand and led me to the rug in front of the fireplace. It was warm so I didn't waste any time and took off my sweater. Ben brought over two wine glasses and a bottle of red, then settled beside me and poured the wine.

I touched my glass against his. "To us."

I took a sip, though I wasn't going to need it. The flames from the fire were hot against the bare skin of my arm and I was burning up on the inside too. We'd been together for a long time and had been through a lot.

The time was right. Ben was right. Everything was right.

Taking the wine from Ben's hand, I placed the two glasses carefully to the side. I slipped my hands under his collar, drew him close and kissed him. One by one, I undid the buttons on his shirt and slid the fabric from his shoulders.

I peppered little kisses on his neck and across to his shoulder, my fingertips skimming his chest. So strong. He'd trained and worked for those muscles. So smart too.

My heart swelled. Felt as if it might explode. I stood up and got rid of the rest of my clothes, all of them. There was no sexy striptease. Just me.

His hands on my hips, he drew me close and kissed my belly. I lay down on the rug. Hoped Ben could see how much I wanted him. Hoped he knew how much I loved him.

He shucked off his jeans. Took off everything and lay down in front of me. He kissed me gently, one hand running over my hips, my waist, my breasts, my skin sizzling wherever he touched it.

"You're so beautiful, Nic," he said. "Everything I could ever want."

He wrapped his arms around me and held me close, our bodies molding against each other. I'd always made sure the two of us were never naked together like this. Always made sure I kept myself safe.

I didn't want to be safe any more. I wanted to be with Ben, show him how much I cared, how much I loved him.

Out of nowhere, a blinding light flashed at the back of my eyelids.

"Ben," I called out.

Pain in my head. Sudden. Intense. So strong it sucked the breath from my body.

No. No. No.

I had a horrible feeling I knew what had happened and where I was. The last place I wanted to be. The one place

I'd vowed never to return to.
    It couldn't be.

CHAPTER FOUR

I couldn't open my eyes. Didn't want to.

Strong arms were still around me. Ben's arms, they had to be. Except it couldn't be him at all.

"Nic." A familiar whisper in my year. "Nic, can you hear me?"

I forced my eyelids open and saw my beautiful Ben. Seconds ago, he'd been staring at me with longing in his eyes. Now his green irises were filled with fear.

I knew the room and the leather chair we were crammed into, both of us naked. Knew the two-way mirror on the wall opposite. Knew exactly where we were. Lucien was bent over, his hands on his knees as he stared at us, not three feet away. Lucien Everett, my captain, my mentor, the man who raised me to be a good soldier, an obedient servant of New Nation.

He was frowning as he straightened. "Welcome."

"Welcome where?" Ben asked, his voice quavering.

I turned to him, his face an inch from mine. "I'm so sorry. I don't know how this has happened."

My heart sank, despair seeping deep into my bones.

Over and over in my head, *no, no, no.*

"This is…" he began. "Is this…?"

I swallowed. "We're in New Nation. And if we've gone to the future, this must be 2120."

I looked across at Lucien for affirmation. He nodded. My worst fears confirmed. "No, no…"

Ben pulled me closer, gripped me as if his life depended on it.

Movement from the corner of the room. Nathan Tyrell stepped closer, his face blank, but then he often looked vacant despite the fact he was a young genius.

"What on earth has happened here?" he asked.

A bolt of anger shot through me. How dare he?

"You had no right." I stared from Nathan to Lucien, fire in my eyes.

Though only around my age, Nathan was the time travel expert. He should know what was going on, not me, not Ben. We shouldn't even be here.

And Lucien? How could he have done this?

I stood, left the warmth of Ben's arms, shoved my hand under Lucien's chin, pushed him back until I'd rammed the back of his head against a wall. "What the hell's going on?"

"Calm down, Nicola," he said through gritted teeth.

"Tell me. *Now.*"

No answer.

"Nic, what's going on?" Ben shouted.

I stepped back, my hands still raised in case I needed to hit someone because that was what I most wanted to do. This was crazy. I was naked. I shouldn't be here. These people shouldn't even know I was still alive.

"Where are my clothes?" A demand, not a question.

Lucien pointed behind me. "At the foot of the chair."

"What about Ben? Where are his clothes?"

Lucien's lips parted but the words didn't come out right away. "This is Ben Tanner?"

As if he couldn't believe it. As if he hadn't brought him here.

Ben looked freaked. More than slightly. My poor Ben.

"That's Ben Tanner!" Nathan's eyes were wide.

"I just told you that," I yelled.

"Get some clothes for him," Lucien told Nathan who stood there like a dummy though he was far from that. "Now."

Nathan left the room while I pulled on the army gear waiting for me – underwear, boots, combat pants and a dull brown tee shirt.

I passed a camouflage jacket to Ben. "Sorry, that's all I've got."

He held it in front of his crotch without saying anything. He was shaking so I put my arm around him.

"What the hell is going on?" he said. "You have to get us out of here."

"Why bring us back?" I asked my former captain.

"We didn't know about Ben," he said.

Louder, this time. "*Why*, Lucien?"

He lowered his head. "I had no choice."

I jabbed a finger in the air. "You always have choices."

He shook his head. "You've been away too long. You've forgotten."

"I forget nothing!"

"Believe me, Nicola, it's better I brought you back than that they did. I couldn't leave you in their hands."

They...I didn't want to think about the superior

officers above me.

Bullshit. That's what this was.

Nathan came back and handed a pile of military clothes to Ben. Stared at him while he fumbled with his clothing. Nervous. In shock.

"What is the matter with you?" Maybe I shouldn't be shouting but I didn't care.

Nathan held my gaze. "Nicola, what you've got to understand is—"

So condescending, so annoying. I shoved him in the shoulder, not too hard but hard enough.

He cleared his throat. "I set the program so it would bring you back. *You*, not Ben Tanner. We've never been able to get a location on him because over the years you've done an excellent job of covering his tracks and eliminating all information about him. I'm still trying to determine how this is possible."

I had a pretty good idea how. Ben and I had been lying in front of the fire. Together. My legs had been intertwined with his, our perspiration mingling. Perhaps the time travel program hadn't been able to differentiate between the two of us so it latched onto both humans, which was much better than bringing back a partial body.

And the travel program only transported organic matter, so they weren't expecting me to be clothed on my return. That was why Lucien had prepared my uniform.

Maybe they'd work it out and maybe they wouldn't. These people didn't have any idea about love and relationships and human emotion. And I wasn't about to illuminate them.

I stared at Lucien. "How did they even know I was still alive?"

He had sent me back to Altabena – for good, I'd thought – yet somehow now my superior officers knew all about me.

"Isn't it obvious?" Lucien replied. "Your geopositrons."

"They're not even my damn geopositrons!"

In New Nation we all had microscopic GPS molecules in our blood so the authorities could know where we were at any time. I'd rid myself of my original geopositrons and later used Reece's so I could time travel when I'd needed to.

After that particular trip, Ben hadn't let me purge myself of the molecules the way I had the first time so I'd done the process bit by bit. Safer but not as effective. Now it turned out it wasn't safe at all.

"Geopositrons only function properly when they reach a critical mass," I said. "There can't be that many still in my system."

"They found a way to locate a smaller mass," Lucien said.

"They?" I glanced at Nathan.

"Not Nathan, someone else."

I sighed. "So how did they know it was me?"

"They worked it out," Lucien said. "They have spies, informants, obedient servants."

My eyes narrowing, I glared at him. "They have *you*."

I paced the floor. Tried to get all this through my head. Lucien had been in league with rebel generals trying to overthrow the government. So who were 'they'? Was there a new rebel force? Or was Lucien a loyal servant of the government?

I stood by Ben, took his hand into mine, my eyes fixed

firmly on Lucien. "If it's such a good thing you brought me back, who is it you're protecting me from?"

Silence.

"Who, Lucien?"

"Supreme Ruler Bartley," he said.

I remembered what happened last time, the jail in which I'd been imprisoned, the justice that had been served to me, the torture they'd put me through. Wondered what they had planned this time.

"Is he going to make an example of me?" I asked.

A curt shake of the head. "You're a hero."

I screwed up my face. "What?"

"Bartley wanted you brought back because you killed the rebel generals who were trying to overthrow the government. That makes you unique, a hero of New Nation, a national hero."

I squeezed Ben's hand tighter, my blood pressure rising. "You know as well as I do that I wasn't the one who did that."

"The truth has nothing to do with it. Not here."

That was my whole problem. I didn't want to be here. And a hero was the last thing I wanted to be.

I glanced at Nathan, then Lucien. "Send us back, both of us, now."

So obvious. It's what I should have demanded in the first place.

Lucien's lips tightened. "No point. They'll get a fix on you and bring you back again. It's out of your hands."

Those damn geopositrons. They'd always find me.

I had to think. Had to work this out. I cupped Ben's jaw in my hand and kissed him on the lips. Hoped he couldn't tell I was shaking.

I dropped my hands. "Then send Ben back."

He grabbed me by the shoulders. "I'm not leaving without you."

"Okay," I said in a small voice.

Ben dropped his hands. Didn't sense that I didn't mean it.

"This is truly remarkable." Nathan's voice came out of nowhere. "Perhaps our only opportunity to study a human from a hundred years ago."

"He's a person," I said. "Not a science experiment."

"A study would not be for the purposes of experimentation, merely research." His response was so cool, so impersonal, so Nathan.

"No way. Forget it."

"Nicola, I can't help but observe alterations in your language, your attitude, even your thought processes. It's quite striking. You've changed in the past months."

"And you haven't."

Lucien stepped closer, staring at me. "You're back in New Nation and you have to deal with it. This is 2120 and you're a soldier, a hero, a loyal servant."

There would always be a soldier inside me, but Nathan was right. I'd changed, no longer the obedient subject of the state. I was exactly what New Nation hated because I'd learnt to think for myself. And I liked it. Liked being able to work things out on my own and feel some sense of self-determination.

"You have to become a corporal again or you won't last." Lucien shifted his gaze to Ben. "And neither will he."

That was the thing about Lucien. He always knew how to get to me because, above all, I had to protect Ben.

"There's only one option," I said. "We have to send

you back, Ben."

His eyes narrowed. "Forget it. We already went through that."

"It's for your own good."

He grabbed my arm, squeezed tight. "I don't know what the hell is going on, only that we have to stick together."

"I'll come back, Ben. Like I did before. We can be together later."

Determination in his eyes. "There's no 'later' Nicola. There's only now. And I'm not leaving you here."

A clunk and the gentle swish of the door behind us cut through the air. This was a high security zone. So who else had access? Who knew we were here? Dread sank deep in my stomach as I felt any chances I may have had slipping away.

Behind me, the shuffle of footsteps, the sound of heavy breathing. I turned around slowly. No sudden movements.

Four beefed-up guards formed a wall, their necks thicker than their heads, their shoulders a barrier. They wore black uniforms and looked like nightclub bouncers, complete with dark sunglasses.

And in front of them a face I recognized all too well.

Supreme Ruler Harrison Bartley.

CHAPTER FIVE

Bartley spread his arms. "Welcome back to New Nation. Your home."

Fear gripped my throat, made my body shake, my legs weak. I had no way of hiding Ben from this man, no idea what to do, but I had to do something. I forced myself to step to the side in front of Ben, blocking him from Bartley.

Bartley's smile might have seemed friendly if it reached his eyes, eyes that were glazed like bright blue ceramics, seemingly fake against his lined face.

He turned to Lucien. "Captain Everett, would you please introduce us."

"Supreme Ruler Bartley, may I present Corporal Nicola Brennan."

My old name. I was Nicola Gray in every way that mattered.

"Returned from the dead." He laughed, the security team behind him snickering because clearly this was hilarious.

This was my fault. I should've got Ben out sooner instead of arguing. I'd wasted so much time being angry and now one false move would cost us dearly. I'd had doubts about Lucien – and still did – but those doubts were so much better than the certainty I felt now.

I nodded, my eyes riveted to Bartley. "Sir."

He turned to the giants standing behind him. "Gentlemen, would you leave us alone for a few moments?"

The guards did as they were told. Not a lot of original thought going on there.

Hands clasped behind his back, Bartley took a few steps, looked around. The man commanded the room. By fear.

My mind was racing, my heart too. I could take Bartley by surprise. Knock him out. Kill him. It wasn't as if I needed a weapon. What then? Ben and I wouldn't last sixty seconds before the guards shot us.

I turned to Ben. Saw fear in his eyes. Hoped he'd keep calm because that was the only thing that would get us through this.

"Nicola," Bartley said. "A pleasure indeed. You are the epitome of everything we strive for in New Nation. A role model for young and old alike. We need more subjects like you."

"Thank you, sir." As I said the words, I felt myself becoming an automaton already.

"Such a healthy specimen," he added. "We do an excellent job of raising our young people here."

He shifted his gaze to Ben, his eyes narrowing. Why wasn't he asking who this was? What did Bartley have in mind?

"You must be so pleased to be back in New Nation safely after your months in exile?" he said to me.

"Yes, sir."

"Very strange that you lost your initial geopositrons."

Such a simple statement and so loaded. I hoped an explanation would come to me, and quick.

Eventually, Bartley added, "I'm curious to hear your response, Corporal."

My lips parted, then it came to me. "I was in a car accident. I suffered mammoth blood loss and can only assume the geopositrons were leached from my body."

I stopped the urge to embellish, to describe the accident that had never happened, the severity of my injuries and the length of my hospital stay. Liars often gave themselves away by talking too much.

"How unfortunate," Bartley said.

I nodded.

"Then you located alternative geopositrons," he said. "How did you manage that?"

"It's a long story, sir."

"How did you know for sure that you'd lost all your geopositrons in the first place?"

"I didn't."

"You're aware these new geopositrons came from another soldier?" He turned to Lucien. "Captain Everett, what became of that young man?"

"We can only assume he is dead," Lucien said.

Better for Reece if they thought that.

Bartley nodded. "I'm glad we've cleared that up. You are indeed innovative and resourceful, Nicola."

Or desperate. And now it seemed he was on first name terms with me.

"You left New Nation a soldier and came back a hero." Bartley was louder now, more emphatic. "We expect all our people to be good citizens but what you've done goes way beyond this."

I lowered my gaze. "I don't feel like a hero, sir."

"Modesty...another exemplary trait. You uncovered a terrorist plot that could potentially have overthrown the government and ruined New Nation. You saw through the aims and methods of the rebel forces, suffered through torture, and didn't rest until you'd eliminated the terrorist leaders. You came through fighting at the end."

He raised a fist in the air, made it sound like an action movie, the sort that weren't even made in New Nation any more. I bit my tongue.

He continued. "If not for your work, our wonderful nation may never have come into existence. The world as we know it would have been shattered. This isn't the time for modesty. This is the time to celebrate, to revel in our achievements, to commemorate our past and future."

Ben's eyes darted from side to side as if he wasn't sure whether this was good or bad. Lucien appeared as composed as ever while Nathan had the expressiveness of a concrete pylon.

I looked at Bartley. "All you have to say is 'thank you' and we can all move on."

The man tossed his head back, the tendons in his neck protruding as he let out a huge howl of laughter. Laughed so heartily that tears came to his eyes and he had to wipe them away. Lucien joined him in a gentle laugh, clearly the tactful thing to do. Even Nathan smiled. While Ben and I tried to work out what the hell was going on.

Bartley calmed down a little. "If you hadn't saved my life, you'd be a dead woman."

I swallowed. Lucien was right when he said I'd been

away too long. This was a warning I couldn't ignore. I had to be more careful.

"You will never be moving on, Nicola," Bartley said. "You will be remembered in New Nation for a very long time. You are part of our history and our future. This is nowhere near finished. We have plans for you."

"What sort of plans?" I asked in a small voice.

Instead of answering, he said to Nathan, "You've done an excellent job, young man. You, too, are a credit to your country." Turning to Lucien, he added, "Captain Everett, you've done your bit for New Nation in training Nicola and supporting her in her quest for justice."

Yes, Lucien had come out of this sparkling clean.

"I have one outstanding question." Bartley gestured toward Ben, his upper lip curling to a sneer. "Who is this man in soldier's clothing and why is he here?"

Ben, with his long wavy hair could never be mistaken for a member of the New Nation military.

Lucien cleared his throat. "We were trying to determine that before you arrived, sir."

"How did he get here?" Bartley asked.

Silence.

Bartley turned to Nathan. "Answer me."

"He and Nicola were transported here together, courtesy of the time travel program," Nathan replied. "We were only expecting to transport one human body, not two, and I do not have a scientific explanation for this particular outcome."

"An error in your calculations?"

"At this stage, I'm not sure, sir," Nathan said.

"If he doesn't belong here, we'll have to get rid of him."

Nathan nodded. "It would not be difficult to transport him to the original coordinates."

Ben's nostrils flared. Fists clenched at his side, he could work out that wasn't what Bartley had in mind.

I stepped forward. "Ben, no…"

Bartley tilted his head. "Ben?"

I hoped my hand on his arm gave him some solace.

"What's your name, young man?" Bartley asked.

He pushed his shoulders back. "Ben Tanner."

Bartley smiled. "When I first saw you, I wondered…then I thought it couldn't be possible, but it seems anything is achievable in our great nation. This is too good to be true." Bartley reached across and shook his hand while Ben stood there in disbelief. "You must be tired, overwhelmed, in shock. This must seem unbelievable, but rest assured we will take care of you throughout this momentous occasion."

Ben pulled his hand back. "I'm fine."

"Nicola, such a coup on your part," Bartley said. "You are an enormous asset to this great country of ours. In fact, I cannot believe my luck." He turned to Lucien and spread his arms. "Why didn't you tell me this right away?"

"We are still trying to come to terms with it ourselves," he said.

"Welcome to New Nation, Ben," Bartley said. "Welcome to the future."

"I don't even know what we're doing here–" Ben's eyes narrowed "–*sir.*"

Bartley didn't notice the slur. "That's perfectly understandable. Naturally you'll want to go back to your own place and time, but you've only just got here. This is an incredible opportunity for me, for you, for all of us. We will have to let you go eventually. And safely, of course. Until then, you will be my guest, my very special guest."

Anxiety set in my stomach like concrete, my throat tight, every nerve in my body on edge. The authorities could erase part of Ben's memory or insert a chip so he wouldn't remember New Nation. That wasn't a problem, but other things worried me.

How long until 'eventually'?

And what else would happen before then?

CHAPTER SIX

I had no idea this section of the army compound even existed. The building was concrete and seemed much like any other from the outside, the interior decorated in the same Spartan style as everything else.

Two guards were stationed outside the room. The public relations woman who was taking care of us stepped out to retrieve some documentation.

Ben had insisted he had to go wherever I went. And Bartley had agreed. Apparently Ben could get whatever he wanted, relatively speaking. So now the two of us were sitting on one side of an enormous desk, staring at an empty chair on the other.

His shoulders were scrunched, the tendons in his neck straining. "What are we going to do, Nicola?"

I lifted a finger to my lips and glanced around the room. Ben's eyes flicked up to a corner of the ceiling where a tiny black camera was perched. He nodded, though there was no way he could understand the extent of surveillance in New Nation or how we were all encouraged to inform on anyone suspected of dissidence.

Here, we expected to be watched. It was part of life.

The media woman, Audrey White, stepped back into the room, sat down and passed some papers across the desk. "Would you please sign here?"

"That depends," I said. "What is it?"

Her hair was pulled back into a tight bun and her empty brown eyes blinked at me from across the table.

"This is the media statement that will be distributed on your behalf," she said.

She made it sound like she was doing me a favor when I didn't want a media statement or a media anything. I lowered my gaze to the papers in front of me.

"What are you doing?" Her voice was sharp.

I glanced up. "Reading."

"You don't need to read this. It has been carefully researched and approved by all the correct authorities."

That was how things worked here. They wouldn't change a single word that was written, no matter the truth, no matter what I said. I ignored her and kept reading while she leaned back in her chair with her arms crossed.

The statement was scarily close to the truth. There was no mention of Ben or my initial mission to eliminate him so he wouldn't go on to create the virus which set Bartley's repressive regime up for success. Instead, it seemed the original plot was for me to go back in time to assassinate an unknown target who was then later revealed to me to be Bartley.

Apparently, that was the point at which I cottoned on that these were rebel forces working against our great government. The rest was surprisingly accurate. The document outlined how I'd hidden in the Badlands before returning to the military compound, how I'd been found and tortured, and finished with the deaths of the rebel generals. I wasn't the one who'd killed them but the authorities didn't know that.

I pushed the papers back across the desk. "You don't need my signature."

Audrey's lips were pursed. "This is most unusual."

I gritted my teeth. Couldn't bring myself to sign on the dotted line as if they owned me.

Audrey glanced at Ben, then back at me. "Is this the sort of example you want to set?"

I shrugged. "That is my statement. You already have it. You don't need me."

A smug smile on her face, she said, "On the contrary, New Nation needs you. You have a live interview scheduled in half an hour and I think you'll find there will be repercussions if you decline."

Bartley had said I wouldn't be moving on, that he had plans for me, and I was starting to understand what he meant.

My pulse raced. "What sort of interview?"

"A live audience and immediate streaming across the country. Your lines have been prepared so all you have to do is read them from the screen when you're asked a question."

I wasn't sure I could do this. "Who's the interviewer?"

"Guildford Lee."

The biggest name in modern media and also a puppet of the state who maintained the party line about the greatness of New Nation and the Bartley government. My nerve endings skittered, my stomach uneasy.

Audrey stood and walked toward the door. "We wouldn't want to be late."

Ben squeezed my hand and helped me up, despite his own nerves. "You can do it, Nic."

I didn't have much choice.

Audrey stood, looking down her nose at Ben. "Your hair is atrocious, young man."

He scowled. "What's that got to do with anything?"

As much as I hated to admit it, she was right.

I pulled him to one side. "I love your hair but it makes you stand out and here, that's not a good thing. It's dangerous."

He raised his eyebrows, didn't look happy. "But it's my hair, part of my personality."

"People around here don't have their own personality. That's the whole point."

"I can arrange a haircut in the prep room while Nicola is there," the media woman said.

Ben's mouth formed a thin line as he looked at me. "Is this what you want?"

The safest option. "Yes."

"Let's go." His hand in the small of my back, he ushered me through the door. The warmth of human touch, Ben's touch, made an enormous difference. It reminded me of my old home and all the things I'd left behind in Altabena.

We were silent as Audrey led us to the prep area, a long room with chairs set up at various stations in front of mirrors lit by blazing light bulbs. Several staff busied themselves tidying the area.

Audrey clicked her fingers and one of the workers snapped to attention. She pointed at the first chair and said, "Ben, sit," then gave instructions.

The woman stylist stood behind Ben, staring in the

mirror wide-eyed as she ran a brush through his hair. "What has happened to you?"

Ben opened his mouth to speak but Audrey said, "Just fix it, please."

The woman reached for a cape, securing it around Ben's neck.

He turned to me. "Nicola, are you sure about this?"

I bit my lower lip. "Sorry, Ben. There's no other way."

It wasn't just his hair that was the problem. I don't think it had sunk in for him just how dangerous our situation was. He hadn't slept – neither of us had – and though most of the time he had his head together, he wasn't coping well, calm one minute, panicked the next.

He sat stony-faced while the stylist picked up the scissors. I couldn't bear to watch.

"We've prepared your uniform." Audrey said to me. She pulled open a curtain revealing khaki jodhpurs and brown knee-high boots, a shirt and tie, and a black jacket layered with medals that were weighing it down.

"I've never worn a uniform like that one before," I said.

"Well, you'll be wearing one now."

In New Nation, my usual clothing was combat gear similar to the outfit I had on. Even our formal military wear didn't look like this.

There was no point arguing so I took off my clothes and pulled on the costume they'd prepared for me, feeling more like a phony with every passing second.

Audrey spoke to a male stylist while I got dressed. We had no privacy in New Nation and undressing in front of each other was the norm.

I stared at the mirror in horror. That wasn't me. I looked like a Nazi or an ugly SS officer, a female Hitler with my hair pulled back in a ponytail.

"Is this really necessary?" I asked.

Audrey's eyes were two warnings. Silence in the room, even the nearby clicking of the scissors ceased.

Ben turned to look at me, disgust etched in his features – not at me, but at what I was being forced to do and wear. His dark hair still hung over his eyes but the sides were cut short. If he could do this, then surely I could too.

Audrey pointed to a nearby chair. "Mason will be doing your make-up."

"Okay." As soon as I said this, the soft, metallic click-click of the scissors formed a soothing background noise. I grit my teeth and sat down. "Since when do we need make-up in New Nation?"

"Since now," Audrey said. "You must look your best for the news program. Nothing less will do." She even smiled at me in the mirror.

Mason tucked tissue paper under my collar to protect my magnificent uniform while I squirmed in my seat. I couldn't stand being a puppet of the state but that's exactly what I was in this outfit. It's what I had to be if I was to survive.

Taking deep breaths, I closed my eyes while Mason applied the make-up that finished off this costume. Audrey droned on in the background, briefing me on the interview. A television interview. We still called it television though it was streamed across computers and PR devices across the country.

Soon, the whole world would know I was a hero. I had to be that person if only for the next half hour. I'd faked being a high school student in Altabena for long enough, so surely I could fake this too.

"I have to speak to the production team now," Audrey said from the doorway. "Mason will direct you to the recording area and I'll be watching from the side."

I nodded as she left. Through the corner of my eye, I saw Ben get up from his chair and stand behind me to one side. Mason was on the other side, dusting translucent powder onto my face.

Ben turned his head, peering at his haircut in the mirror – staring but not admiring. It killed me to see him looking more a soldier than a student. That wasn't my Ben. The only good thing was having his hair off his face brought out the green in his eyes.

"Could be worse." He straightened, forced out the words, then to me, "I've never seen you look like that before."

"Transformation complete." Mason turned to put away his gear.

"He's done a nice job," Ben said. "You still look like Nicola."

"Yeah, if you only look at my face," I muttered.

Nerves settled in my stomach. I wasn't going to be able to make this work, not dressed like little Hitler. I didn't even know the person in the mirror. I looked like one of those cut-outs at an amusement park where you placed your face over the hole, only now I had the body of a military dictator.

I took the jacket off and reached for the hanger.

"Nicola, what are you doing?" Ben asked.

"What does it look like?" I loosened the tie.

Mason and the other staff watched, their mouths open.

Seconds later, I was in the combat pants and shirt which, at least, had once been 'me'.

Ben's lips were thin. "Are you sure that's a good idea?"

I nodded, then turned to Mason. "Please lead the way."

Minutes later we were backstage at the studio. Behind us in a control room, camera operators remotely operated the cameras that sat in front of the stage. The audience, a mix of military and regular personnel, waited in tiered seating. Some were pointing at me and chatting, excited expressions on their faced.

And in front of us, television presenter Guildford Lee was talking at a hundred miles an hour. Tall and slim with cropped blond hair and a neat gray suit, he looked like an advertisement for the virtues of the Aryan race.

"All you have to do is relax and read the auto-cue in front of you," he said. "Everything is scripted and scheduled for maximum ease."

His smile was broad against his sculpted features, his teeth Hollywood white which looked so out of place here.

"Very convenient," I said.

"You won't have to think about a thing," he assured me before turning to Ben. "And who are you?"

"No one." Ben shrugged. "I'm just watching."

The smile disappeared from Guildford's face. "That's fine, *No One*, as long as you stay out of the way and don't say a word."

I stepped forward. "You can't–"

Ben grabbed me by the arm. "It's okay, Nic. I wouldn't want to stand in the way of television greatness."

Maybe Guildford Lee had never heard of sarcasm because he seemed satisfied with that, his smile back exactly where it had been before. It was as if a switch had been flicked, and maybe that was what I had to do too. Flick a switch to survive. For the next half hour I had to be an actor, an obedient soldier, a servant of our great nation. That was my role.

He pressed his fingers to his earpiece. "It's time."

Behind the stage, they'd projected an enormous image of the *Capitale* with its white façade and Doric columns topped with a majestic dome. It reminded me where I was and why I was here.

The audience roared with applause as Guildford ushered me toward one of the two chairs on stage. He sat down, placing a G-Top on the coffee table in front of him as if he needed to look up important things on the computer during the interview.

Studio lights burned on my face. Rows and rows of people stared at me. Cameras perched in front turned toward me. I felt as if there was no escape, nowhere to run or hide.

Guildford launched into a speech about how I'd foiled a serious terrorist attack that put the very fabric of New Nation in danger. I stared at the faces in the audience, people riveted to his words, then glanced to the side to see Ben nodding at me, a reassuring smile on his face. Beside him, Audrey looked me up and down, sneering because I wasn't wearing the chosen outfit.

I shot my head back toward the audience. Better not to look at her.

"Nicola." Guildford's smile was so broad, it consumed most of his face. "What was it like traveling to the past?"

I looked at the autocue. *The past is a backward and desolate place. We have come so far since then. I am fortunate to be a subject of New Nation and I owe everything to this great country of ours.*

"The p-past..." I couldn't say the scripted words out loud, not sincerely, not anywhere near sincerely. This wasn't going to work. I stared at the faces in the audience, silent, anxious, waiting. "The past is not particularly relevant because we live in the present, and that's what counts."

Knowing nods from the audience.

Guildford went into detail about the plot against our government by two evil rebel generals. Our lifestyle was under threat; Supreme Ruler Bartley's life was in danger; the world as we knew it was on the brink. Gasps from the audience.

He followed with details about how I'd been tortured. More gasps. He didn't mention it was our own New Nation government that had tortured me. Silence in the audience as he informed them how I was about to be executed, then managed to overthrow my oppressors.

"Can you tell us a bit about that please, Nicola?" he asked.

But he'd already said everything there was to say. I looked at the autocue. It came up with more garbage about the greatness of New Nation and our esteemed Supreme Ruler Bartley.

I was way out of my league. "Well... I foiled and they failed."

The audience chuckled.

Guildford flicked his eyes toward the autocue, fire in his eyes for a moment before returning to his usual persona. "Let's get back to the rebel generals so you can tell us about their plot."

The autocue. I read the first words out loud. "They were twisted evil men with an agenda."

That much was true. Guildford's shoulders relaxed.

Their plot was the most heinous of all — to overthrow our great Supreme Ruler and send New Nation back to the dark ages. We have come so far and our nation is so great that I could not let that happen.

That wasn't the heinous part, nowhere near it.

"They used me," I said. "They manipulated me and had no regard for my life or anyone else's. Everything they told me was lies. Everything I thought was true was false. I couldn't go through with their plan after I found that out. My only regret is that I wish I'd found out sooner."

Guildford cleared his throat. Stared. At me. "Our very own Supreme Ruler Bartley has said you are a hero and that if it weren't for your efforts, our great nation would be in tatters. Soon you will receive the Bartley Medal, the highest honor for any solider or citizen."

I didn't know what to say or feel. There was a time that would have been beyond my dreams and now it was my nightmare. And no one had even bothered to tell me about it.

My eyes widened. "Really?"

The audience snickered, but not because they were laughing at me. The expressions on their faces told me they found this endearing.

"As I said..." Guildford glared at me, then once again flicked his eyes toward the autocue. He repeated the words he'd just said, but I couldn't bring myself to look up.

"I'm not a hero," I said. "I'm a lot of things but not that. I just did what I had to do."

A single clap from the audience. Then a second.

Followed by the roar of applause.

After it quieted down, Guildford said, "So modest. Such a credit to New Nation. Speaking of which, you must be glad to be back in New Nation, to be serving our Supreme Ruler, to be surrounded by loyal comrades."

I glanced up at the ceiling. "You wouldn't believe my sentiments at the moment."

Perspiration beaded on Guildford's brow. "You learnt everything you know at the military academy through years of tutelage and mentoring from great minds and experts. Can you tell us about these skills that were key to your survival?"

The autocue came up with a speech about the virtues of the system that raised children in military school and created obedient soldiers.

"Training is everything," I said. "If not for my training, I wouldn't have survived. It taught me to fight for what I believe in."

A glimmer in Guildford's eye. "For New Nation?"

The autocue was blank. No words came up. I glanced back at Guildford. The hint of a smirk on his lips, he was trying to get back at me. And he'd taken me by surprise.

He raised his eyebrows. "What were you fighting for?"

I glanced at the audience, expectant, waiting. He had me cornered.

"For our great nation." My voice quavered as I said the words.

"Thank you for your time. That was Nicola Brennan, my comrades." He turned to me, the sparkling teeth gritted together. "We look forward to seeing more of you."

Applause filled the air. Guildford stood, gesturing to the side of the stage, so I got up too.

He kept smiling until we were off stage, then threw the G-Top in his hand to the floor and stamped on it, his face aflame against his pale hair.

"Do you know who I am?" He shook his finger. "Do you have any idea what you've just done?"

Audrey placed a hand on his shoulder. "The people of New Nation will love her. They already do."

"You say that like it's a good thing." He spat the words out.

Audrey pointed a finger at me. "Don't you dare do that again!"

"Then don't interview me," I said.

She turned and stormed off, which was exactly what I wanted to do. Get away. Far away.

CHAPTER SEVEN

Of all the times I'd dreamt about spending the night with Ben, I never imagined it would be in the top bunk of a small room in the barracks of the military compound while he slept below.

Still, by New Nation military standards a room to ourselves was an unheard of luxury. When I'd lived here as a child, there'd been twenty of us in a dormitory and then, when I was older, my room had been a bed partitioned off from the others in what was effectively a long corridor of beds. I hadn't even known rooms like this existed. Earlier, Ben and I showered in the small private bathroom, something else I hadn't known existed.

He'd already dressed in the uniform he'd been given. Similar to mine, it was formal but a far cry from the SS-style outfit they'd tried to make me wear yesterday.

I sat slumped on the bottom bunk in my underwear, the least sexy sort there was, military underwear.

We were invited to a celebratory lunch at the *Capitale*, the sort of invitation we couldn't refuse, not when I was the guest of honor.

"You need to get dressed, Nic," Ben said.

Despite the fact he was still in shock at being here, he had his head together when I needed him the most. He was also right. I needed to get dressed and be someone I wasn't.

I buttoned up the black shirt, adjusted the epaulettes and pulled on a pair of khaki pants. The only action the brown boots had seen was at the end of a brush as they were being polished.

With his short hair and broad shoulders, Ben looked like a natural in his uniform, except for the hesitation in his eyes. Seeing him like this broke my heart.

"Your hair is messy." He pressed a few strands back and leaned close to whisper in my ear. "Can we talk?"

"No."

"Who can we trust?"

"No one," I said in a low voice.

"Lucien?"

I shook my head. Long before I'd arrived here, Lucien had told the authorities *I* was the one who'd killed the two generals. A cover story if I'd ever heard one. It was only by sheer luck things had turned out this way, that I was a hero not a terrorist, alive instead of executed.

Ben raised his eyebrows. "You haven't forgotten what was going down back home?"

"No."

The police coming after Lauren, the cabin, the protest…it all seemed like it was a hundred years ago. And it was.

"How are we going to get back, Nic?" he asked.

Ben was doing what he was told because he'd started to understand how important that was. I had a feeling the seriousness of our situation was starting to sink in.

I glanced up at the camera. "They'll send you back, Ben."

"Altabena is my home," he said, his voice pained. "Dad and Celia and even Josh are there."

Yep, even Josh, the brother he didn't particularly like. Ben longed to be with his family. I could see how he felt about Celia in the thin sheen of tears in his eyes.

Pain gripped my chest as I thought about my parents in Altabena and how I yearned to see them again, ached to be part of their lives, to be the daughter they always wanted. Funny how love could hurt this much.

Ben needed me to be strong or we'd never get out of here. I threw my arms around him and held him close, regardless of whether this was being caught on camera.

A knock at the door. It was pushed open by a female soldier in regular uniform, her expression blank. Three others stood behind her.

"We're here to escort you to the *Capitale*," she said.

"No kidding," I said.

"No, I'm not kidding," she replied. "I'm Corporal Amanda Szabo."

Ben and I walked out of the compound with them. Outside, the light was dull and even, not like the striking sunshine we were used to in Altabena. Clouds hung low in the sky, the air thick and gray, something I'd barely noticed when I used to live here. We had sunshine in New Nation sometimes too. It's just that we never expected it.

Anyway, the dullness seemed to fit with our surroundings, concrete paths, concrete buildings, concrete everything.

C Dock, the major hub for above- and below-ground

transportation wasn't far, so we kept walking past the training stadium toward the edge of the compound walls.

Further along, a gleaming, burgundy pod stood out among the grimy surroundings. Computer controlled pods were an efficient way of getting around, and this was one of the more modern ones that flew low to the ground.

I took Ben by the arm as we stepped on. "Our transport."

Ben and I sat on the back seat, one soldier beside me while the three others faced us. They didn't seem taken aback by the embossed leather seats, thick carpet or the plush interior. Maybe they were used to this but I wasn't.

Ben looked around. "You never told me about this."

"I've never been in a pod like this until now."

"I guess you weren't a hero before."

After a while, the pod went through a tunnel, then slowed down before coming to a halt. Outside the window, Lucien waited for us on an underground dock and I realized this must be a private entrance under the *Capitale*, hence the tunnel.

The doors opened and two soldiers got out, then Ben and me, followed by the other two soldiers. I felt as if I was stuck in a sandwich.

"Come along," Lucien said.

We followed him along the concrete station and, still surrounded by soldiers, stepped into an elevator that had an enclosed waterfall on one wall. Weird, to say the least and not at all what I was expecting. The sound of trickling water should have been soothing but put me on edge. I squeezed Ben's hand, his grasp reassuring.

We stepped out of the lift.

"You won't have seen anything like this before,

Nicola," Lucien said.

"More waterfalls?" I asked.

"Lunch will be a formal affair."

"Glad I didn't get all dressed up for nothing," I said under my breath.

We stopped outside enormous, carved wooden doors where two guards stood. Lucien sidled closer to me as the three of us stepped inside, leaving the other soldiers behind.

"And you will behave accordingly," he said.

I nodded, looked around and saw we were in a different world. I'd stepped back not one but two centuries into an opulent palace. A huge room with high ceilings, the walls were covered in Renaissance-style murals and ornate plasterwork. A domed skylight took pride of place high above us, while glittering chandeliers hung from the rest of the ceiling. The room was filled with several long tables lined with guests.

I couldn't believe this was New Nation. It was about as far from concrete and utilitarian as you could get.

A dozen butlers who were taking care of the guests meandered through the room, while one led us to our table at the far end. I sat between Ben and Lucien, an empty seat beside Ben.

In the next spot, a young man not much older than us reached across to shake Ben's hand. "So pleased to meet you both. I'm Carson Jones."

His sandy hair was swept over one eye which was unusual to say the least in New Nation, the land of neatness and haircuts.

A rumble through the room grabbed our attention and everyone stood. We did too, then the oversized doors at the other end of the room opened and Supreme Ruler Bartley stepped in to an enormous round of applause. Gritting my teeth, I put my hands together too and Ben followed suit.

Bartley was wearing full military uniform, complete with medals, which struck me as strange since he wasn't in the army and never had been. He held his hands out and everyone sat back down.

Before I knew it Bartley was behind us, a butler pulling out his chair. Ben stood, so I did too. He'd been raised to be polite.

Our Supreme Ruler shook Ben's hand. "No need to stand for me. You're our guest of honor." He turned to me. "As are you."

Words that only made me more anxious. I was so far out of my element it wasn't funny. We sat down again.

Bartley was deep in conversation with Carson. The young man's smoky brown eyes were animated and he was exaggerating his hand gestures and agreeing with everything Bartley said. Which was probably what I should do too. Still, something seemed odd even if I couldn't put my finger on it.

Eventually, Bartley leaned back and spread his arms. "Tell me, Ben, have you ever seen anything like this where you came from?"

"No, sir, can't say I have." Ben scanned the room and it occurred to me that his politeness and good manners might help keep him alive.

"Magnificent, isn't it?"

Ben nodded. "Certainly is."

Bartley leaned across to speak to me. "You do realize this is just the beginning of our celebrations?"

"There's more?" I regained my composure and added, "I mean, this is such a salubrious beginning that I can't imagine what else might be to come."

"We will take very good care of you, Nicola." Bartley sounded almost fatherly. "You too, Ben. One day you are going to be a great doctor and medical researcher. We still have diseases and problems here in New Nation but one disease we don't have is cancer. And that's down to you."

"Me?" Ben put a hand on his chest as if this was the first time he'd heard this.

"Yes, son, you're going to go on to create a cure for cancer."

"No way!" Ben grinned. It bothered me how natural he looked, how comfortable, how well he fit into this role. "Are you serious?"

"Yes, that's why we have to send you back to your own time, back to where you belong. In due course."

I cut in. "But you could do that now. You could send him back any time."

Bartley placed a hand on Ben's shoulder. "This is an amazing opportunity for me, for everyone in the room. That's why we want to keep you here a little longer."

Ben raised his eyebrows. "So these people all know I'm going to create a cure for cancer?"

Bartley smile's broadened. "Some of them. You have good reason to be proud of your achievements."

"That's kind of cool." The grin on Ben's face was real. Perhaps he was delirious or perhaps I was wrong in thinking he understood our situation. It sent a shiver up my spine.

"There's nothing for you to be worried about," Bartley said. "No one outside this room knows your true identity.

You'll be safe. We'll make sure of it and then you'll be sent back to continue your work with Max Alonzo."

"With Dr. Alonzo?" Genuine surprise on Ben's face. "You're kidding. So I'm going to work with him?"

Back in Altabena, Ben had hoped to head off for a two-week internship with the man. That seemed so long ago now.

"I believe so." Bartley nodded, then turned to me. "And, Nicola, for you the best is still to come."

Ben couldn't wipe the smile from his face. "Did you hear that? They think I'm some sort of lifesaver!"

I leaned close to him. "You need to keep your wits about you."

His eyes glittered with pride. "This feels so much more real now. Kind of weird, though. So strange to be honored for something I haven't done yet."

Surely he couldn't like this. Any of it. It must be a side-effect of the shock.

One of the butlers was behind Ben and Bartley, opening a bottle of champagne, something else I'd never seen in New Nation. I guess there were a lot of things I hadn't known existed here. The bottle slipped from the butler's hands, champagne soaking through the arm of Bartley's jacket.

There were gasps from around the table and apologies from the butler. Bartley reached for a napkin and blotted the liquid from his jacket.

"Nothing to worry about." He handed the wet napkin to the butler.

"I'm so, so sorry, sir," the man said.

Bartley reassured him and the butler left quietly only to be replaced by another who started moving around the table filling glasses. Bartley excused himself and stood. He was standing behind me when an official appeared out of nowhere.

"Get rid of him," Bartley said to the man.

"Sir?"

"The butler. Eliminate him."

My gut froze into a solid block but as I turned to Ben, I wasn't sure if he'd heard or not.

Carson slid over onto Bartley's seat. "Such an honor for you two to be talking to Harrison."

Ben nodded. "Yes."

Harrison… I would never dare refer to the Supreme Ruler by his first name.

I thought about the butler, how calm Bartley had been, how ordering an execution seemed mundane. I stared at the other officials at the table. Maybe they didn't want to know and maybe they didn't want to think they could end up the same way.

But I was more realistic. I had to find a way out of here and I needed information.

"Carson, you're not military," I said. Not in a million years. "What's your role here?"

He glanced at Bartley now on the other side of the table, then looked at me through lustrous lashes, his lips curling to a sultry smile. I couldn't believe it. We didn't do 'sultry' in New Nation.

"We all have our role to play," he said.

Ben's eyes widened. "So you two…?"

He reached for Ben's hand. "Let's just say I have an important supporting role."

"Okay," Ben said. "I didn't realize."

Solemn now, Carson said, "It stays in this room. It's

not public information."

It wasn't so much that homosexuality was frowned upon in New Nation, more that having feelings and emotions was a sign of weakness. Now it seemed Harrison Bartley was as 'weak' as the next man.

Our Supreme Ruler was the third Harrison Bartley to hold that position. It had been handed down from father to son through the decades, only now it appeared there wouldn't be another son.

Carson became more bubbly. "Harrison couldn't stop talking about you. He'd keep you here longer if he could."

That was the only positive thing about our situation – the fact Bartley recognized he had to send Ben back.

Carson kept babbling. "He has told me so much about the virus, how many people were killed, how our world changed and how important those events were for the government. There used to be seven or eight billion people in the world. Can you believe it?"

Ben's mouth fell open.

"Of course, this was all after your time," Carson said. "The population was shattered. We didn't have enough people and too many cities were left to go to rack and ruin. You've never seen any of this, have you?"

Ben shrugged. "How could I?"

Carson pulled up his sleeve and removed a PR device that hardened as soon as he pulled it off. "I'll show you."

He gave a voice command and tilted the device so Ben could see footage of abandoned cities, dilapidated buildings, trees growing in the streets.

Ben's face clouded over. "This is real, isn't it?"

"Absolutely, my dear friend." Carson's eyes were on his PR. "I can show you what else the virus did too."

Another voice command and footage appeared of bodies piled in streets, hospital corridors overflowing with patients, people sobbing. This was followed by a series of shots of people with deformities caused by the virus, bulbous heads, huge growths covering their bodies, babies born with missing limbs or extra appendages.

I'd told Ben about all of this but maybe it was different seeing it on the screen. I rubbed his shoulder, tried to console him.

Animated, Carson was on a roll. "Three generations ago we had the first Harrison Bartley. Word is that there was some sort of discontent, that the people weren't happy." He leaned closer. "I only know this because of my close relationship with Harrison. But everything changed when the virus swept through the country and then the rest of the world. People needed food, farmers to grow crops, clean drinking water and infrastructure to support them. So they stopped their silly complaints with the government and finally started to appreciate the fact that the first Harrison Bartley was going to take care of them. He gave them order and an organized society, food and water, all the things they needed."

Ben seemed too stunned to speak so I stepped in. "So the virus helped the government survive?"

"Absolutely," Carson said. "Without the virus, there'd be no New Nation, no Bartley government, no order. Harrison has told me as much himself." Carson cupped his mouth with one hand as if revealing a secret. "So you can see why he owes so much to you, Ben."

Ben's eyes were blank but he was concentrating as if trying to understand. I'd told him about the virus and how it consolidated Bartley's power. I guess it hadn't made sense then. How could it have seemed real when it was so far in the future for him?

"What's that got to do with me?" Ben asked.

"Naturally Harrison is excited to meet the man who created the virus. This means so much to him."

Ben's green eyes widened. *"That's* why he wants me here?"

Carson nodded, kept babbling.

I reached for Ben's hand and clasped it within my own. His hand was warm but his eyes, as he turned to me, were not. I couldn't blame Ben for something he hadn't done yet or for what Bartley had done. For one thing, I still didn't believe Ben created the virus as well as the cancer cure though, apparently, the two were linked.

Until now, I'd wanted to keep Ben safe. And myself too. But that wasn't enough, not nearly enough, not with the devastation that was coming with the virus, the devastation that paved the way for the Bartley government.

Now I'd come back to the future, I couldn't hide my head in the sand any longer. Before, I'd been stuck in Altabena and there was only so much I'd been able to do, but now I was in New Nation in 2120 and there were other things I could do, other possibilities. Time travel for one. If I could go back to the right time, maybe I could prevent some of these things from happening.

It wasn't enough to save Ben.

I had to stop the virus.

CHAPTER EIGHT

Ben held his hands out. "I'm not putting that poison into my system."

"You are mistaken." Nathan was standing with a glass of murky liquid in his hand, his expression as blank as ever. "Geopositrons are microscopic, man-made location devices, not poisonous or toxic in any way."

Ben stood, circled around Nathan. "No way. It's not happening."

The two of us had been told to wait in this room, part laboratory, part doctor's office. No one had mentioned who we were waiting for or what was supposed to be happening, only that we had to report here before receiving directions for a parade in my honor. Mine and Bartley's, of course.

Now this.

I stood between the two of them. "Ben's right."

"I have my orders," Nathan said.

"You don't understand." I didn't like being caught off guard. I needed time, a plan, a way out.

"I don't see what the problem is," Nathan said.

"Firstly, geopositrons are ingested orally, an easy process. This is a standard part of life here as you well know, Nicola. Besides, their presence will greatly facilitate the time travel process."

I wasn't quite sure about this. "But Ben managed to arrive here without them."

Nathan looked official in his formal uniform. We were in full uniform too, ready for the parade.

He was as matter-of-fact as ever. "I still don't have an explanation as to how that happened, though further research would no doubt provide the answer. If it was possible once, that would indicate it could be done again. Even so, I'm not sure I could replicate the process and certainly not with the required accuracy."

We glared at Nathan.

He added, "In layman's terms, the geopositrons will enable me to get a fix on Ben so I can transport him through time for his return home."

A clap of thunder made me glance toward the window. This was closely followed by another low rumble that sounded like a warning, then the sky gave way as it poured with rain. It was going to rain on my parade. Literally.

"Nicola…" Ben's voice quavered.

"Maybe he's right after all," I said. "It'll help you get back to Altabena."

As far as I could tell, Nathan's motivation was scientific and rational. I needed his help if we were to travel to another time so we could destroy the virus. It wasn't something I could do on my own, as much as I wished it was.

Ben shook his head. "There must be another way."

"There is," Nathan said, "but the likely result is that

your molecules would be scattered across the universe."

After what had happened in the past, it wasn't surprising Ben couldn't handle filling his body with geopositrons. I wasn't sure I could face it either but it seemed like the only way.

Ben held my gaze. "Nicola?"

I couldn't see a way out. "If you refuse now, the authorities will force this upon you by injection and there'll be nothing you can do about it. They won't let it pass. You don't have a choice, Ben."

He looked from me to Nathan, then dropped to a chair and held his hand out to Nathan who passed the glass to him. Ben's hand shook as he brought the glass to his lips, paused for a moment, then knocked back the contents in several long gulps.

As he wiped his mouth with the back of his hand, I wasn't sure if I was relieved or even more worried than before. What had I done? Was this the right decision? Damn it, I hated lowering him to my level and that of everyone else in New Nation when he shouldn't even be here at all.

There was a knock at the door and four soldiers appeared, ready to escort us. I was never going to get used to this, not after so long in Altabena. Taking Ben's arm, I helped him up.

"Where's Lucien?" I asked Nathan as we stepped out of the door.

"He's at the event already. Said he wasn't needed here."

The downpour had stopped by the time we walked the corridors of the military building and stepped outside. Ben walked in front of us, a soldier on ether side of him, the smell of damp concrete filling the air.

"You know that Lucien taught me everything I know?" I said to Nathan. "He was my teacher too."

He lifted his eyebrows as we walked. "There's very little that's of relevance to the scientific program that Lucien could teach me."

"You seem very faithful to him."

"Lucien has enabled me to do so many things here. My research into time travel wouldn't have been possible without his assistance."

"All you need now is more suckers like me to travel through time."

Nathan nodded. "It would indeed be useful to have more willing participants. I'm working on a new, experimental program that has much more flexibility than the current approach. I've said repeatedly to Lucien that these advances will take us to a new level."

The current time travel program was rigid, so if you traveled back in time and stayed away for two weeks, the same length of time would have passed in the future. I wondered if this could be changing.

"And what does Lucien say?" I asked.

"He is reluctant to give approval for the necessary trials. There's no logical explanation for this and it's quite frustrating."

I sidled closer to him, my voice low. "You don't always have to follow the rules so closely, Nathan. You need subjects to experiment with and I'm willing to time travel. It's not like I haven't done it before."

Surprise in his eyes. And thoughtfulness. Hopefully, I'd planted a seed in his mind.

We walked along C Dock past the masses waiting for

transportation until we reached the executive pod that had been ordered for us. The pod held surveillance equipment so that meant this conversation was over. For now.

I took a seat beside Ben. I wanted everything to be right and had no idea how to get there. Maybe that was why it felt like there was a concrete block in my gut.

Ben brushed his hand against mine, his touch reassuring and unnerving at the same time because he shouldn't be here.

After we arrived at the *Capitale*, we got out of the pod and into the ridiculous elevator with the waterfall. Ben shot me a knowing glance, as if to say "how tacky".

We were passed on to a different set of guards in formal uniforms who continued the tradition of giving us minimal information other than that we were to be part of the parade later on, which we already knew.

Eventually we stopped outside a door. One of the guards pushed it open, revealing a room with white walls, leather chairs and dark wood furnishings. Though this was much more ornate than even the best rooms at the military academy, it was a far cry from the palatial surroundings we'd been shown last night.

Two people stood at the other end of the room. My parents.

It took my breath away. I turned to stare at the guards. Couldn't they have told me this? Maybe given me some notice?

Two guards motioned for us to go ahead, following us into the room. Sensing my reluctance, Ben took my arm as we ambled toward the front.

My father – my biological father – took my hand into both of his to give it a good shake. The two of them were in formal, non-military, navy uniforms. I'd never seen them dressed like this and, besides, it had been a long time.

"We're so proud," my mother said as she, too, shook my hand while I stood there mute.

These people were strangers to me. I hadn't been raised by them, didn't look like them, wasn't even particularly well acquainted with them. I loved my parents in Altabena. Jan and Philip Gray were my parents in every way that mattered.

So why did I feel this strange niggling inside, this sense of loss and longing? I wasn't sure what I felt but in New Nation, I wasn't supposed to feel anything, and I had to remember that.

Ben shot me a sideways glance. "N-Nicola?"

"I'd like you to meet my parents," I said, pleased I could actually speak.

Surprise in his voice. "Your parents?"

I nodded. "Imelda and Marshall Brennan."

"Brennan?"

Surely he'd heard my name before, my New Nation name, though maybe it'd been too much to take in at the time.

"Your parents?" He frowned. "And you were shaking their hands?"

This must be hard for him to understand when at home he often had Celia clambering over him and I'd seen him bear hug his father enough times. So different from this.

"Yes," I said. "May I introduce Ben Tanner." No one said anything so I added, "A soldier. Like me."

My parents shook his hand while I desperately tried to think of something to say and enquired into their health. It ate away at me that these were my parents and this was the best I could come up with.

"You've been gone a long time," my mother said.

I nodded. "It feels like a hundred years."

"Have you heard about your brother?"

I barely knew him, hardly at all, in fact. We'd led separate lives at the academy but I also knew more about him than my parents did.

My mouth fell open and my face froze into place. Imelda must've taken that as a 'no' because she continued.

"He died in the line of duty. I'm sorry if this is a shock to you but I thought you should know."

That wasn't how he'd died at all. Still it was probably better this way, certainly easier for me because I had enough to deal with at the moment.

My throat tight, I swallowed. "I'm sorry, too."

If I wasn't mistaken, tears glittered in her eyes. "It's so good to see you, to know you're safe, to have you back. I can't tell you how much it means to us, especially after we've lost one child. He died for New Nation. Still, he died."

"Everything he did was for our great country," I said, spouting the party line.

She held my gaze. "Take care of yourself, Nicola. Nothing is more important to us than that."

Maybe I'd been wrong about my parents. Maybe they loved me in their own way. For all I knew, maybe they loved each other too.

My mother stepped closer to me, the closest I could ever remember her being. She nodded toward Ben and whispered, "He's...different."

"A bit shell-shocked," I said, "after his last tour of

duty."

Commotion from the front of the room made us turn as Bartley, in full military regalia, made his entrance. The bodyguards in black suits followed him, scanned the area and signaled to the other guards in the room before receiving a signal from Bartley and leaving. I'd bet he didn't spend a minute of his time without some sort of security staff.

"So pleased you could make it." He strode to the front of the room toward my parents.

Their mouths fell open as they extended their arms for handshakes.

"We're honored," my father said. "We certainly weren't expecting this."

"Nonsense." Bartley gave a little wave of his hand. "We're all friends here, all servants of New Nation and we all want what's best for our country. There's no need for formalities with me."

My father nodded. "How generous."

I remembered how 'generous' Bartley had been with the butler who'd spilt his drink.

"The pleasure is all mine," Bartley said. "We're honoring Nicola today and you've played a significant role in her life and the way she turned out. You were chosen to be breeders and you've done an excellent job."

My mother gestured toward me. "We gave the military academy our child and they gave us a fine young woman, an excellent soldier, a credit to New Nation."

"No, they gave you a hero." Bartley placed his hand on my shoulder which, I guessed, was meant to be an honor. "Because that's what she is. A hero."

There was a time I would have coveted an honor like

this. Not any more.

I smiled. Hoped my face didn't crack from the pressure. Because I had to play the game.

"You don't have to do anything special today," Bartley said to my parents. "Just stand to the rear during the ceremony."

Imelda pressed a hand to her chest. "You mean we're to stand on the podium with you?"

Bartley grinned, so natural in this role. "I wouldn't have it any other way. This is a big day for you too, something we should share."

She reached for my father's hand, making me wonder if there was something between them, some genuine affection.

"Such a great honor for us," my father said.

"For me too." Bartley was so charming he actually sounded like he meant it. "Now the guards will escort you to a waiting area and then lead you to the podium."

Beaming with pride, the Brennans left the room, making me wonder if they were my parents or if they were strangers. It was surprising how close the two things could be.

Bartley turned to Ben. "You'll have to stay in the background but I'm pleased to have you on the podium and then as part of the parade. For me, this is personal, very personal, and I want you to be part of it."

Ben nodded and I figured the less he said, the better.

I'd been to many of these parades, always as a spectator. Thousands of us would line the streets. Buildings would be decked out with the red, black and white banners of New Nation. The crowd would thrill to get a glimpse of our Supreme Ruler as he rode along the boulevards in an open-topped pod.

Which made me wonder whether that was safe. I'd seen ancient footage of JFK's assassination.

"Aren't you worried someone might try to shoot you?" I asked.

Bartley spread his hands. "My people love me."

"They do. We all do." I quickly corrected myself. "But what if there was some deranged person or an evil psychopath?"

"Nicola, you've been away a long time but don't worry, you'll get used to things here again in no time."

I nodded. I wasn't getting used to anything.

"I've learnt from past mistakes," he said, walking to the door. "I use a plithium cloak."

I'd heard of them. Their fabric was so fine it couldn't be seen by the naked eye, but the weave provided protection from bullets and lasers.

"They really exist?" I asked.

He nodded. "Only for specialized use. I'm always careful. Years ago, there was a serious assassination attempt on my grandfather's life, the first Harrison Bartley. A sniper took aim from the top of the Bryson Building. I believe it's still there. Needless to say, the man failed. Someone else spotted and shot him. That was before my time but it's a lesson I took into account."

"You mean the Bryson Building in Altabena?" I asked.

I knew the building because my dad – my Altabena dad – had once said they should never knock it down because it was a fine example of art deco.

"Of course you remember it. For you, that was not so long ago." He chuckled. "You're right. It was during a demonstration in your very own town." His eyes two warnings, he added, "We don't talk about demonstrations or discontent here, though."

I looked straight ahead. "Of course not."

If there was an assassination attempt on the first Bartley, it certainly hadn't happened during my time in Altabena. But if he was talking about demonstrations, it must be about to happen soon. Very soon. It was hardly surprising someone wanted to kill Bartley.

If only they'd succeeded, there would've been no more Bartleys and maybe democracy would have survived. But that's not the way things turned out.

We were led to the 'podium' as they called it, a large balcony at the front of the *Capitale* building designed for huge addresses like this one. Bartley was a born orator, giving an emphatic speech. I had to hand it to him. He loved the crowd and they loved him.

He motioned toward me. "This young woman embodies all the values of our great nation and everything we strive for. A hero of the people *for* the people."

I gritted my teeth. Every time I heard that word, it reminded me what a fake I was, and what would happen if I was found out. The applause was a shock to my system as I looked out at a sea of faithful faces. How many people were here? Thousands?

"I am pleased to present the Bartley Medal to the People's Hero," he said.

He pinned the medal to my jacket because, apparently, I was now the People's Hero.

Bartley finished with more meaningful words, his oratory receiving another round of roaring applause. This was his stage and these were his people and, unlike my television appearance, I wasn't being given a chance to speak.

I couldn't speak and had no clue what I'd say anyway. I didn't belong in New Nation, yet here I was. Ben was nearby, standing close to my so-called parents, and I was stuck in the middle of these worlds that were colliding.

When the ceremony finished, I turned to look at my parents. I felt something, not a connection, not love, but something. They were both beaming with pride, holding hands, which was more affection than I'd ever seen in New Nation. No one else seemed to notice as they released their grip.

I went straight to Ben. We were surrounded by noise and commotion, giving us a rare chance to talk without fear of our conversation being recorded.

Ben got in first, his eyes wide. "Are you sure you want to leave here? You're revered here. You're–"

How could he even be saying this? That was the last thing on my mind.

I put my hand out. "This is all a lie, Ben."

"But they don't know that." His eyes darted around. "Bartley doesn't know."

"I don't want the attention or the adulation."

Whereas Ben seemed to think that was a good thing. He wasn't thinking straight. The shock of our arrival must have got to him. I couldn't think of any other explanation.

"We have to get out of here," I said because he needed reminding. "Nathan's our best chance. Maybe our only chance."

Ahead of us, Nathan was walking by Lucien's side.

"Just tell me when," Ben said.

I only wished I could.

CHAPTER NINE

If there was one thing I liked about New Nation, this was it. And maybe it was only this one thing. Training.

Ben and I had been informed we were to be involved in some training exercises followed by shooting drills. We'd only just been told, of course, because we'd be *told* as soon as we needed to, and not before. Funny how there'd been a time I'd accepted this treatment. Now I resented it.

Lucien was leading us through the military compound, walking much slower than usual, presumably to have more time with us. We were headed for the training arena, a big gray concrete building that looked a lot like all the other big gray concrete buildings. The sun was peeking through the clouds, a good omen perhaps.

"Ben, you'll be sent home in due course," he said. "You know that, don't you?"

"That's good," Ben said, "but I'm not going back on my own. Not without Nicola."

Lucien slowed for some soldiers to pass. "It makes no difference what you want. They *will* send you back."

"So then how are you going to get Nicola back safely

too?"

"I don't know." Lucien added under his breath, "I don't know if I can. It would've been different if Bartley hadn't insisted on bringing you back, Nicola. If only you could've stayed."

The regret in his voice sounded genuine but I wasn't completely convinced. Besides, I wasn't going to stay here. I couldn't.

"There's always a way," I said.

"We've made so many mistakes already and nothing has gone to plan," he said.

"We?"

"I've made more than my share." Regret again.

"Maybe I have too. It's no reason to give up."

"I'm not talking about giving up, Nicola. I'm talking about trying to align with the current society, whether we like it or not, and with what's possible within the current infrastructure."

He wasn't going to throw me with his big words. This might be my only chance to talk openly with him.

"If we could go back in time and stop the virus being created, we could prevent Bartley's rise to power," I said. "It's an idea, a possibility."

Lucien pulled over to the side of the path. "In theory, perhaps, but that would be extremely complex. There are too many factors, too many people involved. This is exactly the sort of thing we should avoid."

"Ben's involved," I said. "He can help."

Lucien stepped closer, towering over me. "Ben created the virus. What are you going to do? Kill him? I'll give you the laser from my belt and you can do it now."

I held his gaze, stepped off so I was between him and

Ben. "That's not what I'm talking about and you know it."

He eased away. "Don't worry, Ben. I won't hurt you. That's the last thing I want."

I reached behind me for Ben. "And you know I'd never hurt him."

Lucien's eyes narrowed. "This is too dangerous, not just for you, but for society, for everyone. There could be dire consequences. We don't know what might happen."

My heart was racing. "You did it before. You and the two generals sent me back in time to eliminate Ben before he could create the virus or the cancer cure or anything else. Or have you forgotten already?"

"And I'm sorry I did it. Sorry I got involved. That was very wrong in so many ways."

Had he forgotten that the last time was here, he'd told me the reason he'd sent me back in time was for a new start? No wonder I didn't trust him, not completely, even if he was all I had.

Meanwhile, he was somehow making me feel like a hard ass because I was the one with these revolutionary ideas. Well, maybe that was what I needed to be.

"What's done is done." Fed up, I added, "We should head to the arena."

"Nicola, you don't have any choice. Bartley wants you here. You're a symbol of his success and he won't let you go. If you try to go back to Altabena, he'll send soldiers and scouts to find you. Even if you flush out your geopositrons, he'll still find a way. He won't give up."

All true. All things holding me back. And none of them was a reason to stay.

I'd die here if I stayed. Every day I would think about Ben and the people I loved in Altabena and every day a little piece of me would dissolve. I could pretend to be a soldier again, just like I could pretend to believe in New Nation, but I could never have an honest life here. I had felt too much with my heart to live the rest of my life as a lie.

"Maybe the best way to handle this is one day at a time," I said.

The old cliché did the trick, as Lucien led the way to the training arena.

The concrete entry to the building seemed familiar and reassuring. My heart rate was rising in a good way at the thought of training and sharing the one good part of this world with Ben.

Problem was, I couldn't throw my arms around him and hold him close the way I wanted to. That'd be all wrong here, so I hoped the warmth in my eyes as I looked at him would show how much I cared.

He leaned closer as we walked. "Was that what you were expecting from Lucien?"

I wasn't sure. "I'm not giving up. There's still Nathan."

We stood in the doorway of the arena, a roomful of soldiers in martial arts uniform gathered on the floor. A climbing wall took pride of place at the far end. There were two boxing rings, punching bags, climbing ropes and a weights area, everything a girl could want.

I breathed in the smell of stale bacteria that always lingered in these places and it all came back to me, the hours of training, the challenge, the success.

Lucien ushered me ahead. "A two-hour seminar. They're all yours."

I stopped in my tracks. "Excuse me?"

"You're presenting. You're their teacher for this

afternoon. Weren't you told?"

Even for New Nation, this was bad. They were throwing me in at the deep end, not because they were disorganized or because they didn't know. Not even because they were testing me. But simply because they could.

"Fine." I knew better than to disobey. "Ben, stay behind and hang to the side."

He did so. As I stood in front of a sea of expectant faces – expectant soldiers, no less – I told myself it could've been worse. There could've been a bigger crowd. I could have to teach them macramé or something I knew nothing about. Or I could be in my pajamas.

I tuned out during Lucien's introduction because I didn't want to hear it and I had to think about how I was going to manage a hundred eager soldiers for two hours. What on earth would I teach them?

I wasn't a hero. I was an anti-hero.

"Thank you," I said to Lucien and watched him leave. I looked at my audience, silent, obedient, waiting. I paced to one side of the room, then the other, hoping for a miracle.

I looked out at the sea of soldiers. "If you're waiting for words of wisdom, I don't have any. If you're after stories of valor and savior, I have none of those either. If you want inspiration, you'll have to find it from within. Training is everything. Sometimes it's all you've got. This is training, so we're going to train. Time to fight."

I split them up into two groups, those who were experienced in groundwork and wrestling, and those who preferred kickboxing and stand-up. Ben was a gun at Brazilian Ju Jitsu so he headed for the wrestlers, but I motioned for him to stop.

"I need two leaders to manage the training," I said. A couple of hands shot up from each side of the room and I asked those people to come to the front. "We're swapping it around. Wrestlers, you're training stand-up fighting today. Kickboxers, you're doing groundwork. This is about being uncomfortable. If you're not good at one aspect of your training, the only way to get better is to work at it. And that's what we're going to do. Go!"

These were soldiers, all well trained, and I didn't need to ask them twice. As soon as they got started, I joined Ben at one side of the room.

"Impressive," he said. "You really know what you're doing."

I shook my head. "You think so?"

I was in over my head though I may have been treading water. For now. I had to get through this and make it to the shooting session. That was the part I was looking forward to.

Ben helped me out when it came to giving the wrestlers some drills and tips. Maybe I should've followed my own advice and spent more time on my ground game, but I much preferred fighting stand up so I headed to that side of the room as soon as I could.

I started off easy to check their skill level first but that didn't last long and soon I had them smashing the pads. I suggested some technical aspects for them to work on with their punches and kicks because I believed in intelligent training. Intelligent smashing was always the way to go.

One thing led to another and I gave them some drills using elbows and knees, two of my favorite weapons. Hell, everything was my favorite weapon. I hammered them.

Couldn't help it because 'hard' was the only way I knew how to train. We pushed each other around a bit, did some footwork and movement, then an idea came to me.

I set the guys up with some clinch work and chokes, and separated the girls for a slightly different session. They gathered around me.

I motioned to the males and to Ben standing beside me. "They're always going to be bigger than you, more muscular, more powerful. Nothing you can do about that, but remember, there's *always* something you can do. If you're attacked, there's absolutely no reason you have to play fair."

Expectant faces around me. These young women were so obedient and had probably never even thought about breaking the rules.

"Soft targets," I said. "Go for the eyes, throat and groin."

"But guys will always be expecting a strike to the groin," Ben said.

I used Ben as my target, shadowing the moves. "Eye gouge. Strike to the throat. *Then* go for the groin. The guy will be in so much pain by then that he won't be protecting his crotch."

A wide-eyed young soldier put up her hand. "But that's not a fair fight."

"What's your name?" I asked.

"Ash."

"Is it fair that they're bigger than you to start with, Ash? Is that a level playing field? Is it fair that someone attacks you?" I shook my head. "Get in first. Do whatever you have to do. And get out of there."

We ran through some drills because talking about this

was one thing and training it in was another. I hoped these tips might help these women one day, and I was enjoying helping them.

No point kidding myself. I also liked the rush that came with training and martial arts. I was strong and powerful and I could do this. Whatever it took.

It struck me that maybe this surprise two-hour teaching session wasn't such a bad thing after all.

At the end of the drills, Ash came up to me. "Aren't you going to teach the same things to the boys?"

I glanced across at the group of big guys, all jostling with one another. "That's their problem."

She laughed. Maybe she got it after all. Maybe I'd made a difference.

The session over, I stood at the front of the group who were once again sitting obediently in front of me, only now they were much sweatier than before. I was supposed to say something meaningful.

I paced because I seemed to be good at that. "I can teach you martial arts. I can't teach you 'life'. Life is something you have to find out for yourself. Trust yourself. Trust your gut."

A moment's silence. I wondered if I'd gone too far. Then, an enormous round of applause, excitement in the faces of the soldiers as they considered what I was saying. No one had ever told them to trust their instincts, not in this place, just as I'd never been told either.

They'd only ever been told to trust their superior officers; trust New Nation; trust Supreme Ruler Bartley; revere Supreme Ruler Bartley; put him on a pedestal. These guys were soldiers and warriors, extremely well trained – to believe they were nothing without New

Nation.

Maybe I should take my own advice and trust my gut more.

It was the only thing that was going to get me through this and out of here.

CHAPTER TEN

My day was getting better. How long had it been since I'd shot a rifle?

We'd just been to the pistol range which Ben said looked like something out of a movie. He was right. Concrete floor, black walls, rows of soldiers pointing guns, targets lined up at the other end – some things had barely changed in the last hundred years.

After a short session there, we'd moved to the outdoor shooting range for long distance and sniper training. This was what I'd been waiting for. I loved the challenge of distance shooting, the small target, the discipline required.

I loaded the cartridge into the rifle as I stood by the firing line.

Ben was beside me. "That looks a lot like an AR-15."

"You're close. It's an AR-19. Do you want to see what it feels like?"

I passed it to him. He lifted it up, kept the nozzle pointing down range, but he'd already said he'd had enough shooting for one day. Ben wasn't a military man, far from it.

As he handed the rifle back to me, I said, "The AR-19 isn't that different from its predecessors. There have been slight refinements to the design but no major changes because there was no need."

Ben pointed to the soldiers lined up to my right. "What are they using?"

"Laser rifles," I said. "New technology. They're lighter and barely make a sound which can be a benefit in a combat situation. There's also no ricochet."

"Then why doesn't everyone use them?"

"They're not better. Just different. We still haven't found anything that supersedes old-fashioned guns when it comes to efficiency."

I used the computer panel at my station to set up the first target for 100 meters, or 109 yards in imperial measurement.

It all came back to me as I took aim. My pulse was rising so I took deep, slow breaths to calm myself. I liked staring at the target, the weight of the rifle, the way it felt.

As I squeezed the trigger, I got off on the cracking sound of gunfire and the kickback too. I kept concentrating because this wasn't a game. Nine more shots, then I took a rest.

I turned to Ben. "How am I doing?"

The computer screen had a close-up of the target with statistical information below it, however this was a case where a picture told a thousand words.

"Every shot was a bulls-eye," he said. "I don't believe it. You didn't just hit the target. You hit the middle every time. How did you do it?"

"Practice. I've got a steady hand and a good eye, but I wouldn't have got anywhere without lots of practice.

Training is everything." I'd been a soldier for a long time before I arrived in Altabena. There was something else I'd never mentioned to him. "I wasn't the top student at the academy for nothing, you know."

Ben nodded. "I always knew you were good. Guess I didn't know how good."

"This'll be the real test."

I pressed the numbers into the computer to adjust the target. The 100 meter target dropped down and, further back, the 250 meter target sprung up.

I got down on one knee, my preferred position for the longer range shots, because I felt more stable with a lower center of gravity. My heart rate was rising, my brow beading with perspiration.

It flashed before my eyes, my one act of heroism, the day I acted to save a room full of schoolchildren at the mercy of two crazed gunmen. It hadn't felt like heroism. At the time, it had simply been what I had to do. Two shots. Two men down. To save innocent lives.

Afterwards the magnitude had hit me. While it was happening, I'd had no chance to think, but I had plenty of time afterwards. Too much. I didn't like living with the fact I'd killed two men and hadn't coped well psychologically, something I couldn't admit to anyone because I was a soldier.

I'd have made exactly the same choices if I'd been thrown into that same situation again, and knowing I'd made the right decision helped. It didn't make it easy though. Didn't get rid of the guilt completely. Or the nightmares.

My pulse was rising, my heart rate going crazy. And I wasn't even in a combat situation. I couldn't shoot while I was in this state, couldn't do anything, so I took slow breaths until I had my body in check.

When I was shooting, I had to be aware of everything. It wasn't enough to be aware of my target, what was behind and around that, of any movement. I had to be aware of myself too and how my heartbeat was influencing my aim.

Control – that was the name of the game. I had control of my breathing and now I had to take responsibility for my trigger pull. I was in the zone so I fired. When I was ready, I fired again. Then again. Only when I was ready. Only when I knew I had it.

I stopped before I was exhausted. It was no good to keep going and compromise my shooting.

As I stood and turned, I saw Nathan was there with Ben, which made me think maybe I should be aware of what was going on behind me too. Or maybe that wasn't possible.

Ben pointed to the computer screen. "Nicola, you hit the target very time. At this distance, that's amazing."

Nathan nodded, his expression somber. "It is indeed remarkable."

"Were you ever a sniper?" Ben's voice was low.

"No," I said. "I got out of it."

Though I didn't say more, I hoped he understood. Snipers were trained to shoot people whereas I wanted to shoot targets, not human beings, despite everything I'd been taught in the military.

Ben motioned toward some other soldiers. "I'm starting to get it now. I look around and I can see where you came from, the training, the treatment, what you went through." He glanced down at the computer. "I'm still amazed."

"Hmmm." I looked at the screen. He was right but I'd hit the bulls eye only once. There was always room for improvement.

Ben put a hand on my shoulder. "I know what you're thinking, Nic. This is success. Make the most of it."

Success... I had to succeed, and the one person who could help was standing right here. "Nathan, I didn't think this was the sort of action you were interested in."

He straightened. "On the contrary, scientific 'action' covers a plethora of items."

"Really?"

"I've been active in many areas. My work has been instrumental in several fields including arms creation, atomic explosives—"

That got my attention. "You're talking about molecular bombs, aren't you?"

"Of course. I made significant advances in the destructive capacity of the explosives in reducing targets to the smallest particles. Since then, I've been working on remote timing mechanisms."

My mind was racing. He'd been working for generals Tan and Willis. Had he created the molecular bomb that blew up the school? Did I even want to know?

I had to focus. "And now you've come here. To the range?"

"That is correct. I was curious."

He was more than curious. He'd come here for a reason, hopefully because I'd planted a seed in his mind and he'd been thinking about what I said.

"How's your latest research going?" I asked. "Into the time travel program, that is."

He picked up where we'd left off last time in discussing the rigidity of the time travel program, only this time the facts seemed to be sinking in for Ben.

He reached for my hand. "So if we're here for a few days, that same number of days will have passed in Altabena?" His eyes widened. "Time is passing and my family doesn't know where I am?"

I nodded, my heart going out to him. The last thing Ben wanted to do was upset his dad and Celia.

"That's not necessarily true any more," Nathan said. "I've been working on enhancements that may alter this radically. I believe it's possible to send people back to any coordinate in time and return them to any coordinate of my choice."

This was what Nathan had been talking about to me before. It was why he was here now. Because government authorities were holding him back and wouldn't let him complete his experiments to confirm his findings.

"We can help you," I said. "You need subjects to travel back in time and we're willing. Help me and I'll help you."

Silence.

"Your work is important, Nathan. It could lead to great things, but you need to test it out or none of this will happen. How long will they keep you waiting?"

"I don't know," he said.

"Has anyone even explained why they *don't* want you enhancing the time travel program?"

"No."

Because it was the New Nation way to keep people in the dark and withhold information.

I said, "The government wouldn't have let you

experiment with time travel in the first place either. You know that, don't you? It wasn't government officials who allowed you to do that. It was generals Tan and Will who gave the go-ahead and that's because they were working against the government."

Nathan was weakening. I could see it, not in his eyes because they never gave anything away, but in the slight slump of his shoulders.

He was an expert, a leader in his field, a scientific genius being held back by bureaucracy. Surely he wanted this as much as we did. He had to. Or all his work would've been for nothing. I was banking on it.

"How confident are you that your program will work?" I asked.

"Very."

"Then send us back," I said. "When we're done, you can return us to New Nation, back to a time that's only minutes after we left. No one will know we were gone or what you did. This is your big chance to verify whether your program works."

"An interesting proposition."

"Nathan, you've been working on this for years. This might be your *only* chance."

He paused. Thinking. "You're not interested in scientific breakthroughs, so what's your motivation?"

Nothing to lose. "We want to go back to just before the virus broke out."

"Why?"

"So we can find out more about how the virus was created. Who knows? We may even be able to stop it."

"You wish to return to Altabena in 2041?"

"Not quite. We want to go back to the place Ben was

doing his medical research."

"Nicola, surely you're aware that information is not available. I believe you did a stellar job of covering your tracks and also Ben's. At least that's what I was told."

"I know where." Ben had been silent for so long that the sound of his voice surprised me. "Take us back to Dr. Alonzo's research facility outside San Francisco. That's where I would've been."

"Are you sure?" I asked.

"As sure as I can be." Ben turned to me. "Are we going to need anything else?"

There were a lot of things we needed – a better plan for one. Instead I said to Nathan, "Clothes would be good."

"I can arrange for their transportation immediately after your arrival." He stepped back, held his hand out and I hoped he wasn't changing his mind. "I mean, I'll have to give this serious consideration and think about the possible repercussions. If we're to go ahead, there are arrangements to be made."

If...

"I'll be in touch," he said.

I didn't like the lack of certainty. I was used to doing things with great precision. Instead it was time to trust my gut.

CHAPTER ELEVEN

"If we're going to do this, Nic, then let's go." Ben strode down the corridor at my side.

Nathan had made his decision. He was going to help. We were going to do this, so Ben and I were on our way to the transportation room to meet him. We'd already discussed our destination and the exact timing of our visit and return.

If we succeeded we'd be back in New Nation so soon that no one would know we'd been gone. Or we might not succeed. Something else might happen, something we couldn't predict.

Ben hadn't wanted to go back to Altabena on his own straight after we first got here, but now he was willing to travel to a different time and place with me, more than willing, judging by his walking pace. And I was glad to have him at my side because I couldn't do this on my own.

Nathan was waiting in the transportation room to let us in. The door opened and I stepped in, my eyes riveted to the center of the room.

It came back to me, the first time I'd sat in that chair,

my trepidation when Lucien had left me alone as I was leaving on my mission, my resolve to do whatever was best for New Nation. I was a different person then.

Time travel had given me so much – Ben, family, friends, freedom and all the other benefits of living in Altabena. My life had become so much richer. Then time travel had taken that away from me and brought me back here.

It was also the only thing that could get me and Ben back to Altabena where we belonged.

Nathan shook my hand, then Ben's. "At least now you can see the need for your geopositrons. I couldn't successfully complete the transportation without them. The process would be much more dangerous."

Which made me wonder whether he had been under instruction from his superiors to inject Ben with geopositrons or if he'd been planning this himself all along. I'd thought Nathan was transparent rather than manipulative, but perhaps he was cleverer than I'd given him credit for.

"Take a seat," he said.

Ben sat down first and I wedged myself in beside him, half-sitting in his knee. This was the way we'd arrived and it'd be the way we would leave too.

"Good luck." Nathan turned toward the door.

"No final instructions?" I asked.

"No."

I guess he wasn't the type for a motivational send-off. Nathan left the room to go to the control panel behind the two-way mirror. Though we couldn't see him, he had his eyes on us. For now, that was, until the transportation worked. Then we'd disappear.

It was time.

The light was blinding, the pain too, so I pressed my eyes shut. Seconds ago, my arms had been wrapped around Ben but now I didn't know where he was any more. Or where I was. I'd lost my sense of body positioning. Had no idea where my limbs were.

I opened my eyes into slits but the light was no longer bright. Quite the opposite. There was a moaning sound. So close. I felt a body writhing beside mine, a warm body, and saw Ben had his hands wrapped around his head.

Sitting up, I placed a hand on his bare shoulder. "Ben?"

He stretched out on his side. "My head…is killing me."

"It'll pass soon," I said quietly.

I gave him a few moments while I tried to get oriented. We were on the floor in what appeared to be a bedroom. If only we'd landed on the bed on the other side of the room, we might have had a softer landing.

The room felt familiar and strange at the same time. The furniture was different, giving the feel of a guest room rather than a bedroom but this was the same room, my bedroom. I was sure of it. The window and built-in closet were in the same place and the room had exactly the same proportions.

Ben sat up, his head in his hands.

"Are you okay?" I asked.

"Better. Where are we?"

I stood up. "Nathan has made a mistake. This is my bedroom."

His head stayed down. "It could be worse. At least you'll have clothes."

I opened the closet door. Two guitar cases took up most of the hanging space and the shelves to the left held an assortment of things from blankets and sheets to a toaster and kettle and a box labeled Lego. This looked like somewhere people stored their old stuff, perhaps the spare room, but who were these people? If this was my home, someone else was living here in 2041.

Ben looked around. "You sure this is your room?"

I nodded. "I can feel it. Something's wrong, though."

He glanced around, disoriented.

"You're right about one thing," I said. "We need to find some clothes."

Kneeling beside Ben, I wrapped my arms around him for a hug. Though we were both naked, this was the least sexy situation I'd ever been in. I checked my arm and hip, the usual places I kept my PR device. Nothing. I groped the floor around us in the hope Nathan had transported a device so we could communicate with him. No such luck. We were on our own.

Swallowing back my nerves, I told Ben my theory about our landing and suggested we move carefully while we checked out the rest of the house and searched for something to wear.

We made it to the master bedroom. The bed was in the same place as when my parents were here, only my mom would never have chosen the elaborate, carved bedhead or the peacock feather bedspread. The bed had been slept in. A light on a bedside clock flashed 1.15am.

"Even if my parents don't live here any more," I whispered, "where are these people? Out clubbing?"

"I don't think so." Ben picked up a framed photo from the nightstand and showed it to me. A silver-haired couple looked to camera, both of them beaming. Definitely not my parents, no matter how many years may have passed.

He opened the closet door, then shifted over to make room for me. "That looks like the lady's side."

The floaty dresses hanging in the closet were indeed far too ladylike for me. Ben was still searching his side of the closet while I found a pair of three-quarter pants and a floral top, the best I could do. Floral would not have been my first choice but it seemed the owner of these clothes didn't own anything plain. Underwear would've been nice too but I didn't want to rifle through an old woman's lingerie drawer. For one thing, it might be even scarier than her closet.

I slipped on the clothes which weren't such a bad fit and also found a pair of Birkenstock sandals among the pile of sensible footwear at the bottom of the closet. Not so bad. Better than being naked, anyway.

Ben wasn't having much luck. He was wearing a checked shirt and had found a pair of black trousers that were way too big and kept slipping down his thighs.

He threw his hands up. "Doesn't the guy have any belts?"

I chose a pair of suspenders from the selection hanging inside the closet door. "Nope. These will have to do."

"You've got to be kidding?"

"I'm wearing a floral top. Do I look like I'm kidding?"

I attached the suspenders at the back of Ben's pants and passed the straps over his shoulders. He clipped them on while I searched for a pair of men's shoes. I was getting worried because all I could find were Velcro-strapped sneakers, sensible walking shoes and leather loafers when I spotted a pair of Converse at the bottom of the pile. They must've been there by mistake. Perhaps a present from a relative who didn't know the man's taste.

We headed for the door. I held it open for Ben.

"Ladies first." Perhaps the sneakers had made him happy because he was smiling, even if it was a little grimly.

I stepped through the door even though I hated being a lady, then stopped and put a finger to my lips. Strange sounds carried from downstairs, that of shuffling or footsteps and whimpering. Yes, that was definitely whimpering.

A big thwack rang through the air followed by a yell of pain. A fist on flesh. The sound wasn't like in the movies, not as loud, and with a squelching that sent a shudder up my spine.

Ben reached for my hand, leaned in close. I held back the anxiety simmering in my stomach.

"Might be a burglary," I said quietly. If that was the case, we had one big advantage over a burglar. We knew the house. "We'll move in slowly, survey the situation first."

He nodded.

We padded down the stairs and peered into the living room. A burgundy velveteen sofa was in the same place my parents had placed ours when we lived here. The coffee table had been pushed over. One lamp had been knocked over and another had been switched on.

From here we could see the light was on in the kitchen, but not the people who were there. As soon as we walked into the living room, those people would be able to see us. A risk we had to take.

We were close now, close enough to hear what was going on.

"Where's the safe, old man?"

"We don't have one."

More sounds of punching, kicking, someone being beaten. Another person trying to call out, the scream getting stuck in the person's throat.

This was our big chance. A distraction. *Now.* Ben and I stepped into the living room where we had a good view. An old woman in patterned pajamas was gagged and tied to a chair in the kitchen, my kitchen, the same place I would eat meals with my parents.

I saw red, anger bubbling in my stomach. Took a breath. Waited.

Cable ties lay on the kitchen table. A man in black had his back to us, a knife blade glinting in his hand. An old guy, also in pajamas, was curled into a ball at the man's feet as he kicked him in the side, making him yell in pain.

"Go around the back," I whispered to Ben. "The kitchen door."

We couldn't walk off and leave these people like this, no way. He nodded and left while I crept forward. If the man in black turned, he'd see me. Simple as that. He had a knife. Not so simple.

He kicked the old guy again. The woman glanced up at me. She must've seen movement. I put a finger to my lips, then pointed to her husband and her attacker. She got the message.

She was gagged and couldn't yell but she kept her eyes on the man in black, struggled against her bindings, moaned as much as she could through the gag and rocked on the chair to make some noise. A distraction.

I was close now. So close.

The man in black kicked the old guy again. *No you don't.* I slammed my fist into the side of the attacker's face. He didn't know what hit him. I was good at distracting too.

He was bent over, reeling, but not unconscious. No time to think. I wrapped my arm around his neck from behind, secured my hold using my own shoulder, and pressed his head down into the bent V of my arm so he was choking.

I had to be quick. He still had the knife. I dragged him back so he didn't have his footing, kept him moving. I had the choke and I squeezed. He was big. I couldn't let him get one up on me.

Suddenly limp in my arms, his knees buckled. I held on as he crumpled to the floor, taking me with him. He was out. Unconscious, not dead.

I scuttled back, my instinct to get away from him. My eyes were on the floor, looking for the knife that must've slipped from his hands.

The kitchen door flew open. Ben looked around, saw I was okay and went to help the old lady. Meanwhile the old man got up and staggered in my direction. He'd seen what I hadn't and picked up the knife. He was heading straight for his attacker.

I stood, put my hand out. "No, you don't want to do that."

The attacker was out. For now. There was a big difference between unconscious and dead, and I didn't want this poor fellow to live with another man's blood on his hands. Right now it might seem like a good idea but it wouldn't make him feel better and it wouldn't be justice. It wouldn't be self-defense either.

His mouth gaping, shaking with fear, the old guy stepped back and dropped the knife. I picked it up carefully, placed it on the kitchen table and grabbed the cable ties the burglar had no doubt brought with him. He was still out, so I rolled him over and tied his hands behind his back, then his feet.

In the kitchen, Ben had found a knife and was untying the old woman. The old guy looked across at his wife. His eyes brimming with tears, he padded across, collapsed to his knees and took her in his arms.

They stayed like that, sobbing and shaking in each others' arms while Ben and I looked on, not wishing to interrupt.

Eventually the old woman broke off the embrace and looked up. "Where did you come from? How did you know?"

"We didn't," I said.

"Why are you wearing my clothes?"

I stepped closer to Ben. "We've got to get out of here."

The woman shook her head. "It's okay. I don't care about the clothes. You saved our lives…"

The old man was muttering something I couldn't quite make out.

"You should've just given him the combination," the woman said to him.

"I was going to, but…" He broke off, sobbing again. "…but I couldn't speak."

She wrapped one arm around him. "You silly old thing."

A burglary turned bad, very bad. What were the

chances we'd be transported to this exact time and place? It was lucky for this couple.

Despite everything, I was glad we'd been here to help. The injustice of it ate away at me. Two old people attacked, and for what? Money? Valuables in a safe? These were human lives we were talking about, and these poor people wouldn't get over this in a hurry. They'd be shattered by what had happened.

"Thank you," the woman said. "How can we ever thank you?"

"What's the date?" I asked

She told me.

"The year?"

She gave me a strange look. "2007."

I clapped a hand over my mouth. Nathan was supposed to send us back to the future. Instead he'd sent us to the past to a time before I'd arrived in Altabena, before my parents had arrived too. These must be the people who'd lived here before my family.

Panic ripped through me, my heart racing, my breaths coming short and fast. If that had been a miscalculation, what else would go wrong? Would we be able to get out of here?

Ben grabbed my arm. "We've got to go, Nicola."

He was right. I was glad one of us was thinking straight.

The old guy said, "Don't leave. We have got to call the police. You can tell them what happened."

The last thing we needed was the police after us when we couldn't explain who we were or what we were doing here.

Ben looked down at his checked shirt. "Shit, they'll

spot us in an instant in these outfits."

"No, they won't," the woman said. "You don't want to be found?"

I nodded.

"Then you were never here." She turned to her husband. "Gerald, you fought the man off on your own. No one else needs to know. You're my hero anyway. You know that, don't you?"

Gerald was shaking, his mouth open, unable to speak. The woman was shaken too but there was no mistaking the love in her eyes.

Ben pulled me back.

"Wait." The woman stood. "You can't go like this. Do you need anything? Money? Drink? Food?"

She must've seen the look in my face because she reached into the fridge for two bottles of water and a package wrapped in foil that she shoved into our hands.

"Roast chicken," she explained.

"Call the police after we've left," I said. "Paramedics too."

The woman nodded. "Thank you. I can't thank you enough, both of you."

As we left, an image was imprinted on my mind. An old woman standing in pale patterned pajamas in her kitchen which would one day be my kitchen, her husband still kneeling by the chair. Stranger things had probably happened but I couldn't think of any of them now.

Ben held my hand, leading me down the street. I was glad he had direction because I felt lost. "Where are we going?"

"The Wilsons' cubby house," he said.

"Who are the Wilsons?" I asked as we rushed off.

"They moved out before you came to Altabena but I used to play at their place."

"Play?"

"You know, when I was little. That's what kids do. They play. The Wilsons have a cubby, a big one. We'll be safe there."

After we reached the house, Ben led me down a side path to the cubby at the rear, ushering me ahead of him.

I stepped through the door. "I thought you said this was big."

Ben squeezed in behind me, looked around. "It was when I was a kid."

"It's okay," I said. "We can snuggle."

A built-in bench that ran along one wall was covered in cushioned seating and rugs. A toy truck, plastic buckets and other assorted paraphernalia was scattered around the room. I made some space and settled onto the floor, pulling down a few cushions and blankets to make a bed so we had somewhere to spend the night.

I lay down, desperate to feel safe, but we weren't. We shouldn't even be here. My insides were shaking, my head spinning, while on the outside I tried to hold it together.

So many things felt wrong but when Ben wrapped his arms around me, it felt right. He pressed his lips against mine, gently at first, then passionately. I was desperate to get close to him too, to have things back the way they were, to be where we belonged.

His hand was on my waist. He didn't let it wander. Not so long ago, sex was on his mind all the time. On mine too. But this wasn't the time.

Eventually, he pulled back. "What do we do now, Nic?"

I forced myself to sound calm. "Wait for Nathan to get a fix and transport us back. He said the program was experimental."

"Do you have any way of communicating with him?" he asked.

"No."

"What if we're stuck here?"

"We won't be," I said with mock confidence.

He pressed another kiss to my lips. "At least we've got each other."

"We'll work something out. Nathan will find us."

And perhaps if I kept saying that, I'd convince myself.

"I know exactly what we can have for breakfast," Ben said.

"What?"

"Roast chicken."

"Delicious."

His expression serious, he held my gaze. "There's something else. If this is 2007, my mom is still alive."

My heart went out to him. "Oh, Ben."

"I have to see her," he said.

He'd lived with this loss since he was twelve years old. Suddenly it made sense – his composure when we were leaving the old couple, his determination to find a safe place for the night, the fact he wasn't shaking with fear at our situation. As soon as he found out what year this was, he must've known, must've felt it in his heart.

I'd put him through so much that I had to help with this. It was the least I could do.

CHAPTER TWELVE

At least when I first arrived in Altabena, I'd had no idea how out of place I looked. I'd worn the school uniform, only I had it all wrong with a long skirt, my shirt tucked in and boring black school shoes.

Whereas now I knew exactly how dorky I looked.

Ben and I were walking through suburban Altabena. I was dressed like an old woman in three-quarter pants and a floral blouse while Ben was resplendent in a checked shirt, over-sized pants and the *piece de resistance*, suspenders to hold them up. We were taking nerdy to new levels.

He took my hand into his as we stopped outside his house, which looked pretty much the same, except the trees were smaller and the garden beds held different plants. A strange sense of *déjà vu* overcame me. The streets we'd walked along had been like this too – the same but different – only this was personal. It was Ben's house with Ben's family in it.

"What are we going to do?" I asked. "Knock on the door?"

His gaze was riveted to his old home. "Why not?" He

squeezed my hand. "I have to see her, Nic. I have to do this."

His father would be at work. In 2007, Ben was seven years old so he'd be at school, as would his older brother Josh. His little sister, Celia wasn't even born yet so if all went well, his mother should be alone. So far, not much was going well.

"Won't she recognize you?" I asked. "That'll freak her out."

"How? She doesn't know what I'm going to end up looking like. She hasn't seen photos of me in the future."

Ben strode to the door and rang the bell. Apparently he wasn't fazed by looking like a senior-citizen-country-bumpkin-gone-wrong. No, that wasn't the part that bothered him, but he was anxious, standing ram-rod straight, his shoulders stiff.

A woman pulled open the door and smiled. Green eyes sparkled at us, eyes that were the same as Ben's, that could be filled with emotion but didn't have even a glimmer of recognition in them now. It tugged at my heart, and I could only imagine what it was doing to Ben.

Still, she looked exactly like the pictures I'd seen. Her clothes were simple, a tee shirt and jeans. No make-up, no pretensions.

"Hello," she said.

Ben's mouth fell open, his shoulders slumped as he stared, longing in his eyes.

"Hi," I said in my brightest voice.

"H-hello," he said.

His mom kept up the smile. "How can I help you?"

I nudged Ben.

He straightened. "We're staying with the Hendersons,

Bob and Jo. I-I'm their nephew, Ben." She looked at me expectantly so he added, "And this is Nicola."

"Lovely to meet you both." She didn't budge from the doorway.

Ben let out a long sigh. "It's so good to see you…to meet you too, I mean."

Not surprisingly, his mom gave him a strange look. I would've stepped in if I could think of anything to save the day, but my mind went blank as I glanced at Ben. He wanted to stay and drink her in.

"Not many young men have their hair so short," she said to him. "Are you in the army or something?"

"No, not the army," he said. "We're here on vacation. We'd like to make ourselves useful. You know, if there's anything you need done around the house. Any odd jobs."

"And you're Bob and Jo's nephew?"

He nodded, looking rather like an eager puppy. "So, are there any jobs you *don't* like doing? We can take care of them for you."

She looked at me, then Ben. "Actually, I *hate* cleaning the windows."

Ben spread his arms. "That's fantastic! I mean, sure, we can do windows. Can't we, Nicola?"

"Absolutely," I said, thinking it was good that at least one of us could speak like a normal person.

She stepped aside, pulling the door open for us. "The windows at the back of the house need doing. I'll pay you of course."

Ben swatted his hand. "No, you don't have to."

Closing the door behind us, she looked us up and down. "Look, if you don't mind me asking, what's with the get-ups?"

"The get-ups?" he said.

I jumped in. "It was a dare."

She raised her eyebrows. "A dare?"

Ben nodded vigorously. "Yep, only a few more hours and we get back into our normal clothes."

She shook his hand, didn't look particularly convinced. "I'm Heather. Sorry, I should have said."

"H-Heather," Ben spluttered. "I should call you Heather?"

"Well, yes, that's my name."

I grabbed Ben's arm. "Come on, we have windows to wash."

His mom led us down the hall, explaining how she often worked from home, then added, "You won't believe this. I have a son called Ben."

"Oh, I'd believe it," he said.

She glanced across. "Pardon?"

"Good choice of name, that's all."

We stood in the doorway leading to the living room which felt as comfortable as I remembered it, yet something felt odd. Ben's mom was working from home but there was Lego on the table, along with a couple of milk-stained plastic glasses, and cartoons were playing on the television.

Two heads bobbed up from the other side of the sofa, two cute little boys staring at us. That was the same Ben I'd seen in old family photos and the bigger boy had to be Josh. Heather made the introductions, and Ben seemed to be back to the blubbering mess he'd been at the door.

"Hi guys," I said to the kids while nudging Ben.

"Ben, look at you..." he said.

Seven-year-old Ben did exactly that, staring back with

those familiar green eyes. His hair was much lighter then, wavier too, his cheeks chubbier.

"Let's shake hands, little fella."

The boy stretched out his skinny arm for a handshake, then watched intently as Ben shook Josh's hand too.

"They're home from school, sick with colds." Heather shook her head. "I'm not getting a lot of work done today."

Ben did the puppy dog thing again as he stared at his younger self. "You're not well. I'm sorry to hear that."

"They'll survive," Heather said. "As long as they don't end up killing each other. They've been at it all morning."

Ben nodded. "I bet."

He didn't seem to notice the querying look his mother gave him, so I said, "We should make a start on the windows."

"Windows. Oh yeah, the windows."

He took a step in the direction of the laundry but I stopped him. "Heather, perhaps you could show us where the cleaning things are."

"Wait here," she said. "I'll be right back."

Josh went back to watching the television and young Ben got back to staring at big Ben. Was it possible the boy could sense something?

Heather came back with a bucket, a couple of squeegees, cleaning spray and some rags. After I took them from her, she settled at the dining table where a laptop and some papers were waiting for her.

I explained to Ben that we should start at opposite ends of the French doors and meet in the middle. If he didn't get into gear, his mom was likely to kick us out of the house and I wouldn't blame her.

Our work was disturbed by intermittent bickering between the kids. Ben would turn to look at them at every opportunity. Suddenly a ball came sailing over his head, hit the glass and plopped into the bucket of water on the floor. Josh howled with laughter while young Ben covered his mouth.

Heather stood, her hands on her hips. "Okay, that's it. Josh, you can go and rest in your room."

"No way." Josh crossed his arms, puffed out his chest. "How come he gets to stay here and I have to go to my room?"

Ben picked the ball from the bucket and dried it with a rag. It was one of those soft, spongy ones, not the sort to break a window, only annoy a window cleaner. Meanwhile Heather excused herself and escorted Josh to his room. He wasn't exactly kicking and screaming. It was more like what the police would describe as 'under duress'.

Ben was still crouched on the floor, his eyes on young Ben. "Hey, I bet you're good at catching and throwing."

The boy nodded, his eyes lighting up.

Ben came closer, sat on the floor and tossed the ball. "Good catch."

Young Ben's face lit up. Even at seven, he had that same killer grin. He tossed the ball back.

"You've got a strong arm too," Ben said.

I was still cleaning the windows when Heather strode back into the room, then slowed, a smile on her face, as she took in the scene.

"Sorry, Mmm, Heather," Ben said. "It's a soft ball. I hope it's okay if we throw it in the house."

"Sure." She turned to her young son. "You'll be careful won't you, Pumpkin?"

Young Ben nodded. "Yes, Mom."

"Pumpkin." Ben glanced back at me, that faraway look in his eyes again, then back at his mother. "You called him Pumpkin."

She gave him a quizzical look. "Anything wrong with that?"

"I'd forgotten," he said.

"Forgotten what?"

"Hey, it's your turn to throw," young Ben yelled.

"Yep, my turn."

Lucky for Ben he'd been saved. He threw the ball and they continued their game of catch. I'd turn when I heard the occasional giggle – from young Ben, not my boyfriend. Still, I was wondering who was the bigger of the two kids. Heather would glance up occasionally, a loving smile on her face when her gaze landed on her son.

I finished cleaning the inside of the kitchen window, then came back into the living room to see Ben sliding across on his side to catch the ball in his fingertips. He was lying on the floor, the hand with the ball raised inches from the ground in victory.

"Wow!" Young Ben's green eyes widened. "You're a really good catch. I bet not many people can catch as good as you."

Ben got back into a sitting position. "Well, I bet you'll be every bit as good as me one day."

I placed a hand on his shoulder. "We should get started outside."

"Outside?" He stood. "Sure, no problem." Turning to his mother, he added. "We'll be just outside."

"I heard." Head down, she got on with her work.

On the patio, we continued with what must've been

the world's slowest window washing or rather, I cleaned while Ben dithered, a cleaning rag in his hand.

"You were so cute," I said, glancing inside at young Ben.

"This is all a bit freaky," he said.

I gave him a sympathetic look. "I know."

"I wanted to see my mom, *needed* to see her. She's just how I remember her, only I haven't seen her for years and this is too weird for words." He swallowed. "The scene inside is exactly how things used to be. Mom would work part-time and look after us. Josh would be a pain in the neck and pick fights with me. Dad was always at work…"

A wistful look filled Ben's eyes.

"And?" I said.

"That's how I remember Dad from when I was younger. Always working. Absent, mostly. Makes me wonder if he wasn't there for Mom or whether she was always going to get sick anyway. After she died, Dad spent more time at home, looked after us, did the best he could. Her death brought us closer together." A furrow formed in his brow. "Further apart too."

I nodded. Ben had issues with the way his dad dealt with the loss and his refusal to talk about it.

His mom came outside, a large plastic bag in her hand, a smile on her face. Ben pretended to clean a speck from the glass. His eyes were on her as she headed for the large trash can by the side path and tipped out the contents of the bag.

"Hey!" Ben rushed across and pointed inside the trash can. "They're my…I got those for my…I mean, they look like perfectly good toys that you're throwing out."

Her brow furrowed. "They're toy guns and, yes, I'm

throwing them out. Someone gave them to Ben for his birthday and I don't want him playing with toys like this. Is that a problem?"

Ben held his hands out. "Nope, no problem at all."

"I appreciate your concern but I'm like any other mom. I love my boys and it's my job to take care of them."

He nodded. "Absolutely. I was just wondering. How would you feel if your boys took up martial arts?"

She rolled her eyes. "I think Josh already has. He's more than happy to fight with his brother."

"And Ben?"

"I don't have a problem with martial arts. That involves practice and discipline. It's violence I have a problem with."

Ben put a hand on his chest. "Oh yeah, me too."

"You know you seem strangely familiar." She tilted her head. "Are you sure we haven't met before? Maybe another time when you were visiting Bob and Jo?"

"No, I'd definitely remember."

"You ask a lot of strange questions."

"I do." Ben backed off. "I'm sorry. I'll get back to the windows."

"Strange doesn't mean bad." She stopped by the door, the hint of a smile on her lips. "You're great with Ben. It's nice to see."

"He's a good kid."

Ben nodded and waited until his mom had gone inside, then couldn't help himself any longer. "I always wondered what happened to those toy guns. I loved them. Thought they were the best thing. I got them for my birthday and one day they just disappeared."

I held his gaze. "That's not it though, is it?"

Tears glimmered in his eyes, his expression pained. "I couldn't see it when I was twelve and she died, but I can see it now. She was happy once. And then she wasn't."

"She had depression, Ben," I said. "You told me it got worse after she had Celia. Post-natal."

"I know but I'm seeing her in a new light." He spread his arms. "Seeing her like this makes me realize she wouldn't have left it all behind, wouldn't have left *us* behind, not if she could help it."

Any death was hard to handle and I suspected suicide made it harder still. It had certainly been rough on Ben. Left him scarred.

"It's not the way I thought it would be." His voice shook as he spoke.

"The way what would be?"

"My Mom, her death, the way she went. I understand it so much better now. It's as if there are different levels of knowing. Before, I understood it with my head and all I felt inside was my own pain. I have a deeper understanding now. I feel it with my heart."

"I'm sorry about your mom, Ben, really I am."

"This seals it for me. I have to become a doctor. I have to help people, maybe those with depression, maybe people with other diseases. It's what I'm here for."

"I'm glad, Ben," I said. "Are you with me?"

"Of course."

My throat was tight because I felt for him. I also knew I had to get us back on track.

"Are you really with me? Because we have to leave here. We have to go to a time before the virus and we have to stop that devastation. We're the only ones who can do it."

"Then what are we doing here, Nic? Do we just wait until Nathan works it out?"

I shrugged. "It could happen any time."

Or it might not happen. The unthinkable. My gut twisted into a knot.

A knock on the glass from inside the French doors grabbed our attention. Young Ben was waving as he came out to join us.

"My mom says it's okay if I get some fresh air and watch you guys." He looked even cuter than before, a shy expression on his face, his hands behind his back.

"You can help if you like," big Ben suggested.

The boy shook his head. Instead Ben showed him how to spin the squeegee on its handle so it became a spinning top and also how a dirty rag rolled tightly could function as a ball. Sometimes I admired Ben's maturity. This wasn't one of those times, and it made me love him all the more, a pang in my heart as I watched.

The two boys started a game of hide and seek – and I think it was safe to call them both boys – while I finished off the windows. I didn't mind. After all, how many people got an opportunity like Ben had?

"You can join in now too," young Ben announced when I was done.

"I know the perfect spot." Ben put his arm around me, his eyes on his younger self. "You'll never find us."

The boy smacked his hands together. "Bet I will." Then he turned, shuffled to the wall, covered his eyes and started counting.

Ben motioned toward the trash can near the side path. We crouched down beside it, Ben's arm around me. And that was when it hit.

No, not now.
I pressed my eyes shut against the blinding light.
And knew what was coming.

CHAPTER THIRTEEN

"I didn't get to say goodbye." Ben's voice.

Was the sound in my head? Where were we?

I opened my eyes. Found I could see after all, the pain in my head subsiding. Ben was huddled beside me, his head in his hands, elbows resting on his knees. I put my arm around his shoulders and drew him in close. We were both naked after the transportation, only unlike before, it was daylight and I could see what was around me.

We were in my old room again except it wasn't my room yet, and that meant we'd gone back to the wrong time again.

"I didn't get to say goodbye." This time I heard the pain in his voice.

"To young Ben?" I asked.

"To him too."

Seven-year-old Ben might quickly forget the window washer who played ball with him and then disappeared. But that wasn't the person Ben was talking about.

"I had my big chance and didn't even say goodbye to her," he said.

"But you did. You've said goodbye in so many ways. When you were twelve at the funeral and when your Dad baked a cake on your mom's birthday every year, you were saying goodbye. And when you took me to her grave and told her you loved her. Most of all, then."

"The morning she died, I didn't say goodbye." Ben's voice was soft, loaded with regret. "We'd had an argument about something stupid. She'd said I couldn't go to two parties on the weekend, and twelve-year-old me thought I should be able to do whatever I wanted. I left for school in a huff. Slammed the door behind me without saying another word."

I kept my arm secured around him. "Ben, she didn't kill herself because you didn't say goodbye."

"But just then, when we were back home, I could've made her feel special, told her it was obvious how much her kids adored her, said something meaningful."

"You made an impression."

"Yeah, as a bumbling idiot."

"You were a beautiful, brilliant bumbling idiot. A memorable one. And I'm sure she could see something exceptional inside you."

Ben smiled wanly which was what I'd wanted all along. To make him feel better.

"She knows you loved her," I added. "You saw how she was with young Ben and Josh. She loved you guys."

He raked a hand through the hair that wasn't there any more. "I didn't even get to hug her."

"Hang on." I forced a smile. "She already thought you were weird enough without you trying to hug her."

Ben broke into a nervous laugh. "Yeah, she might've called the police."

"Or maybe young Ben would've tried some commando moves on you."

He rolled his eyes. "Josh certainly would."

Ben needed some space, so we stayed huddled on the floor together while I looked around and tried to sort out what to do next. We were naked. Again. Seemed to be the story of my life lately. There probably wouldn't be any clothes in this room so we might have to raid the old people's wardrobe and end up looking like hobos. Again.

Suddenly a pile of folded clothing appeared on the floor next to Ben, which was what I'd expected the first time we landed here, only it never came. Now I couldn't believe my luck. It grabbed Ben's attention too. Snapped him out of it.

Nathan had thought of everything including socks and underwear for which I was extremely grateful. We pulled on black tee shirts, jeans and combat boots, New Nation's version of casual.

"Glad I don't need suspenders," Ben said. "What now?"

I groped around on the floor, lifting a couple of boxes to search under them.

"What are you looking for?" Ben asked.

"A PR device."

We needed to be able get in touch with Nathan. Without the comms device, we could be stuck here indefinitely or, if things went like last time, we wouldn't be stuck here long at all. I didn't know what was going on any more, or what year we'd landed in.

"Let's head downstairs, get oriented and gather as much information as we can," I said.

Ben held my gaze, doubt glimmering in his eyes. It

wasn't much of a plan but it was all we had.

Last time we'd been here, it'd been dark. Somehow the daylight made me feel more vulnerable and exposed despite the familiar surroundings. We trod carefully down the stairs, stopping at the bottom. Memories of the last time we were here came back to me, grabbed me by the gut.

"Let's just get out of here," I said.

Movement through the corner of my eye. There was a flash of floral as a silver-haired woman stepped in the doorway to the living room. Her hands came up, her eyes wide, a natural fear reflex.

I held my hands out. "It's okay."

"Oh, my goodness." She gasped.

"We'll leave you alone."

"I can't believe it." The woman's face lit up as if she was seeing her long-lost children. Not a frightened I-can't-believe-it shocked expression. It was more like she couldn't believe her good luck.

"I thought I'd heard something." She came forward, took both of my hands into hers, held them tightly. "It's you! After all this time."

Not the reaction I was expecting, not when we'd appeared out of nowhere. Literally.

She still had a firm grip on me. "Nicola."

"You remembered…"

"I'm Shirley." She let go, only to grab Ben's hands with equal enthusiasm.

"Ben," he said.

She stepped back, looked us up and down. "So pleased to finally meet you. I thought I'd never see you again."

"Well, here we are," I said. Uncomfortable was being

taken to new levels. "Just leaving."

"You've got your own clothes this time." She nodded. "That's nice, not that I minded you borrowing our things before. You two are such a mystery. We never let on about you, even when the police badgered us. They didn't believe Gerald had fought off the attacker. They thought there was more to it."

"You didn't tell anyone?"

"I thought you deserved some privacy," Shirley said. "Gerald and I had plenty of time to talk about that night. I've thought about the two of you a lot over the years."

I nodded, wondered if her husband was at work, though I'd have thought he must be retired. Wondered how many years had passed.

She said, "You saved our lives and you did so much more. You saved Gerald from living with the guilt of having taken another human life. My husband was a carpenter, not a killer." She tilted her head. "You were so mature, so quick and thoughtful. It was almost as if you were trained for that sort of thing."

She was right and wrong at the same time. I was trained and I was also struggling with a lot of things.

"There's something else," she said. "You probably don't know how much danger you put yourself in when you saved us."

"Actually, I have a pretty good idea."

"No, no, it was much worse." Her brow furrowed. "That man was no ordinary burglar. The police told us he was fresh out of jail on a murder charge. A ruthless killer. If it wasn't for you, we would've died that night."

I shuddered at the thought of the two of them dead at the hands of a psycho. Nathan had stuffed up, sent us back to the wrong time, but at least one good thing had come out of it.

A hand on her chest, she added, "You deserve a lot more than we could give you. I don't know why you came back after all this time and it doesn't matter. You've done so much for me and I've done nothing." She grabbed Ben by the arm. "Come into the kitchen for something to eat."

"Thanks, but…" I said.

Ben implored me with his eyes. "The least we do is grab a bite if it'll make the lady feel better."

We needed food, after all. Ben was a big guy and probably needed it more than me.

I took a deep breath. "Thank you."

In the kitchen, Shirley cut slices of quiche and ripped off chunks of crusty French bread for us. I couldn't remember the last time we'd eaten. Ben was right about staying.

She was pottering by the sink. "It's a dish I make all the time for the grandkids."

"Delicious," I said between mouthfuls.

Weird was being taken to new levels. I felt as if I couldn't get my footing, the ground constantly moving beneath me, another tremor imminent.

I swallowed. "There's something I wanted to ask. How do you know you can trust us?"

She leaned against the cupboards. "I've got good instincts. You didn't save me and Gerald so you could come back years later and hurt me."

How many years? That was the question. The kitchen clock said 2.00pm which wasn't much help.

"Can you please tell me the date?" I asked and she did. I followed up with, "The year?"

Shirley's expression was strange. Expectant. "You asked that the first time around too."

I didn't have a good response to that. Ben pointed to the newspaper on the table. This was one year before my original arrival in New Nation. I tried to take it all in. Ben would be sixteen years old. Lauren and all my old friends would be here, but they wouldn't know me because they hadn't met me yet. They'd be at school doing all the normal things I longed to get back to.

And my parents? A pang cut through my heart. We hadn't even met yet, so I was nothing to them. And they were everything to me.

I pressed a hand to my temple. Surely Nathan wouldn't have delivered us to this time and place intentionally. He'd said changes to the time travel program were still at the experimental stage and now it occurred to me that maybe there was a good reason Lucien hadn't wanted him to proceed through the testing phase. Because it was too dangerous.

We couldn't stay here. This wasn't our time. And if we didn't complete our mission, the whole world would suffer.

Ben pointed to a rack of hats proudly on display on the wall. "Cool baseball caps."

Shirley's expression softened. "Gerald's collection. I couldn't bear to take them down after he died."

"He passed away?" I put my fork down. Even Ben stopped eating. "I'm sorry. We had no idea."

Perhaps I should have been more thoughtful. Meanwhile, Shirley grabbed two black caps with logos from the rack. "You know what? Gerald would've wanted you to have these."

"I'm sorry about your husband," Ben said. "And thank you. For everything."

Having finished eating, we stood, baseball caps in our hands even though we didn't have a clue what we were doing. I hated feeling lost, yet I was the one who was supposed to know what to do.

Shirley walked us to the door. "Maybe you need somewhere to stay. You can come back tonight."

I opened my mouth to protest, then stopped myself. "That's very kind."

She nodded. "I'll leave the kitchen door unlocked."

"Are you sure?" I said. "That wouldn't be safe."

"I think I'll be safe with my two bodyguards coming back." She laughed. "Besides, you might find it easier than climbing up the tree and through the window in the spare room."

So that was how she thought we'd made it here. I'd got in to my bedroom that way before. It wasn't so bad, but she was right. The door was more convenient.

Ben and I strode down the street in silence, then turned a corner and slowed down. There was one place he'd spent many years, though my time there had been shorter, only one place we could go.

I took his hand into mine. "Are you thinking what I'm thinking?"

"It's funny," he said. "It wasn't that long ago that I couldn't wait for exams to be over, couldn't wait to be done with school and celebrate at the cabin."

Except that hadn't turned out to be the celebration we'd planned and we'd been through so much in a short time.

"Now I can't wait to go back," Ben said.

VALIDATION

And school would be out soon.

CHAPTER FOURTEEN

Was I seeing things? Maybe time travel was screwing with my mind.

"Did you see that guy walking into the convenience store?"

Ben nodded as he walked. "Looked a lot like Reece."

We crossed the road to go into the store. Inside, a young clerk was behind the counter speaking politely to two middle-aged women who were marveling at how he'd grown. Unfortunately he hadn't had much luck with the moustache he was trying to grow.

Ben and I pretended to look at some magazines while trying not to stare at Reece. His afro hair, bleached and dark at the roots, was still in its infancy and hadn't grown to its full craziness. He was wearing jeans, a tee shirt and a scruffy grey coat.

The Reece we knew was slightly cocky whereas now he had air-of-homeless-person about him, which is exactly what he'd been when he first arrived in Altabena. Even though I knew he was a trained soldier, I felt for him. I knew what it was like to feel lost.

He wandered down the food aisles while Ben and I stepped past him. I glanced at him, looked away, then back again. He was very quick as he pocketed some canned goods. If I didn't know what to look out for, there's no way I would've spotted it.

Seconds later, Reece was at the door.

"Hey you!" the clerk called out to him, a suspicious look on his face.

The two middle-aged ladies turned to see what was going on.

I strode to the front, waving to attract the clerk's attention. "Excuse me, do you have Cheetos?"

He looked at me as if I was an idiot. "Of course. Aisle two."

"Thanks," I said in my brightest voice.

My distraction had worked and Reece had left, so Ben and I turned to leave too.

"What about the Cheetos?" the clerk yelled when we reached the door.

"I prefer chips," I said.

He rolled his eyes as we walked out.

"What was all that about?" Ben asked. "With Reece."

I was sure I'd told him the story about Reece's arrival, but maybe he'd forgotten or most likely it hadn't sunk in. I told him again how the authorities hadn't set Reece up with an identity here so he'd had to fend for himself, living on the streets until Connie had taken him in. Life became better for him quickly after that.

"That was tough," Ben said when I finished.

The two of them had always had their differences. It wouldn't hurt for Ben to better understand where Reece was coming from.

We pulled the baseball caps down lower as we walked. They weren't much of a disguise but they were all we had, not that we had too much to worry about. We were only here to survey the school.

As we got nearer, we saw Ben walking on the other side of the street. Sixteen-year-old Ben, that is. His wavy hair hung over his eyes and he was wearing the school uniform of a white shirt and dark blue pants.

Somehow it didn't feel natural. Didn't seem right. It felt as if we were balancing on a tightrope.

Ben stopped, grabbed my hand. If this was weird for me, it would be something else altogether for him.

"That's me." He gasped. "Shit, Nicola, I can't…We can't…"

"It's best to leave it."

"Okay."

Aside from anything else, the sight of his doppelganger would freak the poor guy out. There'd be no way of explaining it.

"Why is he…?" I corrected myself. "Why were you rushing?"

"Probably hurrying home to take Celia to dance class." He gazed at me. "Celia…"

"She's fine," I said. "Because sixteen-year-old Ben is taking care of her, driving her to dance class and doing all those things. Your family is okay."

"I miss her." Emotion glimmered in his eyes. "My dad too."

"If you love them, you'll let them be."

He sighed. "We'll just look around. We've got to do something while we're here."

Glancing up, I saw Lauren heading in our direction

and quickly lowered my head. I stepped closer to Ben, as if I could hide him from her, as if she wouldn't notice. Still, I couldn't stop myself from peeking.

"Ben!" She put a hand on his arm, pulling him back from me. "What's happened to your hair? You look like you've joined the army or something."

"Now there's an idea," he mumbled.

"You'll have to take the baseball cap off sooner or later." Her eyes wide, Lauren didn't seem to be heading anywhere in a hurry. She screwed up her face. "You're going in the wrong direction. Where's your uniform? You were at school today, weren't you?"

"I got changed," he said.

She tilted her head. "I haven't interrupted anything, have I? You two seem pretty cozy."

"You're asking lots of questions," Ben said.

"You're acting really strange," she replied. "So who's your friend?"

"I'm Nicola." I remembered the first time I'd met Lauren and how I'd tried to shake her hand, which had clearly been the dorky thing to do. A mistake I wasn't making again.

Only maybe that wasn't the first time I met Lauren. Maybe this was. The thought was doing my head in.

"We have to go," I said before I got more confused.

"See you around, then," she called as we left.

"You will," I said over my shoulder.

We kept walking past the school, an ocean of students heading toward their cars or the buses further down the street. We'd been part of that mass exodus once too. Every day, in fact.

It was a lengthy walk back to Shirley's house, or maybe

it was my house. We didn't want to backtrack and risk bumping into Lauren or anyone else so we took the long way.

I was relieved to find Shirley wasn't there and that she'd left the back door unlocked as promised.

"What now?" Ben asked.

I wished I knew. Out of habit, I went up the stairs to my room which wasn't my room at all, hoping I'd feel at home there. I opened the door for Ben to go ahead of me. He slumped down against the wall near the spot where we'd arrived.

"Ben," I said. "Move over. No, that way."

Nudging him across, I saw it. The PR device I'd been expecting earlier was now waiting for us. Maybe there'd been a delay. Nathan must have sent this after he'd transported the clothing, only Ben and I hadn't waited around long enough for it.

Ben grinned as I nuzzled closer to him on the floor.

"About time," he said.

A message on the PR device read: *Please respond immediately to confirm your arrival.*

I shot back a missive right away. As did Nathan: *Why did you not respond to the message sent on the first PR device?*

The first one? Was it possible Nathan had transported a PR device to this room when we'd arrived in 2007? Perhaps the transportation had taken a while for some reason, by which time we'd left to spend the night in a cubby house and then visit Ben's mom.

Too many questions. Too many unknowns. It'd be easier if I could simply talk to Nathan and clear a few things up, but voice communications didn't work across the time spectrum. I had to get to the point.

I wrote: *Do you have a fix on us?*

His reply: *Yes, apologies for problems with the previous transports. Are you ready to be transported to 2041 to the required location?*

Problems with the previous transports — an understatement if I'd ever heard one.

My response: *We didn't receive the previous PR device. This time, can you send the device at the same time as our clothes?*

Nathan: *Certainly.*

I looked at Ben expectantly. "Are you ready?"

"Nathan can send us to the right time and location?" he asked.

I nodded. Ben didn't say anything. This place was familiar to him. Shirley had been kind to us. He had friends here, family he hadn't seen yet. And right now there were two teenage Ben Tanners in Altabena, something no one would understand.

"We have to go, Ben," I said.

He raised his eyebrows. "We can't say goodbye?"

I squeezed his hand. "It's better this way."

This was it. We were going to 2041 to do what we'd planned in the first place.

Ben nodded and I typed in my reply. One word.

Yes.

CHAPTER FIFTEEN

Pain ripped through my head, my eyes squeezed shut. You'd think I'd be getting used to this. Instead my heart was racing so fast it was crashing into my chest walls. I took long breaths to slow my pulse and found my sense of awareness returning. I was sitting, my head in my hands, but sitting where?

My eyes opened. Ben was beside me, his eyes wide as he looked around the room. Nerves filled my stomach – at our situation, at what I'd done to Ben, at the magnitude of our mission.

He reached out for me. "Are you okay?"

"I should be asking you that," I said.

The floor was linoleum. There was a big wooden desk in front of us and a green filing cabinet further along the wall. No windows. Shelves behind us held textbooks, anatomical models and electronic data storage devices.

Ben turned and grabbed one of the books. "*Gray's Anatomy*, a classic." He put it back. "Maybe some things haven't changed that much after all."

In fact, I was getting to see rather a lot of Ben's

anatomy, since we arrived naked at every landing. Funny how something so natural could seem unnatural too. Seconds later, our clothes appeared on the floor beside us, a PR device placed on top where we couldn't miss it.

"Thank you, Nathan," I mumbled as we dressed. This time he'd given us white tee shirts to go with our jeans. A wise choice.

"I think we made it," Ben said.

He sounded matter of fact, but he must be in shock after everything we'd been through. Maybe he was good at covering it up.

A message was waiting for us on the PR device: *Please confirm your safe arrival.*

"Let's work out the year and date first." I kept hold of the PR device as we surveyed our surroundings. "Do you think this is your office? I mean, your office in the future."

"If we're in the future, then this is *now*," Ben said. I hated it when he was logical. "It's an office but it's not my office."

"How do you know?"

He pointed to a framed photo on the desk of someone else's family, an African American family.

Leaning over, I tapped on a computer sitting on a Perspex stand. The lid rolled open and glowed to life while I checked the date.

"2041. We made it."

I kept the quaver from my voice because I had to be strong. We may have arrived but that was only the beginning.

And we had to do this.

Ben's eyes widened. "Is that thing a laptop?"

I nodded. "Plithium technology. That's why it's wafer

thin, highly responsive too. It's the same technology that's behind PR devices, though they haven't been invented yet."

"Impressive."

To him, maybe. For me, this was just the way things were. And it was much easier to speak matter-of-factly about this stuff to Ben than take the next steps and work out what to do.

I sucked in a deep breath, messaged Nathan to let him know we'd reached the correct time zone, then placed the device on my forearm where it melded with my skin so it was imperceptible. It would only harden when I peeled it off.

"Do you think this is the research facility?" I motioned toward the door. "That's the first thing we should work out."

As we stepped out into a corridor, a man was approaching, so Ben closed the door and pretended to fiddle with the handle until he left. We wandered slowly along the hallway, peering into offices in the vain hope that adult Ben might be sitting behind one of the desks.

Eventually we found a sign that gave directions to genetics, microbiology and other fields.

"We could try to find a reception desk," I suggested. "Then ask them to page Ben Tanner."

"Or they might kick us out."

"Yeah, there is that."

Two older women were deep in dialogue, staring at us as they passed, which made me realize how much we stood out and not just because of our clothes. We were way too young to be research scientists.

A man was coming toward us, his tie askew, shirt

untucked, his head down, deep in concentration. The top of his head was bald with bushy hair at the sides. He had the 'crazy professor' look in spades and I hoped he might be one of those genius types who wasn't big on common sense.

"Excuse me," I said. "Can you please tell us where we can find Ben Tanner?"

The man stopped. "Do you have a pass?"

I didn't have an answer.

"We dropped it," Ben said.

"Teenagers!" The man rolled his eyes. "Who were you looking for again?"

"Ben Tanner."

The man's brow furrowed as he stared at Ben. "That's what I thought you said. And you are…?"

"Ben's nephew."

He took off his glasses, wiping them on the tail of his shirt. Handy it was untucked. "Ben's nephew. Why didn't you say so in the first place? What's your name, son?"

"James." His middle name.

The crazy professor put his glasses back on and stared some more. "You know, you look a lot like your uncle."

"You think so?" Ben shrugged. "I can't see it."

He motioned for us to follow. "This way."

Just as well we could use the family resemblance to our advantage or we would've been kicked out of here.

We followed the man down several corridors and onto a covered walkway that led to an adjacent building. Luckily, he wasn't big on talking. He tapped his security card on a scanner outside a large laboratory and told us to wait.

Windows looked onto the lab where Ben had his head

down, concentrating – an older version of Ben but definitely still him. It sent a ripple through me, a surge so strong I had trouble holding back the swell inside me. A real person. My Ben in the future.

I glanced at Ben beside me, his mouth gaping, eyes glued to the scene in front of him. I couldn't tell what was going through his head. Or his heart. What was this like for him?

Ben-in-2041 looked up from his work, shock in his eyes at first, then composure. Somehow observing the scene unfold through the glass made it feel unreal, as if I was watching a movie.

Adult Ben strode through the laboratory, shaking the crazy professor's hand when they reached the door.

"Thank you, Ralph," he said as if this was the most normal thing in the world, then waited for him to leave. He looked at me first, then Ben, shock turning to exasperation. "What are you doing here?"

Beside me, my Ben looked as if his life was shattering before his eyes.

I had to take control. "It's a long story. We'll explain later."

"Let's go to my office."

Adult Ben led us back to the other building and into a bland office that looked much like the one we'd landed in. This must be the business side of Ben because there wasn't a lot of personality happening here.

Ushering us ahead, he closed the door behind him. "If you're here, I can only assume there's a good reason for it."

"There is," I said.

My boyfriend looked as if he was about to collapse so

I motioned for him to sit. Suddenly regret flooded through me. Maybe I should have thought this through, done this on my own, found another way.

Adult Ben covered his chin with one hand. "There are a few things I have to organize. I need to call Nicola, for one thing. She'll be as shocked as I am."

"Maybe not as much as you." I knew the way my mind worked.

He shook his head. "This is beyond weird."

Beside me, Ben leaned back in his chair with a thump. "You're telling me!"

His adult self paced the room. "You know, you're such a teenager."

"Yes," Ben said. "I am."

The pacing stopped. "Look, stay right here. Don't move. Don't talk to anyone."

"We won't," Ben and I said in unison.

"I'll be back." He closed the door behind him as he left.

"How is this even possible?" Ben threw up his hands. "Shouldn't meeting my adult self cause a rift in the space-time continuum or something?"

"Clearly not," I said. "I'm sure Ben knows what he's doing. We'll wait."

I hated keeping still, so I started looking around the office for further information or anything that could be useful. I found Ben's address, memorized it.

Adult Ben came back into the room and grabbed a jacket from the coat rack in the corner. "Let's go."

"Where?" I asked.

"I've found a place for you to stay. You can both rest, explain why you've come and then we'll work out what to do."

Sounded like a plan. I hadn't given consideration to where we'd stay though, if anything, I'd assumed we could stay with our adult selves.

Ben led us to a basement car park, then we drove off in his electric car, old but reliable and very quiet.

There was a big world out there. I didn't recognize the streets because the research institute was outside San Francisco and I'd never been there before. A sense of hope washed over me. Or maybe that was just the sunshine.

We pulled up outside an art deco apartment block and got out. Adult Ben strode to the double leadlight doors that fronted the building, then punched in a security code and held the doors open for us. Inside, he led us to an apartment on the third floor.

The living room was plain, decorated in shades of cream and white, though it'd be more correct to say it wasn't decorated at all. Bland was being taken to new levels, the leadlight glass in the window the only ornamentation in the room.

Ben told us to take a seat on the sofa, came back with glasses of cold water and sat down on the other side of a small coffee table.

"Nicola is on her way," he said.

I brightened. "Really?"

He nodded. "She's bringing food and a few things you might need."

"Whose place is this?" I asked.

"It belongs to a friend who's out of town at a conference. He travels a lot so I keep an eye on the place for him." Adult Ben looked at his younger self, then back at me. "Do you want to tell me what's going on?"

"You know the K-virus is going to wreak havoc and kill off most of the population," I said.

"Yes."

"We have to make sure the virus is never created," I said.

Adult Ben shot me a condescending look I'd seen many times before – from adults and others who thought they were superior – never from Ben.

He raised his eyebrows. "Really?"

A buzzer rang and he got up to let Nicola into the building, then waited. He gave her a kiss as she walked in, and took the bags from her arms to deposit them in the kitchen.

Nicola closed the door, gazing at the two of us sitting on the sofa. It was the strangest sensation, nerves nestling in my stomach, as I looked up at myself. That was me, yet somehow it wasn't, and none of this felt real.

"I don't believe it." She rushed across to give me a big hug, then made her way over to Ben who looked overwhelmed as she cupped his face in her hands.

"Ben, Ben, look at you," she muttered before throwing her arms around him.

She came across as part mother, part old friend, yet she was so much like me, which shouldn't be surprising but was blowing me away. Still, one thing had clearly changed. I'd come a long way from my days in the military when I'd suppressed all emotion.

I poked my finger at her leg. The skin bounced back. Then I pinched her thigh.

"In case you're wondering," she said, magnificently composed. "That hurts."

I rubbed the skin. "Just testing."

She smiled. "I'd have thought Ben would be the one conducting scientific experiments."

Adult Ben stood in the doorway, a bottle in his hands. "Wine. You brought them wine? What were you thinking?"

Nicola didn't flinch. "I happen to know that Nicola here is going to enjoy a glass of red."

Ben shook his head, ducked back into the kitchen and came back into the room to sit on the chair opposite us, *sans* bottle. Nicola got up, perching on the arm of his chair.

He didn't waste any time. "You two need to get back to where you belong."

I didn't appreciate his disapproving look. "Do you really think we'd have come if we didn't have to?"

"I think you're taking physics and nature and the world into your own hands and acting dangerously."

My eyes narrowed. "I did this once before, Ben. I traveled through time and saved your life. You wouldn't be here if I hadn't *acted dangerously*."

He was like a rock, a giant boulder that wasn't going to budge.

"There are practical aspects as well," he said. "The guy who owns the apartment will be back in a few days."

"Couldn't we stay with you?" I asked.

Nicola glared, silencing me with her stare. I must've asked the wrong thing, but it seemed anything I said was the wrong thing.

"Has Ben told you about his work at the institute and how close he is to discovering a cure for cancer?" she asked.

"Not yet," I said. "I'm sure he will, though."

Nicola looked at young Ben. "You know how you always wanted to work for the *great* Dr. Max Alonzo? Well, you do."

Ben grinned. "That's cool. That was my dream."

"Nicola," I said, though it was strange to say my own name. "Why the sarcasm? Does that mean he's great or he's not?"

Her eyes narrowed. "It means he's not as great as he thinks he is. Also, that Ben's discoveries are more monumental than anything Max has ever come up with." Adult Ben opened his mouth to say something, but she put out her hand. "Ben is the great mind, not Max, but you'd never think that to hear him talk."

"You've never liked him," adult Ben said.

"That's true. It's also true that you don't listen when I voice an opinion against him."

"Because it's always down to a bad feeling you get from him. You don't have to like the man. That's fine. I don't always like him either. But I admire what he's doing."

I couldn't believe this. "What? Twenty years on and we're still having the same argument." Turning to them, I added, "Haven't we moved on from that?"

"Apparently not," Nicola said.

"You've got it wrong," Ben said. "It's a case of agreeing to disagree. And it's not relevant right now. We've got bigger things to worry about. You must have a PR device. That means you can communicate with the authorities and arrange to be sent back."

"No." I glared. "We can't."

If only things were that straightforward. We'd already explained our reasons for being here to Ben, and I explained them again to Nicola. She'd grown up in New Nation, seen the future and had a good idea of the devastation caused by the virus. She would understand.

"We know all that," adult Ben said.

Nicola leaned forward. "Of course we'll stop the virus being created."

She made it sound so easy. As if they had everything under control.

Beside me, Ben pointed a finger at the two of them. "But that's exactly why we're here."

Surprise in their eyes. Nicola's mouth fell open.

"Because you *don't* stop the virus."

CHAPTER SIXTEEN

How long had it been since were alone, just the two of us? We were constantly being pulled in one direction, then another, never left so things could progress between us naturally.

Ben tipped more wine into my glass and passed it to me. This was my boyfriend, my Ben, the same Ben who'd cooked a simple dinner for us.

I sipped my wine. "Nicola was right. I'm getting a taste for this stuff."

Earlier, I'd brought the comforter from the bedroom, laid it on the floorboards and covered it with a blanket to keep it clean. We were lounging around by the hearth in the living room in front of a fireplace with a gas insert. Gas heating was practical. Too practical for my liking.

Cross-legged on the floor, I stared at the small flickering flames. "Are you okay with this? With our being here?"

Ben put his arm around me. "We have to be okay with this."

"We could leave right now," I said. "I could message

Nathan and he'd transport us back. I could probably convince him to send us both back to Altabena too, back to our time, back to where we belong."

"But that wouldn't be the right thing to do," Ben whispered.

And it wouldn't solve our problems. Ben could stay in Altabena but there was no way Supreme Ruler Bartley would leave me be. He'd track me down one way or another.

"We're here now," Ben said. "We've made it part of the way."

I clinked glasses with him. "And we have wine."

He smiled. "Nicola thought of everything."

"It's kind of weird. She's me and she isn't."

"At least, she's nicer than I turned out to be."

I nodded. "Ben was a bit of a grumble guts."

"Great." He smiled grimly. "We've seen the future and I'm a grumble guts."

We were making light of our situation but underneath I'm sure Ben was just as nervous as I was. Anxiety was simmering beneath the surface and that wouldn't change. Unless we succeeded.

I held his gaze. "You can always make me smile."

He kissed me gently. "I hope so."

We sat like that for a while, enjoying the moment and each other's company. It was unlike Ben to be so mellow. Usually when we were alone, he'd start making out with me and wouldn't stop, whereas tonight I didn't want him to stop and couldn't get him to start.

"It wasn't that long ago we were in our room at the cabin drinking wine," I said.

"No, but it feels like years," he said.

It did. "That was so romantic. I'm sorry it didn't work out the way we planned."

The gold streaks in his green eyes glimmered. "I'm not an expert on romance but I don't think the gas fire is cutting it."

I placed my wine glass on the hearth. "I don't need a log fire or candles or silk sheets if I have you. You're everything I've ever wanted."

"Back at the cabin, that was meant to be our perfect time together."

"There'll never be a perfect time." I reached for his hand. "We have each other. We have now."

I didn't feel safe and I didn't care. Because I had Ben. And I ached for him, longed to be with him. In every way.

Whereas he was probably feeling something else. He must be, because the Ben I knew would be grasping at any opportunity to get my clothes off and wouldn't care about anything else that was going on.

"Before we got here, I was scared of the unknown," I said. "I still am."

He didn't say anything. I took the wine glass from his hand and placed it to one side. Cupping his face in my hands, I kissed him in the same gentle way he'd kissed me a few minutes ago.

I gazed into his eyes. "But I've done much scarier things. And sometimes the only way is to just do it."

Then I kissed him the way I wanted to, our tongues rolling against each other, and he kissed me back. Hooking my fingers under the hem of his tee shirt, I pulled it over his head and admired the muscles of his chest.

"You'll always have me, Ben," I whispered.

I pulled my tee shirt off, unhooked my bra and tossed

it aside. Ben's eyes widened as he placed a hand on my breast and his mouth on mine.

Getting undressed wasn't dangerous. Going all the way wasn't deadly. We were in this together.

This was right. We weren't being brainwashed by the New Nation government or being forced back in time on a mission. This was everything it should be.

And if there was danger ahead, that was all the more reason to do this now. Something might happen tomorrow. Our plans could go wrong. The next transport might not work properly.

But we would always have tonight and this time together. No one could take that away from us.

My hand on his chest, I pushed Ben back until he was lying on the comforter. I stood and took off my jeans and pants. There was no sexy strip tease. Only me. Naked before him. Telling him I was ready.

I loved him and now was the time to show him. I always knew we were going to end up together. We'd traveled to 2041 and here we were. Together. But now I knew it in another way. In my heart.

We'd both grown so much, shared so many experiences, and we were on the edge of something momentous. We were planning on saving the world from a killer virus. That was big. As big as it could get.

Emotions could be big too. That's what this was about – about being alive and in love and true to ourselves.

I slid my body on top of his. I'd never been more ready, never felt more alive. Ben wrapped his arms around my waist and rolled me over.

Tomorrow, we might save the world. Or we might not. But tonight was for us.

CHAPTER SEVENTEEN

We were back at the research institute where the important work seemed to be happening. After last night, I was even more certain of what we had to do and where we were headed. There was only one way.

Adult Ben had found a place for us in a back corner of the room, far enough away from the others for privacy, close enough for access to microscopes and tissue samples and whatever else he was showing my Ben.

He'd given his younger self a baseball hat to keep pulled down over his face. Not that the other medical researchers were paying him any attention. They were all concentrating on their own tasks, working at their stations or speaking quietly with colleagues.

Adult Ben found some journals, opened them up to the correct page and placed them on the bench in front of us. "I'm going through all this so you can see how I've been working on a cure for cancer, not developing a killer virus. You've got this all wrong."

Boyfriend Ben scanned the journals. "That seems to be what these articles are about."

"Immunotherapy was in its infancy in your time." Adult Ben leaned over the bench on the other side of us. "We've made huge progress since then. Scientists were always baffled by the way the body accepted cancer cells instead of fighting them. For whatever reason, the body's immune system sees cancer mutations, yet doesn't attack them in the same way it would attack a virus or another invader. Somehow the cancer fools the immune system into thinking it's a friend, rather than a foe. The cancer then grows, multiplies and spreads. Basically, the cancer can do what it wants because there's nothing stopping it."

"So why doesn't the body's immune system kick in?" my Ben asked.

"We're on the verge of working that out. We'll have an answer soon, I'm sure of it. Our main aim at the moment is to analyze these cancer mutations using DNA sequencing methods, then to introduce vaccines containing the cancer mutations into another part of the body so that they go on the attack, shrink the tumor and get rid of the cancer."

"Like re-training the body's immune system to do what it was supposed to do in the first place?"

"Pretty much," adult Ben said. "Our goal is a vaccine that induces tumor shrinkage, cancer cell elimination and eventually a return to good health."

"And you're close?"

"Very close. When we can link the DNA of the cancer cells to the reaction of the vaccine, the process should be complete."

"How far are you through the trials and testing?"

"We've progressed through all the other stages and are now going through human trials. More specifically, we're looking at the best methods of vaccine design and delivery."

"You sound very confident."

Adult Ben nodded. "I am."

The two of them seemed to be on the same wavelength. It was hardly surprising they thought the same way.

Meanwhile, I was on a different planet completely. They were in a little bubble where they were only looking at the mechanics of the cancer and the cure and the related medical aspects, while I was considering the bigger picture.

We stopped talking as someone approached. It was the crazy professor dude we'd met yesterday. He didn't seem to notice his bow tie was crooked or his shirt stained, and he wasn't shy about approaching us.

"Max would like to see you later," he said.

"Did he say what it was about?" Ben asked.

"Something to do with increased government funding." The man frowned. "I wouldn't know. Money is not my specialty."

The crazy professor turned away, then stopped as if remembering something. "I forgot to say good morning to you all." His eyes narrowed as he looked at the two Bens. "The family resemblance to your uncle is remarkable, James. I'd go as far as to say it's astounding."

Young Ben grinned. "Except I'm better looking than him."

The crazy professor nodded. "Ah, a joke. Interesting."

Adult Ben gave him a pointed stare. "Thanks, Ralph."

He shuffled away.

Adult Ben raised his eyebrows. "James?"

Young Ben spread his hands. "Benjamin James

Tanner. I had to come up with something quickly. What's wrong with that?"

"No one calls you Benjamin. Not since Mom…"

Adult Ben's voice trembled, while my Ben's eyes glimmered with pain, both of them still feeling the loss.

I placed my hand on Ben's arm. "That was a long time ago. A lot has happened since then."

He nodded. "And we came here for a reason."

I leaned across to look at adult Ben. "The scientific progress you've described is amazing – truly it is – but I'd like to step back a bit and look at this from a different angle. Are you telling me you can't see any potential problems with what you've said?"

A deadpan stare. "Actually, one of the problems is with Max Alonzo. He takes care of a lot of things, the funding for one thing."

"That's good, isn't it?"

"He's always boasting about the size of his budget. Nicola says he's a control freak and she's right, but he's also the one who enables me to do the work that I do."

"They're not the sort of problems I meant," I said. "I've only heard the term 'DNA sequencing' in passing and I still don't understand what it involves. I'm not an expert."

Adult Ben looked down his nose at me. "No, you're not."

I ignored the pointed comment. "But I know a lot of things about the future and where we're headed and you'd be a fool not to listen. From what you've said, there's a good chance the K-virus uses the same DNA sequencing as the cancers. The virus is airborne and had always existed without being a problem until, at some point, it learnt to 'latch on' to humans without our immune system rejecting it."

Adult Ben raised his eyebrows. "So what are you saying?"

"That the K-virus does the same thing that cancers are doing at the moment. It convinces the body's immune system that there's no need for it to go on the attack, then the body makes no attempt to evict the invaders.

"The K-virus models itself on the cancers." I stared at adult Ben. "The next step of your research will be when the virus will be developed and released. Your work is what enables that to happen."

He leaned back, drummed his fingers on the bench.

My Ben covered his chin. "Whoa."

His lips thin, adult Ben stood. "Come on."

"Come on what?" I asked.

"We're going to my office," he said. "We can't have this conversation here."

I felt like a kid being summoned to the principal's office. Still, he might be right that we couldn't talk openly in the laboratory.

He led us into the next building and ushered us ahead of him into his office. There were only two chairs so I took the spare seat while younger Ben sat behind the desk.

Adult Ben remained standing, his arms crossed as he leaned against a wall. "You were way out of line, then. In one fell swoop, you tried to crap all over years of work that's gone into something magnificent. Creating a cure for cancer."

My pulse was rising. "I voiced a theory. That's all. I didn't crap over anybody. We have freedom of speech in this country. *For now.*"

"Of course." His voice was thick with sarcasm. "Because you know what's going to happen in the future."

Adult Ben and I hadn't known each other for long and at the same time, we knew each other inside out. He was just as riled as I was.

"You seem offended," I said.

"With good reason."

"That's where you're wrong. Just because you're offended doesn't mean I've said something wrong. I think you're worried because deep down – or maybe not even that deep inside – you know I'm right."

Silence was probably better than shouting but not by much.

My Ben cut in. "Look, I'm not a great scientific mind and medical genius yet–"

"Neither am I." Adult Ben gave me a pointed look. "I'm just a man doing his job."

"Are you kidding?" My Ben said. "I can only dream of what you're doing. I guess that's where it starts. With a dream. But part of your job is to be open-minded and look at other possibilities and theories."

Older Ben clenched his fist. "I'm so close. I've even written up the results in anticipation. I can't wait to get them published for the whole medical community. I'm on the verge of finalizing a cure for cancer. This is huge."

I stared at him. "Exactly. And that's why you have to consider the ramifications."

"You two can't come here and feed me this information after I've worked so hard. Not for a few months, but for years, my whole adult life. Everything I've ever done has been leading me to these discoveries. You can't tell me to back off now."

I cleared my throat. "That's not what I'm saying. Not exactly."

He spread his hands. "It's not just my work. I'm part of a team. Nothing happens in a vacuum. There are other people involved, from the administrative staff who put together the funding proposals right up to the head of the research institute. Then there's Max Alonzo who's part of the reason I'm here in the first place."

Dr. Max Alonzo again. Why did I think he was a problem?

"Ben," I said. "You have a great scientific mind and that's why you've got this far. All I'm asking is for you to listen, look at what else is going to happen and how this fits."

He banged his fist against the wall and bit his lower lip. Younger Ben flinched. I wouldn't have thought fist banging would ever be his style but maybe I had a lot to learn too.

His fist remained clenched. "You don't get it. I've always known I was going to do this. Since I was seventeen years old, I've known." A pause. "Because *you* told me so."

A pang cut through me – of fear, uncertainty, maybe regret. Had I done the wrong thing? Ben Tanner was always going to create a cure for cancer, regardless of anything I said. But Ben was human and I had a role in this too.

Damn it, life had been easier in New Nation when we'd all followed the rules. It was hard making your own decisions and your own way in life and maybe hurting people.

Adult Ben stared at me with eyes that were older but

they were the same green eyes, Ben's eyes, and they glimmered with emotion.

"Nicola, you came into my life and turned it upside down. Popped in out of nowhere. Literally. You told me I was going to do this great thing."

"I did."

"You can't do that, then come here and tell me to back off."

The phone rang. I'd never been so grateful.

CHAPTER EIGHTEEN

Adult Ben came back into the office after taking the call, and put the phone down. "Nicola is on her way. She'll take you back to the apartment."

I looked up at him, standing uncomfortably. "Trying to get rid of us?"

"No. Yes. You've thrown me. I can't focus with the two of you here. I have work to do, for one thing."

"And that's easier than thinking about the issues we're raising," I said.

Ben stiffened. "They're big issues and this isn't just about me. I can't stop work on the cancer vaccine. Nicola, what about the people who get cured, the lives saved? Do you want to tell those families that, sorry, they're going to lose their loved ones? What about toddlers who develop leukemia? I can help those people. This is life-saving stuff."

"It isn't black and white, and I'm not saying I have all the answers."

"What about your own mother?"

He meant my mother here in Altabena, the mother I

loved. Then there was Dad too. My throat tight, I swallowed back the pain. I couldn't go there, not when I couldn't see them, not when the timing was all wrong.

Adult Ben's gaze hardened. "When you went back to New Nation before, you stole a vial of the cure for her, didn't you? What happens to her if the cure hasn't been invented? Cancer is often a long slow death."

But I'd already stolen the vaccine and administered it to her. That was last year. Done and dusted.

If Ben stopped his research now and the cancer cure was never invented, would that mean I wouldn't have given my mom the vaccine? Would that change what I'd already done?

This was doing my head in. Whichever way I looked at it, I was going around in circles. I wasn't a physics or time travel expert and couldn't work out the chain of events or what would be altered. What *could* be altered, for that matter. Even Nathan would be confused by this and he was much more knowledgeable than me.

"You've definitely got to me now," I said.

Adult Ben raised his eyebrows. "Like you got to me?"

My Ben reached for my hand. "Your mom is okay. We'll make sure she stays that way."

Could I be a hard ass, focus on the big picture and forget about my mom? Could I forget about the other people who would suffer with cancer and die?

Billions of people would perish from the K-virus, many more than would die of cancer, yet I wasn't sure this was a simple matter of mathematics. We were looking at changing the world and I didn't know what was right and wrong any more.

A knock at the door. Adult Ben opened the door a

crack, then relaxed when he saw it was Nicola and let her in.

"There are no free chairs, I'm afraid." He kissed her on the lips. At least his soft side hadn't disappeared.

Ben was still holding my hand. I didn't want him to let go. Ever.

Nicola pressed her back against the door. "Wow, does anyone want to tell me what's going on?"

Adult Ben went back to leaning against the wall with his arms crossed, his favorite position. "I explained the scientific results so far and showed them some of the findings."

"And that went down like a lead balloon, I can see," she said.

I nodded. "We're at a standstill. The big problem is that the cancer cure and the K-virus are inextricably linked. The final steps of the cancer vaccine are going to create the virus. That's what we think, anyway."

Adult Ben looked at Nicola. "And she doesn't believe it's worth saving cancer victims and their families from all that pain."

"That's not what I said. I was going to ask you if it'd be possible to find another method for procuring the cancer cure."

Exasperated now, adult Ben said, "It doesn't work that way, Nicola. I can't go Eeny, Meeny, Miny, Mo and pull another cure out of a hat. Far as we can tell, there *is* no other cure. No other way."

My Ben squeezed my hand. "What's going on here, guys? This is turning into 'us versus them.' Aren't we supposed to be on the same side?"

"I second the motion," Nicola said.

Ben held my gaze, nodded towards the other two. "Those people *are* us. We're looking at ourselves in the future. And we're arguing? How stupid is that?"

Nicola put a hand to her mouth, a nervous laugh escaping her lips.

Adult Ben glared at her. "You don't even know what was being said before you walked in."

"That's right," she said. "I can laugh because I wasn't here. That doesn't change the fact that he's right." Adult Ben kept up the stern look, so she added, "I take it you don't like being outsmarted by a teenager. You were young once too, Ben. Don't forget it."

"Look, I'm smarter than I was then. I'm more experienced and I've learnt a lot over the years."

"That's quite an ego you've got."

His eyes narrowed. "That's got nothing to do with it."

"Sometimes I think Max Alonzo is rubbing off onto you. Now there's one hell of an ego."

"It's hardly surprising." Adult Ben sounded calmer. "When you look at his body of work, his reputation, how long he's been established in the field."

"He's always bragging about something, going on about the Porsche and the European vacations and the jewelry he buys for his wife."

"Not always."

"Only whenever I see him which, thankfully, is not very often. Honestly, I don't know where he gets the money from. Maybe he's selling off medical secrets."

Ben shot her a derisive look. "Now you're being ridiculous."

"I was only joking."

Nicola didn't look like she was joking. She could be

one scary-looking woman. And I liked that about her.

She held my gaze. "Max got angry with Ben about some silly thing, then got all hot headed and started pointing the finger." She jabbed her finger in the air for effect. "He said *I made you and I can break you*. They were his exact words."

He didn't sound like a well-respected name in medical research. Sounded more like a psychopath.

Nicola added, "I don't want anyone talking like that to the man I love, ever. I wanted to go to that man's house and kick his ass. Ben wouldn't let me."

"He apologized," adult Ben said. "Seemed genuinely sorry."

She said in a low voice, "He was showing his true colors."

No wonder Nicola didn't like Max Alonzo. I'd never even met the man and I thought he seemed like a piece of work.

I let out a long sigh, then stood behind my Ben's chair, my hands on his shoulders. "This is driving me crazy. I can't stand being cooped up like this."

Adult Ben didn't miss a beat. "You don't have to stay. You can go back."

I draped my hands over Ben's chest – *my* Ben, that is – hugging him from behind. I wished adult Ben would be more insightful or more cooperative or even go away. I couldn't think straight any more.

"You can't go wandering the streets unaccompanied either," he added. "You're safe at the apartment and that's where you should stay."

This was too much for me. "We came here to the laboratory, didn't we?"

"Because we needed to talk and that was fine while you were with me. Out there, anything could happen. You might get hit by a car and then you won't be able to travel back to where you belong. You might accidentally change something that affects the future."

I hated going around in circles. "We *are* trying to change the future. That's why we're here. To get rid of the virus."

Tightlipped, he said, "You're safest at the apartment."

"We need to get out, go for a walk, maybe get some exercise. You can't keep us locked up."

"Don't be ridiculous. This isn't a prison."

"No, it just feels like it."

Nicola turned to face him. "Ben, you need to take it easy. I'll drive them to the apartment and then I'm giving them the key and the code. They're not six years old. You know what six-year-olds are like. They need a lot of attention."

He gave her a pointed stare.

"Look at them," she said. "They just want to feel like normal people again. There's nothing wrong with that."

"What, exactly, do you think is normal about any of this?" Ben asked.

Nicola could be tightlipped too. "Let's go."

I couldn't get out of there fast enough.

CHAPTER NINETEEN

I needed fresh air and exercise to clear my head. I needed to run and sweat and maybe beat someone or something up.

Nicola had nailed it when she said I wanted a normal life. Unfortunately, that was the one thing I couldn't get.

Ben stepped out of the front door of the apartment building ahead of me. "It was good of Nicola to get us these clothes."

We hadn't even needed to stop at the store on the way back here. She'd already purchased fresh tee shirts, underwear and the shorts we were wearing as we headed out on a run. Luckily she knew my style. Ben's too.

I jogged down the front path. "Yeah, I'm nice, aren't I?"

"Let's just run, okay? I'm not going through that again."

We headed off through the suburban streets at an easy jog. To look around, you'd think the world hadn't changed much over the last twenty years and, in some ways, it hadn't. People still lived in houses or apartments, went to work and came home to their families in the evening.

Changes in technology meant that the way people lived and worked was constantly evolving. But it was still work. And this was still life as we knew it.

We turned a corner. More houses, more trees lining the streets, more people doing their everyday chores. All of this suburbia was reassuring. This might be boring, but 'boring' was fine by me.

Though the sky above us was cloudy, there was a certain clarity in the air. In New Nation, the atmosphere had always felt heavy, as if the sky might fall in, even on the sunniest day.

"I felt a couple of drops of rain," Ben said.

"Me too." I kept jogging. "A bit of water never hurt anyone."

"Do you think the weather is changing here? Getting hotter or colder depending on where you live?"

"I think that started a while ago. This is nothing compared to what's coming."

"Hang on." Ben stopped to tie his shoelace.

In New Nation, the country was ravaged by a series of storms, floods, tornados, you name it. After a while, it wasn't so bad though, mostly because we were set up for it with lots of concrete structures. Living in a bunker became normal.

Traffic increased as we turned onto a main road with cars zooming past. Luckily the sidewalk was wide and people were making way for us so we didn't need to slow down.

"What are those tracks down the middle of the road for?" Ben asked.

"They're for pods, the early ones. At first, they were

mostly used for public transportation."

A large driverless pod passed by. Technically it was a pod because it sat on tracks but it looked like a glorified bus. Later, pods would hang from overhead tracks and, later still, they'd travel through the air. They were computer controlled so accidents and traffic congestion became largely things of the past. Mind you, a huge drop in the population must've done wonders for reducing traffic.

We entered a shopping area with stores lining the streets and people buzzing around, so we slowed to a fast walk, making a beeline for a square that lay ahead. There were trees overhead, a few garden beds and benches that looked out onto a central fountain while, at the rear, tables from a café spilled out onto the square. The rain hadn't eventuated.

A drinking fountain was a welcome sight so we took turns getting a drink, then sat on a nearby bench.

"This feels so normal," I said.

Ben looked around. "Yeah, it does."

I ruffled his nearly non-existent hair and he swatted me away.

"It'll grow," he said.

Two boys aged about ten or eleven took turns splashing each other by the fountain, then running away. A little girl in a pink dress toddled over to them, giggling. The two boys took her by the hand, one on either side, and swung her gently through the air as they walked, which caused even more giggling. Their parents got up from a bench, the man leaning over to pick up the toddler, while the mom spoke to the two boys. I didn't need to make out her words to sense her loving tone.

To think that New Nation had got rid of this, replaced the family unit with a different system, something more efficient. It wasn't progress. It was cruel.

"Do you think about your family, Ben?" I asked.

"Yes." He stared at the parents and kids as they walked away. "I can't wait to get back to Altabena and the way things were."

I squeezed his hand. "We'll get there, Ben."

"The problem is I feel so far away from my family. I mean, I know they're here somewhere but it's not the same."

"What if we could arrange something? Maybe find some way of seeing them from a distance. Your dad, Celia. Josh. They'll all be older but they're probably still living in Altabena. It's not that far."

A curt shake of his head. "I don't want to do that. There might be things I'm better off not knowing. If something happened to Celia, a serious illness, a car crash, I couldn't bear to find out. I'm too scared even to ask adult Ben about them.

"I know how you feel."

Did he think it unfair that I knew so much about future developments and where the world was headed? But I didn't know exactly what would happen to the people I loved. And maybe it was better that way.

Ben raised his eyebrows. "How about you? Do you want to visit your parents?"

"A bit like you," I said. "It's complicated. While I was in Altabena, Jan and Phil Gray were the only parents I knew and I was their daughter." I swallowed the lump in my throat. "But I'm somebody else's daughter too."

"Sorry, Nic, I never asked you about your biological

parents."

I shrugged. "In some ways, there's not much to say. When I was growing up, I didn't feel anything for them. I took the emotion-suppressing pills like everyone else. I thought they were vitamins. And I was brainwashed, like everyone else. But it was different when we came back to New Nation. I felt something."

"That's not a bad thing, though."

"Isn't it? I feel like a traitor." I shook my head. "I don't know what to feel. My Altabena parents are my real family, the only family I've ever known, and now I'm getting all emotional toward my New Nation parents who are practically strangers to me."

Ben slid his hand onto my knee. "Your feelings aren't wrong, Nic. Maybe you feel something for your New Nation parents but that doesn't mean you love your Altabena parents less. It doesn't mean you're two-faced or guilty of anything."

I gazed down at leaves being blown on the pavement. "There's something else. If there's no virus and we change the future, how do I know my biological parents will still meet and be together? How do I know I'll even be born?"

There was also another question I didn't dare raise. If I wasn't born, how could I be sent back?

And if I kept asking myself these questions, I'd go crazy.

"I keep hoping I'm wrong about that," I said. "I saw my biological parents holding hands and wondered if they had some genuine affection for each other. It's not something I'd seen in New Nation, not that I could remember anyway."

"I noticed too, Nic."

Maybe Ben and I were more attuned to that sort of thing. "Which makes me think maybe they're going to be together anyway, regardless of the government."

He shrugged. "Maybe they are."

Too tentative to look up, I pretended the leaves on the ground were riveting. "Sometimes I wonder if I've been a traitor all along. I'm having second thoughts about whether we're doing the right thing. We want to rid the world of the virus and stop Bartley consolidating power, but is that too big? Is it going to have other repercussions that we can't even think of?"

Ben looked at me as if I were an idiot. "Stopping Bartley, preventing the virus and saving billions of lives – when you put it that way, it sounds so noble. You've got me convinced!"

This was why I loved Ben, or one of the reasons. He could always put me back on track and make me feel better. Because he believed in me, sometimes more than I believed in myself.

I also believed that sometimes you needed to pare things down to their simplest level. Life was already complex without making things harder than they needed to be. It was too easy to add complications and then you'd forget what you were doing and where you should be.

I wrapped my arms around Ben's waist and kissed him. He was magnificently sweaty. He was everything I wanted him to be.

His arm around my shoulder, he held me close. "I finally feel as if we belong together."

That was a strange thing to say. Perhaps he sensed my hesitation because he added, "That didn't come out right. I mean, *obviously* we belong together but after last night, it's on another level. As if it's added a layer to our relationship or cemented us even closer."

Having sex with Ben was the one thing about which I had absolutely no doubts. If I pared this down to its simplest level, it was meant to be, and my life was richer for it.

I pressed a quick kiss to his lips. "Cement. That's very romantic."

"Hey, you were the one who said you didn't need candlelight or satin sheets."

It was funny because in some ways sex changed things and in some ways it didn't. I was still basically the same Nicola Gray. Yet I felt committed and Ben felt it too.

Maybe 'cement' wasn't so bad after all.

And maybe last night had been much more than just sex.

CHAPTER TWENTY

I took Ben's hand as I got to my feet. "Time to get going. We need to get warmed up again."

We turned off the main road and started jogging, only in a different direction so we weren't backtracking.

A small mosque on the other side of the road had been burnt out, the white walls blackened and the front fenced off to prevent trespassers.

Neither of us said anything for a while.

"You know what I didn't like about Ben?" Ben asked with absolutely no irony. "He wasn't listening, wasn't open to our ideas or new ways of doing things."

"Yeah," I said.

"As people get older, they get so closed-minded. Not everyone, but lots of people. I just never thought I'd be one of them."

"You don't have to turn out that way."

"But you saw what I was like," he said. "A grumble guts, to use your words."

"Then don't let that happen. My Ben is a wonderful person. You can grow into an even better Ben. You've got choices."

He stopped at a corner. "Let's go down this way."

"Any idea what's down here?"

"We'll find out."

"What other choices have we got?" I asked. "What other ideas?"

"Bartley and the virus..." Ben mumbled as he jogged. "The virus is going to kill billions of people. So we need to stop it happening."

An idea came to me. "You know what the rebel generals would have done? They'd blow up the research institute building with everyone in it. Obliterate the years of research and everything else that went with it."

"Could be fun to blow up a huge building."

"Not so much fun to kill people," I said. "We'd have to evacuate the place first."

"Maybe blow up the mainframe and research records too. Blow up a bunch of stuff."

We kept jogging. These were just ideas. Ideas weren't action. Ideas weren't bad. We weren't really going to blow anything up.

My mind was ticking over. I was in the zone. You couldn't have the cancer cure without the K-virus. That was the way it seemed. We wanted to keep one but not the other.

"The virus is coming," I said. "We know that. Maybe we can cordon off the institute building, stop the virus escaping, prevent it leaking out into the rest of the world."

"It's an airborne virus," Ben said. "We could build a dome around the building."

"Or use some of the concrete we love so much in New Nation."

"Or develop a vaccine for the K-virus before it's released."

A vaccine for the virus. Just because no one had managed it before didn't mean it wasn't possible. Maybe we didn't need to rid the world of the virus if we could find a cure first.

"That's a great idea, Ben." I nudged him around a corner. "There's a park down there. Bartley wants the virus to happen. What if Ben stopped work on the cancer cure now? No cure, no K-virus either."

"Ben isn't going to stop," he said.

"I know. Besides, the cancer cure will be a great thing."

We looked down a side street being blocked by a crane at the far end. A crane with a wrecking ball. Ben motioned for me to follow, closer to where a small crowd had gathered on the sidewalk outside a synagogue. Several men in hard hats and construction clothes were arguing with the people there, or maybe it was the other way around. Voices were raised. Fists were being shaken in the air.

Ben seemed surprised and stopped at the side of the road, a safe distance away.

Police arrived and asked us to move, so we shifted a little further down the street where we could stay in the background. They were busy pushing back the crowd while two men got back into the crane.

Ben screwed up his face. "They're going to knock that building down?"

"Yep."

"Because it's a synagogue?"

"Because it's a place of worship. The sort of religion makes no difference."

Ben pointed and gesticulated. "Isn't that what Hitler did?"

I wasn't sure. "Hitler hated Jews. Bartley hates all religions equally, as far as I know. You saw the burnt out mosque we passed earlier? They started with the easy targets first. Mosques were the first to go. People let it happen because they didn't like Muslims or they thought they were terrorists or had some other stupid reason."

This wasn't quite what the history books had said. At school, we'd been told about bigoted behavior toward some religious groups and how this made people start to reconsider their beliefs. All of which led people to abandon religion. That was the history according to the Bartley government, though now I was interpreting it differently.

"Bartley believed we didn't need religion," I said. "Only a stable system of government. And him, of course."

Ben stared at the crane, its wrecking ball swinging as the crane turned. "We should do something."

I reached for his arm. "We can't. Those people are doing what they can."

"I don't want to watch," he said.

Which was fine by me, so we walked away, an uncomfortable silence between us. I wished we could make everything right, but there was only so much we could do.

When we got to the end of the street, we turned right to head back toward the apartment. I started to jog but Ben reached for my arm and shook his head. Still, his walking pace was fast and that suited me.

"We've been so focused on the virus," he said. "What

if we forgot about that for a while and concentrated on Bartley? What if someone could assassinate him?"

"It's an idea," I said. "Someone tried that once, when the first Bartley was in power."

I told him about the assassination attempt from the top of the Bryson Building, and how I thought it happened not long after the student massacre in Altabena.

"Maybe someone *should* assassinate Bartley," Ben said. "If he died, then there'd be no more Bartleys after him."

His son took over leadership and then his son after him, which sounded a lot like a dictatorship to me. Or perhaps Bartley thought of himself as royalty.

"The second Bartley has already been born by now," I said. "He's going to take over the reins. It's one thing to assassinate a dictator, but could you kill his child as well? A child who hasn't done anything yet?"

Ben didn't answer. "Bartley reminds me so much of Hitler. What if you could go back in time and assassinate Hitler before he took power, before he caused a world war, before he exterminated six million Jews. Would you do it?"

"Maybe. Anyone who'd assassinated Hitler would deserve a medal. But could you kill him *before* he'd done those things?"

"I don't know, Nic. I haven't killed a lot of people."

Killing was hard. Or maybe I wasn't good at it. Maybe I didn't have the guts and determination to do it. Or perhaps too much humanity.

The first time I arrived in Altabena, I'd practically made sure I couldn't kill Ben by falling in love with him instead. I hadn't even cared that I was putting my own life at risk.

Did I have it in me? Was I really a killer?

"There are lots of ways of killing," Ben said. "People hire experts for the job. Contract killers have no problem doing it in cold blood."

I wasn't sure that was even an option. In my wildest dreams, I couldn't imagine we'd get together enough money to pay someone for a job like that.

Also, why would we hire someone when I was such a good shot myself? Seriously good. When it came to targets, anyway.

The apartment building lay ahead. I couldn't call it 'our' apartment because it wasn't. This wasn't our home. Home was so far away it wasn't funny.

We'd come here grossly unprepared. Full of honorable intentions, yes. And between the two of us, Ben and I had brains and a remarkable skill set. We were finally coming up with ideas. There were options.

But ideas didn't achieve results.

Action did.

CHAPTER TWENTY-ONE

Back in the school principal's office again, or at least that was what it felt like. Come to think of it, I'd never been sent to the principal's office the whole time I'd been in Altabena. Yet I'm certain this felt worse.

Adult Ben had been called in to Dr. Max Alonzo's office, which was a lot like the other offices we'd seen at the research institute except it had a window with a view through the trees to a park across the road.

The walls were pale gray, the desk boring brown, the bookshelves immaculately neat, no personal items, no sign of personality anywhere. We were sitting in a small breakout area with padded vinyl chairs that made you sit bolt upright.

"I'm sure you understand, Ben," Max Alonzo said.

Adult Ben acknowledged him with a nod.

Max spread his arms, motioning toward Ben and me. "I had to see this for myself. Besides, it was the only way to assuage Ralph's concerns. You know what he can be like."

At least the man I referred to as the crazy professor

wasn't here. I hadn't thought he seemed the suspicious type, but I'd been wrong. He didn't know where Ben and I were from, though. He couldn't.

Adult Ben had that slightly world-weary, bored look that adults sometimes got. "You have a responsibility to the institute. I don't have a problem with that, but I think Ralph has gone a little overboard."

Max stared at Ben, then back at adult Ben. "The family resemblance is truly remarkable."

"So what if it is?" adult Ben said. "What is it Ralph thinks we've been doing?"

A pause.

"Well?"

Deadpan, Max added, "He said you two looked so alike it's almost as if you're the same person."

I froze in my chair.

Adult Ben rolled his eyes. "That's the most ridiculous thing I've heard."

"I know. He went on about unauthorized experiments and DNA manipulation and cloning and all sorts of things. For a scientist, Ralph was coming out with some wild ideas and accusations."

Maybe Professor Ralph wasn't crazy at all. He could spot that something was odd even if he hadn't put his finger on exactly what.

"It's lucky Ralph hasn't met your wife too, Ben," Max said. "Or he'd be taking this to the ethics board or some higher authority."

Explaining a strong family resemblance on Ben's side of the family was one thing. Having the same striking resemblance on Nicola's side of the family as well made this harder to explain. Perhaps the answer was not to try to explain it.

I cleared my throat. "I hope you don't mind my saying so, but the only strange thing is being called in here and asked to explain our appearance. I can choose my clothes but I can't choose my face. I can't help looking this way and it's not my fault if I look a lot like Aunt Nicola."

"There's no need to get upset," he said. "It's not personal."

"My face feels pretty personal to me."

"I'm sorry, but I have to be seen to have made enquiries and a basic investigation. It's part of my job. Then, if anyone else asks, I can tell them the situation has been dealt with. I didn't intend for this to be an interrogation."

"And it's probably not unless you're at the receiving end." I had to hold my ground. "We came here because we're both very proud of Ben's work and we're interested in what he's doing. Well, actually James understands it whereas I'm mostly tagging along."

Max's shoulders relaxed, his whole demeanor changing, and in an instant he became a different person. "You 'understand' the research we're doing?"

Ben-who-was-now-called-James nodded. "Some of it, yes. It's cutting edge stuff. How could I not be interested?"

Max's eyes lit up. "Really? Which aspects in particular?"

"DNA sequencing for a start."

Max grinned, something I hadn't seen before. The three men had an animated discussion about immunotherapy, cancer mutations, their analysis, DNA sequencing methods and the possibility of introducing vaccines containing the mutations to other parts of the body to shrink tumors.

Their conversation went much deeper than I could understand but I got the gist of it, however unlike our earlier discussions with Ben, there was no mention of the killer virus.

"Are you at college yet?" Max asked my Ben.

"Soon," he said. "I plan on studying medicine."

"Like your uncle." Max nodded. "Excellent. However Ben isn't the only one making exciting discoveries in the field."

"Really?"

"I've also been doing some research of my own into why the body accepts cancer cells without treating them as it does other invaders. Ben's earlier work into DNA sequencing has been instrumental. I've long thought that was where the key lay to a cancer cure."

Something flickered in adult Ben's eyes. "What sort of research?"

Max leaned forward. "I believe it's in the sub-molecular level of the DNA of the cancer cells. For want of a better word, there's a kink in the sequence of the DNA that causes the strands of DNA to react with each other and then with neighboring cells. It's fascinating because the sub-molecules appear perfectly normal on observation but they're programmed to cause a reaction. I believe we're very close to understanding this highly important aspect."

"So this research brings us closer to a cure?" Ben asked.

"There's more." It seemed there was no stopping Max. "I've delegated some other researchers to work on a special project. We've added the same kink to cells bearing diseases that the body traditionally does fight off. As soon as the kink was added, the body's immune system stopped attacking the disease, and the illness took over at great speed."

"You're talking about creating diseases in animals," Ben said.

"We need your expert mind on this, Ben. You've made outstanding discoveries in the past and you can do it again."

Ben stared at the man. "Why didn't you mention any of this to me before?"

"I'm telling you now."

Adult Ben's eyes narrowed. "Research into DNA sequencing to refine a cancer cure is one thing. Using DNA sequencing to experiment with how to encourage diseases to take over the human body is another."

Max glared right back. "Yes, it's a separate but related aspect, one I knew you wouldn't approve of."

"Because it's unethical."

"This project went to the ethics committee and went through the same process as all our other research."

Ben raised his eyebrows. "You can't tell me the committee approved this?"

"It was approved," Max said.

"By whom?"

"This went right to the top to the Secretary of State. And higher. State Ruler Harrison Bartley has personally endorsed this research."

Of course.

Because this was exactly what Bartley wanted.

CHAPTER TWENTY-TWO

Ben and I were back in our apartment, which wasn't our apartment because we didn't have a home any more. If we had a prison, however, this would be it because it felt as if we were under house arrest.

While the two of us stood in the kitchen chopping onions and garlic, adult Ben hovered over us. He was pacing, his hands behind his back, even though there wasn't a lot of room for movement in here.

"You're wrong about Max Alonzo," he said. "The man's a scientist, not a criminal."

I turned from the bench. "I'm sure he's the one who propagates the virus. We need to be very careful with him."

Ben kept pacing. "What about evidence?"

"You heard what he said. Bartley gave approval for the research. He might not yet know this will develop into a killer virus but he's sure as hell going to work that out pretty soon and use it to his benefit."

"Look, Max isn't a bad person. It's early days yet and there are lots of ways this could go."

"That's where you're wrong. There's only one way this will go unless we do something about it."

Ben stopped and stared. "I can't accuse a well-respected medical professional of something he hasn't done, not when we don't even know if you're right. It's just a suspicion."

"I'm not saying we should throw him in jail or eliminate him, only that we need to get him out of the equation."

There were other things we had to get out of the equation – the K-virus, for one. My mind was ticking over. Meanwhile adult Ben seemed to be at a standstill.

Eventually he said, "You're young and you still have a soldier inside you. You spent your first seventeen years in New Nation and that's not something that gets wiped out overnight. You might be able to fool yourself but you're not fooling me. Don't tell me you're not talking about eliminating Max Alonzo because that's exactly what you're talking about."

Adult Ben was wrong. And he was right. I was thinking like a soldier. If there was opposition, you should get rid of it and find safety. The strategy made sense, and maybe that was the best solution in this case. We'd tried coming up with complex ideas and hadn't come up with anything worthwhile.

Keep things simple. What would my superior officers do in a situation like this? They'd probably eliminate Max Alonzo and also Ben because if he was going to create the virus like it said in the history books, we couldn't take any chances. But I couldn't kill the man I loved.

My Ben was beside me. He dropped his knife and turned, anger glimmering in the green eyes I knew so well.

"Nicola and I may be young," he said. "But that's not the problem. We came here with our eyes open."

"No you didn't," his older self said. "You came with good intentions, gunning for action."

"At least we're trying to do something. We're being open-minded. You're supposed to be a man of science yet you won't even look around and think about things a different way."

Tightlipped, adult Ben had the look in his eyes that said *you think you know everything.* "Stay here. Don't do anything stupid. Don't do anything at all. Just wait."

It was a relief when he left.

I slid my arms around my boyfriend's waist, nuzzled my head against his chest and held him close.

Eventually I said, "We could always talk to Nicola. On her own, I mean."

Ben held me at arms' length. "Do you think that would do any good?"

"It's worth a try. Ben can't distance himself from his research. It's not the same with Nicola. She's a different person and she sees things in a particular light."

He smiled. "You've always been...different." Seeing the look on my face, he added, "in the best way possible, of course."

We finished cooking dinner. Actually, Ben did the cooking while I followed instructions, which was the safest way to tackle this. My skills in the kitchen have improved in the last year but Ben was a much better cook.

I stared across the table at him. "How can we act so normal, cooking up a pasta dinner and sitting here as if everything is okay?"

"This is the new normal," he said. "We've got to eat.

Life goes on."

"Or does it?"

Ben ate his meal without speaking. There were some things we didn't need to say. The virus was hard to ignore while we were here – harder than it had been in Altabena – because it was just around the corner. A pang cut through my heart at the thought of our families and friends, and the lives that would be lost.

That's why we were here. To stop that from happening.

I picked up my glass. "A toast. To our success. Because we have to think positive."

Ben touched his glass to mine. "Nicola was smart when she bought us the wine."

I smiled. "I've got to agree."

Though I wasn't a heavy drinker, a glass wouldn't hurt. In fact, a glass made both the dinner and the cleaning up go down more smoothly.

After dinner, Ben was rigid on the sofa beside me and didn't seem himself at all, so I suggested a massage. The muscles of his neck were stiff beneath my fingers. He moaned. In a good way.

"Let's get your shirt off," I said.

He ripped off his tee shirt and I massaged his shoulders and back, my hands working in little circles to press out the knots, then used larger movements to get him relaxed. His skin felt so smooth, the muscles of his back well defined.

I nuzzled closer to him, peppering his neck with little kisses. He smelt like my Ben, fresh and familiar at the same time. I ran my hand over his hair, still so short, so unlike my Ben, something I was never going to get used to. Yet he was still my Ben in every other way. Still the Ben I loved.

He shifted on the sofa, cupped my face in his hands and pressed his lips against mine. His hands were on my waist, under my tee shirt, exploring softly, more gently than I longed for. I lifted my shirt over my head, unhooked my bra and tossed it aside. Snaking my arms around Ben's neck, I drew him closer. Skin on skin. A sizzle shot up my spine.

My mouth found his and we were both hungry for more. I kissed him as if this was the last time, as if I'd never see him again. Could he tell how desperate I was to have him, all of him, to never let him go?

A strange feeling flooded through me. It was as if this was my last day on earth, our final moments together, my last chance to show Ben how much I loved him. If the world crumbled around us, right now there was nowhere I would rather be than here with Ben.

So why did I also feel this sense of desperation dripping from me? As if I could feel him slipping through my fingers.

We kissed and gripped each other tightly, ending up on the floor. The rest of our clothes came off and Ben was on top of me and I'd never wanted anything so badly in my life.

I had him. All of him. He was mine and I was his. As close as we could get. As intense as any experience could be.

Ben didn't know how much this meant to me. He couldn't. I was clinging to him for dear life, for the two of us, for the world that was falling apart around us. Because I had the horrible feeling that if I let him go, I might never have him back again.

Afterwards, the floor on which we lay was hard, something I hadn't noticed before, but I was with my Ben and wasn't ready to let him go just yet.

He held me close and whispered in my ear. "This isn't just sex, Nic. You know that, don't you?"

Did I? The physical side of things meant more to Ben than me. Or they had until recently. He'd been hanging out to take that next step, made that very clear, and I'd been putting it off for a long time.

He pressed a little kiss to my neck. "We were making love. That's what this was all about."

I held him close, saw emotion glimmering in his green eyes, and didn't know what to say.

But Ben did. "I love you, Nic. I've loved you for a long time."

My body – my whole being – was flooded with warmth and contentment. So this was what it felt like. So right, so natural. I was floating, lost in a sea of emotion, sailing toward a magnificent sunset. With Ben. Always with Ben.

I whispered the words because I couldn't say them out loud. "Love you too."

"There are lots of things I've never said."

"You don't have to say them now. You can save them."

"You're always there for me."

I pressed a finger to his lips. There was so much going through my head and many words I couldn't bear to hear right now.

He pulled my hand away. "You're perfect for me. You balance me out. We've been through so much together, things that other people could never understand, and that brings us even closer. I couldn't replace that. I wouldn't want to."

There was a time I would love to have heard these words from him, but not now. A different sort of desperation gripped me.

Trying to make light of it, I said, "Good, because I don't want you to find a replacement."

If only I could stay with Ben like this forever. If only I could be the person he wanted me to be.

He wrapped his arms around me and held me close. This was what I wanted – for him to hold me and never let me go.

"Tomorrow, I want to wake up in your arms," I said. "Like this, though preferably in the bed."

He peppered my neck with little kisses. "That can be arranged."

Tomorrow…and how many other days? Would he still want me the day after that?

Because if worse came to worse, there might only be one way to stop the virus. I might have to eliminate adult Ben so he wouldn't create the cancer cure and the virus.

Maybe my Ben would never accept me again, not when he knew what was coming. And that was probably how it should be. Maybe I didn't deserve him.

I couldn't hurt my Ben. I'd risked everything to be with him, to stay in Altabena. I'd even saved his life.

But could I get rid of adult Ben to save the world?

CHAPTER TWENTY-THREE

Another day, another disaster. That was what it felt like. I shoved my hands into my pockets as I strode down the street. Ben and Nicola's house wasn't far from the apartment – an easy walk, in fact – yet they'd kept us away from it. Not for much longer.

I'd convinced Ben I should talk to Nicola on my own while adult Ben was at work. Woman to woman. Or at least that was the idea. Nicola seemed much more respectful of our opinions and attitudes than adult Ben, and much less likely to write off our ideas.

In the army, I was used to being dismissed and constantly told what to do. I wasn't in the military any more. I was a different person now.

I turned the corner onto a pleasant, suburban, tree-lined street, the street where Nicola and Ben lived. They must be doing okay to live in a good part of town. I felt strangely proud and pleased with myself, then shook off that ridiculous feeling as I strode to the front door. These weren't my achievements. Not yet.

As I walked up the front path, strange shrieking

sounds sailed through the air from the rear of the house. Drawn to them, I followed the noise and headed down the side path.

Not bad noise. These were high-pitched, fun shrieking sounds, the sorts of noises produced when people were playing with each other.

Something made me think of the way I'd been raised and the childhood I'd missed out on, the love I'd never had growing up, the warmth and fun that had never been a part of my life. Nothing wrong with having a bit of fun.

I stood behind a chest-high gate looking out onto a neat yard with a grassed area, flowerbeds and a cubby house tucked into the far corner. A little boy and girl squealed and raced around the yard. They were wearing shorts and tee shirts, both of them blue-eyed with wavy light brown hair. Twins, perhaps. They might've been around six, which made something jump to my mind – Nicola telling Ben six-year-olds need lots of attention.

Nicola was in the yard, her back to me. She was teasing the children, telling them to watch out as she sprayed them intermittently with a hose, which only made them shriek louder.

The little girl pointed in my direction. "A burglar!"

The two kids ran into each other, which made for more giggling and hilarity as they tumbled to the ground.

That was when it hit me. Nicola and Ben had children.

We were going to have kids of our own one day – happy, healthy children who were going to run around the yard and play. My heart swelled in my chest, overflowing with so much emotion it was hard to breathe, hard to think or function.

Nicola turned to me, her eyes two warnings. I knew

the look. She was protecting her children and nothing would stand in her way.

Leaning over to turn off the hose, she smiled at the kids. "Time to go inside now, guys."

The little girl ran inside giggling and squealing while the boy dragged his feet. Nicola tickled him until he steamed ahead.

She came to the gate. "Wait for me at the front of the house. Give me five minutes and don't move."

I nodded, watching her close the door behind her. Maybe I should've thought of this before, but it hadn't occurred to me. Ben and I had wondered about our families, where they were, how they were doing, whether they'd survive the virus that was to come. *This* wasn't the family I'd wondered about. *This* seemed so far into the future it was unfathomable. Well, it was time for me to fathom it now.

I padded back down the side path to the front of the house.

I'd seen Adult Ben and Nicola bickering, seen them stressed, seen how hard Ben must've worked all these years. That was only one side of them. I could so easily have pictured Nicola fending off attackers or pummeling an intruder, yet I would never have pictured this little vision of domestic bliss in the back yard. Now I imagined something different – Ben taking the kids to the park, chasing them, throwing the ball to them.

No way could I mention any of this to my Ben. It'd freak him out like it was freaking me out. Besides, there were some things he didn't need to know. I almost wished I didn't know too.

The front door opened and Nicola stepped out.

"How could you do this?" she said in a low voice. "I thought you'd know better."

"I didn't," I said. "I'm sorry."

Fire in her eyes. "Those kids are the most important thing in the world to me and I refuse to let you see them when it'll only screw them up."

I held my hands out. "I had no clue, no idea at all."

This was why we couldn't stay with adult Ben and Nicola. It was so obvious now. Because there was no way to explain our presence to the children. Kids had good instincts. These two had called out there was a burglar but they hadn't been scared. Though they didn't know who I was, they knew enough not to be afraid.

Nicola shoved her hands into the pockets of her jeans. "The kids are watching a video. You've got five minutes or you can go now."

I got straight to the point. "I'm worried that if we don't do something, the same things are still going to happen. Ben will create the cancer cure, the virus will be a byproduct, the K-virus will take over and Bartley will consolidate power."

Nicola raised her eyebrows. "Can't you leave us to deal with the situation?"

"No, because you don't succeed. We need to stop Ben, if only until we work out what to do."

"He won't stop. His research is too important to him."

"That's what I'm worried about. We've got no control over Max Alonzo but with Ben, we've got a chance."

Nicola ran a hand through her short hair. "We don't have time to talk now."

"When then?"

"I know what you're thinking and you can't do it.

There must be another way. There's always another way."

"What am I thinking?"

Eliminating Ben and Max Alonzo seemed possible in theory but I couldn't bring myself to say it out loud, not in front of her. I couldn't. I would change in the next twenty years. I'd mellow and soften. But there was still a hard ass not far beneath the surface.

"You've got two beautiful children," I said. "How do you know they won't get the K-virus unless we make sure the virus doesn't eventuate?"

Nicola didn't say anything. The blue eyes that could be so stern glimmered with a combination of warmth and worry. I'd hit a nerve.

I took her hand. "They're the most important thing to you, that's what you said. And I believe you."

She glanced toward the road. "There's another reason you can't stay here. You have to go."

A blue sedan pulled up and someone familiar got out, her eyes fixed on the two of us. I'd have recognized her anywhere and that probably meant she'd be able to recognize me too. Lauren.

"Shit, it's too late," Nicola muttered, then more loudly, "Lauren, you're back early."

Lauren ambled up the front path and deposited her shopping bags on the porch as she stared at me, her eyes wide. She looked exactly the same, only her cheeks were more gaunt and her hair was streaked with purple. Good old Lauren, still experimenting with colors.

"Oh my God," she said. "Who is this?"

Nicola said calmly, "I'd like you to meet my niece…Grace."

"You never told me you had a niece." Lauren frowned.

"Hang on, you don't have any brothers or sisters. How can you have a niece?"

"Grace is my cousin's kid."

Lauren's eyes were ready to explode from her head as she looked from Nicola to me and back again. "You've got to be kidding me. She looks just like you. The spitting image. How'd that happen?"

Deadpan, Nicola replied, "A freak of nature."

"That's freaky all right!"

"Hey guys." I waved my hands in front of their faces. "I'm right here."

"So sorry, Grace," Lauren said. "We shouldn't be talking about you as if you're not there."

I shrugged. "When I'm with Nicola, I'm used to it."

"It's incredible," Lauren said. "You even sound just like her."

"Would you like me to stop talking?"

"No, no, I'm sorry."

After this ridiculous rambling we hit a roadblock and there was only silence.

Eventually Nicola said, "Lauren is staying with us for a few days. Grace, I believe you were just leaving."

I stepped back. "Yep, that's right."

Lauren turned to Nicola. "I'm having the weirdest sense of *déjà vu*. Remember when I met you on your first day at Altabena High and I thought I'd met you before. I've got that same feeling now."

There was a good reason for that.

"You were so nerdy," Lauren continued. "You talked like a robot, as if it was your first day on earth, and the worst thing was your boring, black school shoes. What a major fashion mistake."

Nicola shot her a stern look. "Thanks for reminding me."

"You know what," Lauren said. "You should offer yourselves up for some sort of genetic research because the resemblance between you two is like nothing I've seen before."

I placed a hand on my chest. "I'm a girl, not an alien."

"Sorry, I didn't mean that," Lauren said.

"Nicola's right. I have to go."

Or maybe I should never have come.

I was becoming the-girl-who-knew-too-much. Maybe not enough to save the world but enough to ruin some of life's surprises and future joys. People said knowledge was power but that wasn't necessarily true. There were some things it was better not to know.

So I left.

CHAPTER TWENTY-FOUR

Adult Ben's eyes were glued to us through the window as he headed for the laboratory door and opened it from the inside. "How did you get in here?"

As if we'd let a little thing like a secure facility stand in our way.

"Ben tried flirting with the receptionist," I said, a tactic that had worked well for us once before. "Then we got lucky and the crazy professor came by and let us in. He mumbled an apology and was extra nice to us. I think he felt bad about the accusations he'd made earlier."

Adult Ben looked annoyed. "I'm in the middle of something. You can't interrupt my work like this."

"You have to talk to us sooner or later," I said. "We're not going away."

Though he left us in no doubt that was what he wanted.

"Wait here." He left us in the doorway while finished off in the lab and gave instructions to a couple of technicians. "Let's go."

He led us down the hallway and into the next building

where his office was located.

Closing his office door behind him, he said, "You've got five minutes."

I'd heard that before, only I hadn't minded it coming from Nicola.

I leaned against the desk. "And how long does the rest of the world have?"

Ben glared. "I'm under a lot of pressure here and you're not helping."

"You can't hide behind your work and your research," I said, "because that's what you want to do."

His lips went thin. "Don't you dare diminish the importance of what I'm doing."

That wasn't what I was doing at all. Maybe it was time to hit him over the head if that's what it would take.

I said, "Max Alonzo is a big problem and you know it. You heard him yesterday. You can't be in denial about that."

A pause, then, "I need time to think about that. I can't go rushing in, even though I found out some things about Max that give me cause for serious doubts."

"He's going to create the virus. And you know it as well as we do."

Frustrated, he shook his head. "I can't accuse him of something he hasn't done. I can't be judge and jury for an act that hasn't happened."

"Exactly. And we can't wait until disaster is well underway because we do know what's going to happen. It's worse, though, Ben. This is personal. It's not just that Max Alonzo is instrumental in creating the virus. I think he's going to blame you for it. That's why you go down in history as creating both the cancer cure and the K-virus.

You end up the bad guy, not him."

Ben didn't say anything. Maybe he was horrified. Maybe he was thinking. From the look on his face, I couldn't tell.

"Have you ever heard the saying that history is written by the victor?" I asked.

"Of course."

Whoever wins the wars and ends up in power is the one who writes the history books. The Romans conquered other territories, forged their way into other lands, forced their rule onto other people, then wrote the history with themselves as the valiant conquerors bringing civilization to the barbarians. I dare say the people who had their land pillaged saw the situation differently.

Bartley did the same thing when he took over and created New Nation and a dictatorship. Bartley wanted this. He knew the power it could give him.

I said, "In this case, I don't know if the victor is Alonzo or Bartley. I only know you get a bum rap. This sort of thing is always about money and power. Alonzo is probably going to sell the virus to someone, maybe an individual investor or maybe straight to Bartley. He'll take the money and leave you with the blame."

We were still standing. Leaning against the desk, I was probably the most comfortable of the three of us, though I could guarantee no one in the room was relaxed.

Ben dropped down into the chair behind the desk, his head in his hands. "I used to respect Max. That all changed when he bypassed the ethics board and got approval from above for this research into DNA sequencing. That's not the man I used to know."

Progress at last. I shot my Ben a look as if to

acknowledge this. He nodded.

Adult Ben lifted his gaze. "From what he's said, he's on the verge of creating the virus even if he doesn't know it yet. The next step is to get other diseases to act like cancer, and fool the body's immune system into accepting these diseases as a friend. It's dangerous."

"We have to stop him," I said.

"Give me some time."

"That's something we don't have a lot of. You have to stop work on the cancer cure now. And we have to force Alonzo to stop, one way or another."

"It's not just up to me or Alonzo or any one person, though. The cogs are already turning. I've made a certain set of discoveries already and they can't be erased. If it's not me, it's only a matter of time until someone discovers the cancer cure given what has already been done. And only a matter of time until someone else discovers the K-virus."

"You have to find a cure for the virus, then," I said.

He stared at me as if I was an idiot. "Oh really? Do you think it's that easy?"

"Either that or you make sure all work stops on the cancer cure right now."

The tendons in his neck strained. I knew that look. He was ready to blow and I didn't care. Maybe he needed to be pushed.

He shook his finger at me. "You can't tell me what to do. You're only eighteen. Just a kid. I'm the one with the medical degree and the years of research experience. I know a lot more than you do."

I didn't respond well to finger-shaking. Ben may well be brilliant at his work but he was stuck in his medical bubble where his research was the only thing that mattered. He'd forgotten what it felt like to be eighteen and he'd also forgotten there was a big world out there, a present and a future.

I straightened, pulled back my shoulders. "Ben, don't ever underestimate what I can do. Ever."

His lips thin, he clapped a hand over his mouth, maybe to stop himself saying something he'd regret. Meanwhile, my Ben's eyes were wide – with fear, if I wasn't mistaken. He knew me too well. Knew I wouldn't stop.

Adult Ben paced the room, or what there was of it, then stopped. "You've always been a good person, Nicola, never wanton, never bad. What's going on with you?"

I folded my arms. "We don't want the same thing any more."

"You used not to be like this."

A curt shake of my head. "Our situation has changed. Not me. I'm not that different. I want a world free of the virus. At any cost."

"What's that supposed to mean?"

"It means I want an end to this. Maybe it'd be a good thing if you went to the future and saw exactly what it looks like."

Nothing from Ben. No response.

He didn't know what it was like to grow up in a government facility, to be indoctrinated, to be told there was only one way, the New Nation way. He hadn't seen the cities abandoned because we didn't have sufficient population, families devastated by the loss of loved ones, others left with the mutations that resulted from the virus.

I peeled the PR device from my arm. "I'll show you."

It took me only a minute to access the footage I was

looking for. I knew exactly what I was after because Carson, Bartley's young partner, had shown Ben the effects of the virus at the celebratory dinner in New Nation. That felt like so long ago now.

The scale of suffering was undeniable. Bodies were piled in the streets and that had caused further disease and more problems. Grown men were crying uncontrollably. Other shots showed the deformities caused by the virus to those who survived, huge heads, strange growths over once healthy bodies. Then there were shots of the next generation, babies born with missing limbs and extra appendages.

I saw it in adult Ben's eyes. He couldn't bear to watch the footage any more than I could, but this was something we couldn't turn a blind eye to. This was the future and he was part of it.

"How do I even I know this is real?" he asked.

"Of course it's real," I said. "Maybe you don't want to face it."

Disgust in my Ben's eyes. "It's sickening, isn't it?"

"Yes," adult Ben said.

My Ben continued. "I was shocked and revolted when I first saw this footage too, so I know how it feels. In fact, I know exactly how you feel. The K-virus will devastate society and Bartley will take over. I've been there. I saw what it was like. It was a cross between Nazi-style celebrations and some sci-fi movie. And it wasn't pretty."

Adult Ben opened his mouth as if to argue, but didn't. He started pacing again, his expression intense. "There might be something I can do. I'm not sure. It's risky and I've barely given it any thought."

The soldier inside me wanted to get a move on. "We

don't have a lot of time for thinking."

Adult Ben turned to me. "Is this an ultimatum, Nicola? Do it your way or…what?"

"I'm not into threats," I said. "But this isn't going to go away."

And neither was I.

CHAPTER TWENTY-FIVE

Footsteps on the floorboards. I'd been staying in the apartment long enough to recognize the sound. My eyes sprang open, quickly adjusting to the darkness.

I nudged Ben lying in bed beside me and put a finger to my lips, motioning him to be quiet. His eyes opened, suddenly wide with realization. He might not have heard any noises yet but he knew something was up.

Creeping out of the room, I stuck close to the wall and avoided a couple of the floorboards that creaked. Glancing back, I saw Ben standing in the corner by the bedroom doorway, ready to back me up. Ahead of me, a shadowy male figure approached. He hadn't seen me yet. I'd have the element of surprise.

I kept low and leapt at him, my shoulder cutting through his waist as I took him to the ground.

"Nic, no," my boyfriend yelled from behind me. "It's Ben."

I wished he'd told me two seconds sooner. I rolled off adult Ben and got to my feet now I knew there was no assailant. "You could've knocked."

He sat up, rubbing his ribs. "I didn't want to wake you both."

"Well, we're all awake now. Wide awake, I'd say." I took his hand and helped him up. I felt silly standing there in crumpled shorts and a tee shirt, but I'd bet he felt sillier.

"What time is it?" I asked.

"Three in the morning." He grabbed my shoulder to steady himself and whispered in my ear, "I've made a mistake."

My gut told me he was referring to something much bigger than coming in uninvited. A shudder reverberated up my spine.

My Ben came closer. "Are you all right, Nic?"

I nodded. "Someone else might be the worse for wear."

Adult Ben put his hand out. "Okay, I should've been more careful." Even in the dim light, I could see he was pleading with his eyes. "Nicola, I need to talk to you."

My boyfriend motioned toward the bedroom. "Give us a minute to put some clothes on."

"On her own," adult Ben said.

Silence.

He added, "We won't be gone long."

My Ben stopped and turned. I didn't know what was going on any more than he did but I wanted to find out. I took his hand, leading him to the bedroom.

"I don't like this," he muttered. "He breaks into the apartment in the middle of the night and then tries to drag you away."

I pulled on a pair of jeans and grabbed a windbreaker. "I'm not being dragged. I just want to hear what he has to say, that's all."

"So why can't he say it in front of me?"

"I don't know but I can only assume he's got a good reason. If you can trust anyone, you can trust him. This is 'you' in the future."

Ben dropped down onto the bed. "He's stubborn. He's going to let the virus be created. You don't trust him either, not completely."

Leaning over, I drew him close and held him, his head nuzzled against my chest. "I'll be back."

"What am I supposed to do in the meantime?"

"Try to get back to sleep."

"Yeah, right."

I turned to face him from the doorway. "I'll always come back, Ben."

There was only one thing that could keep me from him and that was…no, I wouldn't think the worst.

Adult Ben was waiting in the living room. As soon as he saw me, he reached for the door.

I raised my eyebrows. "Can't we talk here?"

His lips thin, he gave a curt shake of his head. Outside, we got in his car.

He switched on the engine and sat there, his hands on the wheel. "I can't go back to the lab."

Presumably because the facility had security and access was monitored. If my place was out, I figured his was too. And staying in the car for half the night felt too claustrophobic, so I suggested the town square that Ben and I had found when we went jogging.

A few minutes later, we were there. Luckily parking wasn't a problem at three in the morning. The fountains were lit up and flowing, the sound of streaming water soothing. There was no one else around as we sat on one of the benches.

"I've always known the K-virus would be coming." Ben's voice was low so it didn't carry through the night air. "But before you got here, I couldn't create a vaccine because I didn't know quite how the virus would work. There was always something missing. I didn't know how close I was, though, until you talked to me and then the pieces fell into place. It all fit in perfectly with my previous experiments and research, so it was quick. Much quicker than I thought. After you gave me clues about how the virus worked, it expedited the process significantly."

"That's good, isn't?" I said.

"It seemed so clear to me. I knew the virus would act the same way as cancer and that it'd encourage the body's immune system to accept it rather than fight it. They use the same DNA source code and that changed everything. That was the key."

I waited, thinking this sounded positive, with the possible exception of the tone of Ben's voice which sounded more like impending doom.

He rested his elbows on his knees. "I was so confident. With the source code, I got the nullifying agent very quickly."

"So where's the problem?" I asked.

"I narrowed it down to one of two options. I wasn't going to waste time and certainly wasn't going through the ethics board for approvals for testing. I refused to let them or Alonzo or anyone else impede my research." He turned to me. "I thought about you, Nicola, thought about my goal. I wasn't going to let anything get in my way."

My pulse was rising. Though I wasn't sure exactly what was coming, I felt a sense of responsibility for pushing myself into this Ben's life. I nodded for him to continue.

He said, "I had to start somewhere and was extremely confident the first option would be successful. I tested it on myself."

He tested it… Fear gripped my chest.

I swallowed. "Did it work?"

"In a way. I did the DNA testing straight away and can confirm the second option is the one that will produce a vaccine that alters the body's DNA sequencing so the human body rejects the K-virus. I'm on the verge of developing a vaccine, in other words. I knew if the first option didn't work, that would confirm the second option must be it."

I squeezed his hand. It was cold. That was what struck me most about Ben right now – how cold he was in his manner and approach.

"Then the virus won't devastate the world?" I said. "Is that what you're saying?"

"No, it won't. Or I believe it won't. It may have some effect. It may even become a dreaded disease in the same way that cancer is a horrible illness but we should be able to keep it at bay. We have a vaccine. That's huge."

"Then why so glum?"

"The problem is the first option I tested on myself."

"Go on."

"I wasn't just confident, Nicola. I was cocky. The first vaccine I tested turned out to be a potent mutation of the virus, one that digs deep into the DNA. This form of the virus is different, though. It's not infectious or contagious. This isn't the K-virus as it will become known in the future. This is more like a single shot that has affected only me."

"Are you…?"

"I feel fine for now but I don't know how long that will last. My DNA has been irrevocably altered. I've done the tests, seen the results." He paused. "I was so sure of myself. Knew I had a fifty-fifty chance but didn't believe this would really happen to me."

"Ben, are you saying what I think you're saying?"

He nodded. "I've given myself the virus."

CHAPTER TWENTY-SIX

My head was in my hands. *No, no, no.* That couldn't be what he was saying. He must have got it wrong or maybe I was the one who'd got it wrong, but there was no way this could be true.

This was Ben in the future. Did that mean my beautiful Ben only had another twenty or so years ahead of him and then he'd die a slow, agonizing death? No wonder he couldn't tell me this in front of my Ben.

My heart was being ripped from my chest, leaving a great gaping hole and pain like I'd never felt before. Except I had. But, no, this couldn't be happening again. Not again. Not to Ben.

I was only eighteen, and a couple of decades seemed such a long way in the future, but it wasn't when that person was sitting beside me. This wasn't what I wanted for him. It wasn't fair. He deserved so much better.

I sat up, my mouth open, the words stuck in my throat.

"It's not your fault, Nicola," he said.

"Isn't it?"

"I'm an adult, a qualified doctor, a medical researcher. The responsibility was all mine. I knew the risks and repercussions."

His voice cracked. He wasn't talking about himself any more. He was thinking about his family, about Nicola and those two little kids who needed a father. It sent a pang through my heart. They'd be my children too one day. I would love them and they'd be a part of me even if that wasn't how it felt now.

This couldn't be the end. I had to focus.

"The vaccine," I said. "Are you close to finalizing it?"

"Yes, now that I've conducted the first test, I'm ninety-nine percent sure the second option will work. I just have to hope I don't become incapacitated and die first."

Ninety-nine percent wasn't a hundred and this was my Ben we were talking about. He absolutely one hundred percent had to live and thrive and succeed. I didn't want any more statistics. I didn't want hope. I wanted certainty.

"Then you can cure yourself," I said. "You'll be okay."

"I have a different form of the virus," he said. "A mutation with different DNA sequencing. A vaccine won't work against this particular form."

"Are you sure?"

"I'm certain."

Pain gripped my throat but I forced the words out. "You have to keep going. You *have* to get the vaccine."

He looked down at his hands. "I think I can do it."

If only that would be good enough.

Not so long ago, I'd considered killing him to save the world and that had seemed a reasonable course of action. I knew now I'd never have been able to do it. I couldn't eliminate adult Ben any more than I could've eliminated him when I was younger and first landed in Altabena.

Now Ben was confident he was about to find a cure for the K-virus. If he succeeded, this discovery would save billions of lives and change the course of the future. He was on the verge of saving us all, and he was going to die a painful death.

No, I wouldn't have it. Couldn't bear it.

I wanted to scream and yell and shout at the world, but that wasn't what soldiers did. Soldiers took action.

Deep breaths. You can't lose it now, Nicola.

I stood. No, I wasn't going to lose Ben or my temper or anything else. I was selfish and determined and I would have it all. My way. Ben wasn't going to die, not now, not for a long time.

"There's a way," I said. "There's one more thing we can do."

Ben raised his eyebrows. "Really?"

"I'll go back in time twenty hours. It'll be morning, the start of a new day. That day will unfold the way it originally has. Ben and I will come to see you at the lab. We'll argue. You'll tell me I'm a kid and that I can't tell you what to do. I'll know what you're about to say before you say it. You'll also tell me you have doubts about the footage on my PR device."

"And how is any of this going to help?"

"You were already thinking about the two options for testing when we had that discussion, weren't you?"

"Yes," he said.

"I'm going to tell you to abandon the first option, that it's too dangerous, that you'd be about to give yourself the virus. I'll insist you go straight to option two."

Ben covered his chin. "Do you think I'll listen?"

I paced the pavement, my mind ticking over. "Yeah, I do. Remember when I went back in time to just before Altabena High was blown up?"

"Of course. It's not something I'll ever forget, no matter how long ago it was."

"That day, I could tell you exactly what was going to happen, who was going to say what, which car was going to drive by. I could tell you these things before they happened and that was what proved to you that I'd time traveled. We'll do the same thing this time. I'll tell you something that's about to happen as proof that I've gone back in time."

Ben gazed up at me so I stopped pacing.

"I have just the thing," he said. "Elizabeth, our youngest professor, came into the lab at exactly 3.00pm that afternoon and announced she's pregnant. It's a huge surprise because she had a medical problem as a teenager and was told she'd never be able to have children."

"Sounds good."

"There's more. She comes in with an orange cake and a bottle of non-alcoholic sparkling wine that's supposed to be a substitute for champagne."

"And you don't like orange cake," I said.

"Or non-alcoholic wine." A pause. "My thoughts weren't very charitable."

"Perfect."

I sat beside him and peeled the PR device from my arm, so it stiffened immediately. I was about to start my message to Nathan when Ben interrupted.

"Wouldn't it be easier if I traveled with you? If I went back in time, I'd know the mistake I'd made. You wouldn't need to explain it to me."

I shook my head. "Too dangerous. Nathan will be able to lock onto my geopositrons with relative ease. If he can't get your exact location, your transportation would be compromised. I don't want to think about what would happen if that went wrong."

At the moment, my boyfriend and I both had geopositrons in our system. I was working on the assumption that once we got back to Altabena safely we'd rid our bodies of them even if it was a slow process that took years.

He raised his eyebrows. "You're sure you can do this?"

I nodded, though I wasn't sure of anything.

No time to waste. I sent a message to Nathan instructing him to return me to New Nation and to be prepared to send me back to 2041 to twenty hours before the current time. I gave him the coordinates of the apartment as my return location. If all went well, I'd be sent to New Nation briefly so that Nathan could then send me back to my bed at the beginning of a new day. Safer to go to New Nation first, then travel back twenty hours, especially after the previous transportation mishaps.

Then I could warn adult Ben what was about to happen. It all made perfect sense. I sent the message and waited.

After a while, Ben asked, "What happens when the transportation works? Do you just disappear?"

"I presume so."

He nodded.

I was glad for the sound of rushing water from the fountain. It made me feel vaguely normal. Reminded me there was a world where children splashed each other with the water. And that was one of the reasons I was here. For my Ben, yes. And also for future generations. In fact, I would be one of those future generations one day, which was weird to say the least.

Suddenly, the water gushed more loudly but the fountain looked exactly the same. Louder, louder, like the sound of a giant waterfall, not a city fountain.

I covered my ears, except the noise became thunderous. The commotion wasn't outside. It was inside my mind and there was no escape, my skull about to explode. I wrapped my arms around my head and squeezed my eyes shut. It felt as if my brains were being blown out in slow motion.

It was too much to bear.

I couldn't do this...

CHAPTER TWENTY-SEVEN

A robotic voice droned in the background. I couldn't make out what was being said. Wasn't even sure there were actual words. The rushing noise in my head was subsiding, the pain lifting and I was starting to feel human again. I was a million miles from the fountain in the town square. I didn't need to see. I felt it. Another feeling overcame me, a feeling of success.

My eyes opened into slits. Nathan was standing there. It may have been his voice I'd heard. I wasn't sure.

I looked around. Definitely New Nation. The transportation room. The dark walls. The chair with moon-shaped fingernail marks on the arms from where I'd gripped it too tightly.

And I was naked. Typical.

Nathan nodded. "This is truly remarkable. From a scientific viewpoint, I mean."

"Good to see you too, Nathan," I said. "How are you doing?"

"In fact, you should not be enquiring into my health. I should be enquiring into yours. Is the headache passing?

How do you feel?"

The pain or the trip – I wasn't sure which – had taken it out of me like never before. It went beyond pain into another realm where I was on the brink of breaking.

"I'm gutted," I said. "Thanks for asking."

"This is an exciting moment for me."

Though Nathan wasn't exactly one for smiling and laughing, there was the hint of a satisfied smile on his lips. His normally pale skin appeared to be glowing, his eyes beaming, his face lit up with warmth. This was weird. Nathan didn't do warmth or pride or satisfaction. He was a facts person.

I tilted my head to better stare at him. "Are you okay?"

"I'm very okay." This time there was a definite smile on his face. "*Very okay?* How unusual for me to use incorrect grammar. I must indeed be excited."

I raised my eyebrows. "To see me?"

"In a sense. Your presence here confirms that my programming has been successful. I've done it, Nicola. I can transport people through time so they depart and arrive at the pre-programmed time."

"If I'm not mistaken, you look…proud," I said.

"That may be an accurate description. I now have the evidence to prove that the programming is successful. I've been breaking boundaries, opening up new worlds, crossing scientific barriers that were previously unknown."

And re-hashing old clichés too. I didn't say that. Didn't want to ruin his special moment. Besides, I couldn't have done this without him.

Still, I was in New Nation and didn't want to spend any longer here than necessary. I had to go back. I had to join Ben so we could finish what we started. The longer I stayed here the more dangerous it was.

"Are you ready to send me back?" I asked.

"Of course," Nathan said. "In your message, you asked for an immediate return to a time twenty hours before your initial departure. The programming has been completed exactly as you requested."

I could've kissed him. What the hell? I did, then sat back down.

"I gather you're pleased to see me," he said, deadpan.

"Very glad. Now send me back."

"Goodbye again, Nicola."

Nathan left to go to the control panel in the next room. In seconds, he'd be sending me back. Soon I'd get another of those killer headaches and I'd be with my Ben. It'd be early morning and I'd wake up in bed in the apartment.

Pain rocketed through my head. Again. It hit me like a truck, took my breath away, sucked the life out of me. Before, my head had felt as if it was about to explode. Now it felt as if it already had, bits of my cerebellum splattered across the pavement. I wasn't going to recover. There was no coming back from this.

Breathe, Nicola. One breath in – I could do it after all – then one breath out. In fact, that was all I could do. There was no thought in my head. I wasn't capable. There was only this earth-shattering pain.

I had no idea how long it took, where I was or what was going on, but finally the pain started to lift.

My ribs hurt. I was grateful to feel this pain instead of the sort that made me think I'd died. And if I was thinking, I must be alive. *I think, therefore I am.* Someone had said that even if I couldn't remember who.

I was lying on something with defined ridges that were digging into me. I shifted my hand and got a grip on the corner of something. I wasn't lying down, but I was. I couldn't make out my positioning.

I opened my eyes. Tried to lever myself up. Worked out I was draped face-down on some stairs. No wonder it was so uncomfortable, not that I was devastated about a cramp in my ribs under the circumstances.

Sitting up was hard work, but I did it. And I stayed there, my head in my hands as I gathered strength. Gazing around, I recognized the art deco railing. At least I was in the right apartment building though, with my astute powers of observation, I'd worked out I wasn't lying in bed next to Ben as I'd planned.

I was naked, of course. If I wasn't so gutted from the travel process, I might've cared more, however my exhaustion overrode that.

Struggling to my feet, I forced one foot after the other as I headed up the stairs, then stepped on the landing when I saw a door. I stood in front of it, trying to stay upright, trying to focus on the number on the door so I could work out which floor I was on. The first number looked like a 'two' so I only had one more floor to go.

Suddenly the door was pulled open and an old lady with a bag slung over her shoulder was staring at me, open-mouthed and wide-eyed. She slammed the door shut as quickly as she'd opened it, leaving me stunned.

Since this clearly wasn't the right apartment, I backed off to keep going up the stairs. The door opened again, only this time the woman looked less shocked as she stood in the doorway.

"Excuse me," she called out. "Are you okay?"

I turned from the first step. "Yeah."

"You're naked. Can I get you some clothes?"

Very considerate. "No, it's fine. Um, I was sleepwalking. Sorry."

She nodded, closed the door behind her and headed down the stairs, which is where she must've been going in the first place. Meanwhile, I trudged up the steps to the next floor. My eyesight must've been clearing up because I could read the number on the door with ease, so I knocked. This was it.

Ben pulled the door open. "Nicola!"

He wrapped his arms around me, pulled me in and spun around so we were inside the apartment. He smelled like sleep and he smelled like my Ben as I rested my head against his shoulder. Breathing him in, I heard the click of the door closing.

"Told you I'd always come back," I said.

"The banging on the door woke me up." He rubbed my back. "Where were you? Have you been sleepwalking?"

"A common assumption," I mumbled.

He held me at arms' length, looked into my eyes. "Are you drunk or something?"

I shook my head. "Exhausted. Please can you take me to bed and I'll explain later?"

My pathetic look must have been convincing because he scooped me up in his arms and carefully deposited me on the bed. He covered me with the comforter and lay beside me, stroking my hair.

It took all of about five seconds until I was out. I didn't drift into sleep so much as drop straight into it. After a rest that was too magnificent for words, I woke up ready for action.

Together, we had breakfast – or at that time of day, it may have been called lunch – while I filled Ben in on what had happened. His reaction made me appreciate having someone who trusted and believed in me. He was shocked and had trouble taking it all in, but knew I was telling the truth even if the full ramifications hadn't sunk in.

"We know what to do," he said as if this was the most normal thing in the world. "We've got to find Ben at the lab and tell him not to do the experiment."

"Yep."

A strange thought hit me. If there was an older Nicola and Ben here, as well as us, then shouldn't there also be another young Nicola here, the same person who'd time traveled before with Ben? Damn it, I was never going to understand this stuff. It did my head in every time I seriously thought about it.

A strange sense of *déjà vu* overcame me as we headed to the lab and saw one extremely disgruntled Ben Tanner at work, though perhaps it wasn't so strange after all. We had the same argument in his office. Maybe it couldn't be avoided.

The repetition was strangely reassuring, yet at the same time it felt like I'd been sucked into a vortex with the world whirling around me and my life spinning by.

I couldn't let that happen. I remembered.

Time to focus. "I know what you're thinking, Ben. That I can't tell you what to do, that I'm just a kid." His nostrils flared with anger, so I added, "There's a very good reason why I know."

I repeated the words he'd said to me about the research he'd already done and two options he was considering. "You're going to think the first option is the answer." Silence. I added, "And you're going to be wrong."

He tilted his head. "How do you know?"

"Because you told me. You said you had it narrowed down to two options, that you thought it was a fifty-fifty chance. The statistics didn't work in your favor."

Recognition sparked in his eyes. He knew I was telling the truth, I was sure of it, but I hadn't finished yet so I told him about the young professor who was going to announce her pregnancy at 3.00pm.

He seemed to consider this. "But you don't even know Elizabeth."

"No, I don't." I paused. "You can do this, Ben. You said you were very confident."

"You're saying I give myself a death sentence?"

"That's what you did the first time around. You can change that."

He nodded, mumbling something about calculations, then, "Leave it with me. I'll work it out. What are you two going to do in the meantime?"

"We wait," I said. The hardest part because you can never be a hundred per cent sure until after something has happened.

I stepped across the room and took my Ben's hand into mine. His grasp was warm and firm and everything I wanted it to be.

He let my fingers slide out and put his arm around me. I wasn't sure it had fully sunk in for him that adult Ben had given himself the virus and come close to death. And maybe it wasn't possible to understand when he hadn't been there. Besides, he'd have plenty of time to think about it later and we'd have plenty of time together. Soon we could go back to Altabena where we belonged. We were close, so close.

Something else was sinking in for me. I slipped my arm around his waist to draw him in more tightly. This was my Ben and nothing would change that.

However many years he had, no matter what happened, even if adult Ben messed up and things didn't work out...

I'd always choose Ben.

No matter what.

CHAPTER TWENTY-EIGHT

I woke with the realization that adult Ben hadn't woken me at three in the morning to tell me he'd given himself the virus. Such a relief to have succeeded. And that made for a wonderful start to the day.

Instead he'd called at a more civilized time and told us to meet him at his office. Sitting behind his desk, he looked frazzled but in a good way.

"I've been up half the night." He rested his head in his hands. "The second option was successful. It was amazing how quickly it happened, probably because the new information you gave me followed on from my previous research."

I'd heard the last part before but stopped myself from saying it.

"I wrote up a report on the results." Adult Ben sounded so confident and content, and even looked relaxed. "The quickest report I've ever written. I've submitted it to *Medical Research Today* magazine and I've sent copies to several colleagues here and also at other institutions."

"Butt-covering?" I asked.

"Absolutely. I wanted to get the information out there so my work can continue regardless of what happens to me." He put his hand out. "Not that anything will happen to me."

My Ben said, "Make sure it doesn't. You've got to take good care of that body."

Adult Ben grinned, something I hadn't seen since our arrival. I didn't want him to lose that. Ever. I'd have to make sure my Ben kept smiling and enjoying life.

Slipping a folder of notes under his arm, adult Ben stood up. "This is perfect timing. We've got a research meeting this morning. I'm going to announce my findings."

He may have been happy to get rid of us at that point but we followed and waited until his colleagues had gathered together. The meeting room had a large window, the blinds left open so we could see inside.

Though we couldn't hear what was being said, it was obvious the meeting was getting heated. Ben was calm and leaned back in his chair. Meanwhile Max Alonzo's face reddened at regular intervals. Others at the table looked tense to say the least though our old friend the Crazy Professor seemed unfazed.

Inside, Max Alonzo stormed to the door so we moved aside, sticking close to the wall. He pulled the door open and adult Ben was louder than I expected as he yelled from inside that it was too late; he'd already spread the word about the possible virus and the vaccine.

Alonzo paced outside the door, didn't seem to notice Ben and I were there, then others made their way out of the room.

He shook his finger at adult Ben as soon as he made it to the doorway. "You're covering your ass."

"No, my ass is fine." I had to hand it to Ben, cool and calm. "So what's your problem?"

Alonzo had found a way to profit from the virus either financially or professionally, and now Ben was getting in his way. I'd put money on it.

"Excuse me, Max." Crazy Professor Ralph had now joined them in the corridor. "Ben's suspicions are that the cancer cure might instigate a deadly virus. This is a reasonable scientific conclusion that he's backed up with evidence. I concur with him."

Max Alonzo scowled. "This is nothing to do with you, Ralph."

"On the contrary," Ralph said, "as a respected member of the team, you should value my opinion. Besides, this could potentially be a terrible tragedy for humanity and that makes it not only my problem but everybody's problem."

"Thank you for your insight. It has been duly noted." Max Alonzo stared through bushy eyebrows, then shifted his gaze to adult Ben, a muscle in his jaw flinching. "Are you too good for us now? Is that it? You think you're so smart working on a cure for cancer like a great man."

Ben straightened, took a moment, refused to raise his voice. "Are we children in a playground, Max? Why don't you speak to me like an adult, a medical professional...an equal?"

Flecks of white foam formed at the corners of Alonzo's mouth. "You are not my equal and you are fired!"

"You don't have the authority to do that. I'm not

going anywhere. Besides, the scientific community has the information now." Ben stepped closer, his eyes narrowing. "Why, Max? Why is the virus so important to you when it's so deadly for the rest of the world? What's in it for you?"

Max Alonzo started shaking, his face red, lips thin. I thought he might blow so I stepped between them.

Alonzo pointed a finger at us. "What are *they* doing here?"

"Leaving." I grabbed adult Ben's arm, stepped back to stand by my Ben.

"This isn't over till I say so," Alonzo yelled. "You're finished. You can't stay here, not after this."

Ralph placed his hand on Alonzo's arm. "This is extremely unprofessional behavior. You can't–"

Alonzo yanked his arm back and kept ranting while the three of us backed off. We turned and strode down the hallway in the direction of Ben's office.

I stopped and reached for my boyfriend's hand. "That's what we should do, Ben."

He shrugged. "What?"

"Exactly as I told Alonzo. We should leave." My beautiful Ben stared at me without understanding. "The cancer cure will still be created. We don't need to be here to see that. And there'll be a vaccine for the virus. That's the most important part. There's nothing more we can do."

I gave him a few moments for it to sink in. I felt a sense of urgency, a need to get out of here and return to our lives. Perhaps I should've felt a great sense of accomplishment too from completing our mission. We'd finished here. Done as much as we could. Yet somehow it didn't feel finished.

'Home' was a long way away. What would the future hold? There was only one way to find out.

Ben raised his eyebrows. "So it's time…to return to Altabena?"

I nodded. "I'll get in touch with Nathan." Not that I could peel the PR device from my arm in these surroundings.

Adult Ben motioned for us to follow. "Let's go. I'll take you to the apartment. It'll be easier that way."

Fine by me. I could just as easily tell Nathan to use the coordinates for the apartment. We headed for the parking lot.

I stopped by Ben's car. "We can't leave like this. We have to say goodbye to Nicola too."

While we got in the car, adult Ben called her, then we took off. She'd meet us at the apartment. In the meantime, I set up the transport with Nathan. New Nation first, then home. Hopefully. That was the safest route to Altabena.

After we arrived at the apartment, the three of us sat in uncomfortable silence in the living room. Adult Ben had something on his mind, probably had a lot on his mind, and he wasn't the only one.

If we'd saved the world from a deadly virus, why did it feel like such an anti-climax? And if we'd changed the future, what sort of world would we be returning to? I wasn't sure we'd thought this through properly in the first place. I'd been so focused on saving the world from the virus, and Nathan had been so excited about testing the time travel program.

There was a knock at the door so adult Ben got up to let Nicola in, then stood holding her hand as we got up to greet them.

He shook hands with me first, then Ben. "I'm no good at farewells."

My Ben looked into the eyes of his older self. "Goodbye and good luck…with work, life, family, Nicola, with everything you do."

Adult Ben smiled. "I should be the one saying that to you."

This was weird – Ben saying goodbye to Ben. I'd be glad to get back to Altabena where our world made sense. So close and yet so far.

Nicola nudged him aside. "You're hopeless."

She hugged Ben, then me.

"I can't stay long," she whispered in my ear. "The kids are in the car."

"Give them a hug from me," I said quietly.

Hug them and hold them. Because they were important. Ben and Nicola were important. Their families, the people in their lives, the relationships – all of these things were invaluable.

This was what gave our lives meaning. We didn't have one reason to live. We had lots of reasons and, for me and Ben, those reasons were waiting in Altabena. My parents, Ben's dad, Celia, Lauren, Reece and the others. And our future. That was a pretty big reason too.

Adult Ben turned to wave from the doorway. He looked relieved and maybe he had reason to be. Nicola blew us a kiss, a melancholy look on her face.

I ran to her for one last hug. "Why so sad?"

She held me at arms' length. "I'm happy too. It's just…I don't wish I was eighteen again."

I stared at the closed door after she left. She was right.

It was hard being eighteen. Would things ever get easier?

Ben slipped his arms around me. I rested my head against his shoulder, such a comfortable place to be. Except I wasn't comfortable with any of this.

My heart was racing, my gut a concrete block, nerves simmering in my stomach. I didn't know if we'd done the right thing. Didn't know where we were going any more.

Because if we succeeded and there was no more virus, there'd be repercussions. The virus was what allowed Bartley to consolidate his power, to build a dictatorship and a military state, to create New Nation.

Would there be a military time-travel facility for us to return to? And if there wasn't, how could we have been sent back in time in the first place? If our actions had created a different world, would my parents have met and procreated and would I even have been born? I'd like to think they would, but couldn't know for sure.

Maybe this was something we shouldn't have messed with in the first place, but I'd done it before and it hadn't presented this same set of problems, so I'd thought I could handle it. Now I wasn't so sure.

I hoped the headache wouldn't be so bad this time, hoped I'd had enough rest since the last transportation so the physical problems wouldn't be so devastating.

Hoped there'd still be a world I recognized when we got there.

It was time…

CHAPTER TWENTY-NINE

Fear skittered along my nerve endings, my eyes squeezed shut. My head was pounding, only in a good way compared to the previous times when I'd thought my brain would explode.

I reached for my thigh, gripped it, the skin bare. I lifted a hand to my waist. That was bare too. I must be naked again, and that told me something. I was squeezed beside someone in a cramped space, skin on skin, skin on leather, pressed against something. A chair, perhaps. The transportation chair.

"It's okay, Nicola." The voice whispering in my ear was soothing. Ben's voice.

I opened my eyes. Ben had his arms around me, the two of us crammed onto the transportation chair. We'd made it to New Nation.

Nathan strode into the room, two large bags in his hands. He was smiling, not something that happened often, and I remembered his joy the last time I'd seen him. Not joy at seeing me. That would've been too much to ask. No, it had been the joy of scientific success.

He placed the bags on the floor. "Clothes."

"It's good to see you again, Nathan," Ben said.

Nathan merely pointed at the bags.

Relief flooded through me. Nathan...New Nation...I hadn't been sure what would be here when we got back. *If* we got back.

I threw my arms around Nathan, not something I would normally do while naked, or even while fully dressed.

He stepped back and straightened, held his hands out. "Nicola, please."

"We made it!" I turned to Ben who looked as pleased as I felt. We got dressed into the military gear Nathan had prepared for us.

I pulled on pants first, then reached for a shirt. "Are we safe? How long have we been gone?"

Nathan laughed, actually laughed. "Very little time has passed."

"Good."

He raked a hand through his hair, only for it to fall back exactly where it had been. The smile didn't leave his face as he began talking.

"This is magnificent. The two of you have traveled so far and been gone for days, yet time has barely moved on here. It's truly remarkable."

"So no one knows we've been gone?"

"No one." He put a finger to his lips. "No one believed the new program would work. Do you know, there were some highly respected authorities who told me it couldn't be done? They had ridiculous theories about how time couldn't be compressed. Pfft, completely missing the point."

Dressed in full military gear again, Ben smoothed down the front of his pants. "Did we succeed?"

"Of course." Nathan straightened. "That's what I've been trying to tell you."

"The virus...?"

"What about it?" Nathan asked.

My stomach lurched, my heart sinking deeper with each passing moment. He had no idea how much he'd given away with those three small words. The virus still existed.

I grabbed Ben's arm, trying not to think the worst. We'd risked our lives. Changed events from the past. That was the whole point.

I'd told Nathan before we left that our aim was to eradicate the virus. Had he forgotten? Didn't he care? Or was he simply too wrapped up in his own research and his own scientific success?

I stared at him. "Has anything changed?"

"What do you mean?"

A legitimate question. If we'd changed the course of the future and the world was now a different place, he wouldn't know it. He'd only know the world that he knew.

"Let's get this straight." My pulse rose. "Does the K-virus exist?"

"Yes," Nathan said.

Ben turned to me, his hands on my shoulders. "Something went wrong, Nic. We failed. Nothing has changed."

Maybe some things *had* changed. I had to hope.

"How many people died from it?" I asked Nathan.

"Tens of thousands," he said.

Ben dropped his hands. Not billions, not even

millions. The devastation had been reduced to a mere fraction of the original number.

I turned to him. "We did *something*. We had an effect. That's still billions of lives saved. Ben found a vaccine for the virus. He made a difference."

"Of course there's a vaccine," Nathan said as if this was common knowledge, and maybe it was.

"Is Bartley still in power?" I asked.

He nodded. "Of course."

So what kind of place was this? I didn't want to know, yet I had to find out.

"This is New Nation..." My voice tapered off. "There's no more United States of America."

Nathan frowned. "Nicola, even under the circumstances, you're behaving very strangely."

"I need to get this straight. Is this a regimented, highly controlled, organized society where people are raised in government facilities and channeled into the careers for which they show aptitude? Where obedience and loyalty are the greatest virtues? Where no one has any choice?"

"Of course."

"Do people still take emotion-suppressing drugs?"

"Yes."

A muscle in Nathan's cheek twitched. He'd been caught out and he knew it because everyone else might take drugs to control their feelings, but Nathan had somehow avoided it. Anyway, he'd said himself the drugs made very little difference to him, that he didn't need them, which was true. He didn't.

I lifted a hand to my temple. I had to think. Had to find a way out of this.

We'd saved the world from the virus – partly. We'd

done something but we hadn't saved society from the Bartleys' dictatorship and the creation of New Nation.

Bartley…I'd bet I was still the hero who'd overthrown a terrorist plot led by two generals, thereby saving his life. An alleged hero. This was killing me. I was so far from being a hero it wasn't funny.

Ben placed his hands on my shoulders. "I thought we made sure there was no virus and no Bartley in control."

I gazed into his eyes, wished there was more I could say or do. "We did everything we could, Ben."

Nathan interjected. "You succeeded in being sent to the past for several days and returning within minutes. I consider that a great success."

A great *scientific* success, perhaps, but not a success for me and Ben.

The door swished open. I shook Ben off. Reprimanded myself. I should've been more aware. Of everything.

Lucien walked through the door, scowling. I breathed a sigh of relief. Only Lucien. It could've been a lot worse.

Still, I wasn't happy to see him, wasn't sure where I stood with him. Damn it, I'd never been sure I could trust him, not completely.

What's more, he didn't know we'd traveled to the past. No one knew.

He placed his hands on his hips. "What are you doing here?" He looked at me first, then Ben, and rested his gaze on Nathan.

"Actually, sir," Nathan said. "I was going to ask you the same question."

"In an hour, I'm giving Supreme Ruler Bartley a tour of the transportation facility." Lucien walked slowly around the chair to where we were standing. "Does that answer your question?"

Nathan nodded. No one said anything. It wouldn't be long before Lucien worked out where we'd been and what we'd attempted.

What possible excuse could I come up with for our presence here? What explanation would be believable?

"Ben and I are ready to return to Altabena," I said. "I want to go back."

Lucien nodded, looked down his nose at me. "There's no point. We've been through this before."

A muscle in my jaw twitched. I was giving myself away.

His eyes narrowed, realization dawning. "Damn it, you've done something, concocted some plan and gone back in time, haven't you?"

I didn't say anything.

Lucien shifted his gaze to Nathan. "You were so eager to test your new theories and the new time travel program."

"Sir." Nathan did his best impersonation of an obedient officer.

"So confident too." Lucien shook his head. "Nathan, this is serious. The authorities were very clear when they prohibited those time travel experiments. Do you have any idea what will happen if someone suspects you've been tampering with the programs? That sort of disobedience will be punished by death."

Nathan's face remained as blank as ever.

"They'll be ruthless," Lucien said. "They'll give me a death sentence too. And Nicola and Ben...I hate to think what will happen to them."

"It was my decision," Nathan said. "It was my research that enabled this to happen. I wanted to prove the scientific principles, to show the physics was sound, to achieve ground-breaking success. I knew the cost."

There had to be a way out.

"We were only gone for seconds in New Nation time," I said. "No one even knows we left."

Lucien placed a hand on his chest. "*I* know. It didn't take me long to work it out. Do you think I'm the only one who can find out?"

I reached for Ben's arm. "We don't belong here. We've got to get back to Altabena."

To our homes, our old lives, our friends, our families, the people we loved and who loved us back. Had we got this so wrong? We had to escape.

Lucien glared at me. "Bartley will come for you no matter where you try to hide. He will always find you."

I gripped Ben's arm more tightly. Felt the blood rush through my veins, my heart rate rising. I even felt my range of vision narrowing as I focused on one thing, the transportation chair. My body was telling me something. Fight or flight. I was trained to fight but that wasn't necessarily the smart option. The answer flashed in front of me.

"Send us back first," I said. "Then we blow the place up."

It was the only answer.

CHAPTER THIRTY

Lucien paced the floor. "Do you know what you're saying?"

Ben's eye widened – with fear, anticipation, relief, I couldn't tell which. I glanced at Nathan, his expression giving nothing away. A few seconds ago, my pulse had been rising yet now a sense of calm overcame me. A sense of certainty.

I held Lucien's gaze. "Don't tell me you've never thought about it. The time travel mechanism has caused you nothing but trouble since the first time you sent me back. You and the rebel generals."

There were things I hadn't forgotten either, the way he'd sent me on a perilous mission with little regard for my safety or wellbeing. I'd found love and a new life and a lot of things in Altabena, but that wasn't why Lucien had sent me back. That hadn't been the aim. And though his motivations seem to have changed since then, I couldn't be sure. I could never be sure.

Time travel had put him in a difficult position too. Like the one he was in now.

He stopped and stared. "Do you have a strategy?"

I had no plan, no idea, only what I was coming up with on the spot.

Nathan cleared his throat. "You'll be in need of a high power molecular bomb then, I take it?"

Oh, yes we would. Nathan knew all about explosives. I still suspected he'd designed the bomb that blew up Altabena High School, an explosion with which I'd had first-hand experience.

I turned to him. "Why would you help? Why would you blow up your beloved time travel device and equipment?"

"There's the small matter of my execution should my superior officers discover what we've done," he said. "I could destroy the evidence and, as you know, the results of a molecular bomb are very thorough."

The results would be devastating. All affected matter would be reduced to its molecular level. There would be no recognizable remains, no bricks or pieces of building matter. To the naked eye, everything would look like dust.

"But all your work," I said. "Your research. This was your baby."

He straightened, his face as blank as ever. "I took great pleasure in the scientific process and principles. It is of no consequence to me whether others recognize this or not. I did it for the satisfaction, and that is something no one can take from me."

I tilted my head. "You're a strange one."

"On the contrary, I've explained myself and it makes perfect sense."

"Nathan," Lucien said. "We'll need a timing device as well."

"Certainly. The prototype bombs I built are in storage. It's a secure facility, of course, but I have access. I have several prototype timers, though one would need to be tailored so it goes off remotely. It's a relatively straightforward procedure. Should only take a couple of hours."

"You've got sixty minutes, maybe less," Lucien said.

Nathan didn't flinch. "That makes it much less straightforward."

Lucien ran a hand over his bare scalp. "It's the perfect time. That's when we'll do it."

I stepped closer to Ben, squeezed his hand, but didn't dare look at him. I had to concentrate. One more hour and we could be out of here. So close.

"Nathan, the technology will still exist even if we blow everything up," I said. "In computer records on mainframes, in cloud storage, in scientists' minds. New time travel equipment could be built in the future."

He nodded. "I'm confident I can erase the records in all their formats. There's a computer virus that will perform admirably. I can't erase people's minds, however, and therein lies the challenge. I can't predict whether future research into time travel will be successful or how long it will take. I'm confident that a small molecular bomb will obliterate the transportation facility and cause serious damage to the surrounding area. There will, of course, be some collateral damage. The aim is to minimize it."

He was right. It was impossible to avoid the loss of other lives. There might be soldiers who died, and I couldn't let that stand in my way. Couldn't think about it. In fact, when I'd been a loyal New Nation soldier, I hadn't thought about it.

"We need to hurry." Lucien turned to me. "Your parents have been invited on the tour with Supreme Ruler Bartley."

My biological parents. A shudder shot up my spine. They couldn't go the same way Bartley would. They weren't 'collateral' as Nathan had said earlier. They were my flesh and blood even if it hadn't felt that way while I was being raised by the military.

"Do you know where they are now?" I asked.

"I can find out."

He was giving me a warning, being considerate, and it touched me.

"Thank you," I said. "What are you going to do? How will you get out of the tour with Bartley?"

Lucien's expression hardened. "I'm not backing out."

"What do you mean?"

"Nicola, it's not enough to blow up the time travel equipment. Not enough to set the timer. I have to make sure Bartley is there when the bomb goes off. Then he won't be able to send anyone after you. Ever. Because that's what he'd do as soon as the time travel equipment was recreated."

I raised my hands to my temples. "But Lucien…"

His eyes softened. "I have to do this, Nicola. Bartley must be eliminated. It's something that should have been done years ago. The only shame is that someone didn't assassinate the first Bartley years ago so he didn't pass on his leadership to his son who could then pass it on to his son."

"There has to be another way."

"There is no other way, Nicola. The time travel

machinery will be blown up. I have to make sure Bartley dies."

And Lucien would die with him.

CHAPTER THIRTY-ONE

Ben turned to me. "It's his decision."

"This is his life he's talking about," I said. "I can't be indebted like that. I wouldn't be able to live with myself."

"You don't owe me, Nicola," Lucien said. "Don't ever think that, not for a moment. Ben's right. You're not forcing me into this. This is my life, my choice, my gift to you."

And I didn't want it. Couldn't he understand?

Lucien stepped closer. "Nicola, there are things you don't know, things I've never told you. I haven't taken the emotion-suppressing drugs for a long time. Nathan is aware of this. It's something we discussed and kept between ourselves. I'm very good at acting emotionless but that's not the case at all." He swallowed. "I've done some terrible things in my time. Sending you on the mission to Altabena in the first place was one of them. I knew exactly how dangerous that was."

"I worked that out," I said in a small voice. "I blamed you."

"With good reason. So, imagine my joy when I found a

way to turn that around, when you could stay in Altabena and have the life you deserved."

"I want to go back too. Not like this, though."

"You must go." He took one of my hands into his. "Though I may never have been good enough to be your father, I *feel* like I was a parent. And I love you...like a daughter. I'd gladly give up my life for you. What father wouldn't?"

My breath caught in my throat. Tears filled my eyes. All the times I'd doubted Lucien in the last year flashed through my mind, sharp stabs of guilt in my chest.

I wasn't sure if I loved him or not, wasn't sure what was going through my head or my heart. I only knew this would be my last chance to say something to him and I'd regret it for the rest of my life if I didn't.

Throwing my arms around him, I drew him into an embrace. He placed his hands loosely on my back, tilted his head and held me stiffly. The saddest hug I'd ever had. He'd never done this before and didn't know how to hug someone. Tears tumbled down my cheeks.

"I love you, Lucien." Staying close to him, I brushed the tears from my face. "You don't have to do this."

He held me at arms' length. "Yes, I do."

Maybe he and Ben were right and it wasn't my place to tell him what to do. I couldn't tell him what to feel, not when I hadn't even known he had any emotions, certainly not feelings this deep.

Lucien said, "We don't have any time to waste. Nathan, you have work to do. Ben, you need to be careful. Nicola, you must see your parents."

The military complex was huge and I'd need their location. "Where are they?"

"One minute." Lucien stepped back, rolled up his sleeve and peeled off his PR device.

Ben reached for my arm. "How are we going to do this?"

We needed a plan and we needed it fast. "Nathan, where's the bomb storage facility?"

"G Block," he said.

The other side of the complex.

"Can we locate the bomb and bring it here using the time travel facility?" I asked.

"The mechanism isn't made to transport items within the same time zone. That's not how it works."

"How big is the explosive device?"

Nathan held his hands out, showing something slightly bigger than a baseball. "Not large but extremely effective."

"Can we transport the bomb so it arrives a few minutes in the past?" I asked. "Then it can still be here. We won't have to go and get it."

Nathan shook his head. "Too dangerous. If there was a glitch in the system, the effect would be so terrible I couldn't even predict what might happen."

Lucien stepped forward, slapping his PR back onto his arm. "Your parents are waiting in the Rhodes Room until Bartley arrives."

It amazed me that he understood my need to see them one last time, yet there wasn't even a hint of jealousy from him.

I had to hug him again and maybe he sensed that because he put his hand out to stop me coming closer. It sent a pang through my heart but maybe he was right. We didn't have time for feelings.

Lucien looked into my eyes. "I have to go. And you

257

have to find a way."

I gasped. We had so much to do and I wasn't sure we'd be able to complete our mission. We needed all the help we could get. We needed him.

And he couldn't handle any more pain.

Lucien turned from the door. "You can message me if you need anything, but I'd rather you didn't. I'd rather we left it...like this.

"Goodbye, Lucien, and thank you," I called.

The door closed behind him.

I had to be a soldier one last time. After this, it would be over, one way or another.

"G Block is a long way." My head was buzzing, thinking about getting there, seeing my parents, a timer mechanism and anything else I might've missed.

"You and I can go," Ben said. "Break in and get the bomb while Nathan stays here and does his bit."

"Security is a problem, a big one," I said to Nathan. "What protective measures do they have securing the room?"

"There's a security code to get into the general area," he said.

Old fashioned but the security still worked.

I raised my eyebrows. "And?"

"Another numerical code allows entry into the bomb room. Also not a major problem. This room gives you access to the various storage cupboards in which the bombs are stored. The only way to access them is through handprint analysis. The bad news is it has to be *my* handprint that unlocks the door."

I pressed a hand to my temple. "Then that's it. Nathan, you need to go first and unlock the storage cupboard. You can give Ben and me the codes. We'll get over there, steal the bomb and bring it back."

"An interesting plan, Nicola," he said. "But if I get to G Block, I won't have time to build the remote timing device."

"Yes, you will." I slapped my hand on his back. "It'll take Ben and me twenty minutes to get there. You'll be there in nineteen minutes. You can leave now and be back within moments. You're going to time travel, Nathan."

His face lit up, his eyes narrowing with a mischievous gleam. "I've always wanted to do this. My secret dream."

Maybe dreams could come true. Maybe there was more to Nathan than I'd ever thought because he was about to defy the authorities in the biggest way possible.

"You've got to set the time travel program," I said.

"I will, of course." He peeled a PR from his arm, the device hardening immediately. "You need to know where to go once you're inside G Block."

He brought up a map of the building and explained the location of the bomb storage facility and associated security measures. There were three sets of doors in all – one to get through to the main area, then another to get into the inner room. From here, there were four doors behind which the bombs were stored. Nathan would make it easier for us to find by leaving the bomb at the front within easy reach.

"Is the device delicate?" I asked. "What if it gets shaken in the backpack while we're running?"

"That amount of agitation will have no effect," he said. "It has to be set off remotely."

"What if we drop it?"

"Don't! Don't even think about it. Now come with

me." Nathan led us through the door into the control room. Though I'd time traveled on several occasions, I'd never been in this particular area. There'd never been any need.

A long desk lined with computer equipment was on one wall. Screens and monitors were embedded into the desk and a window looked out into the transportation room with its empty chair. One-way glass.

Ben and I stood while Nathan sat at one of the chairs and began programming. It was strange the room was so simple when the physics behind the programming was so amazing.

After a few minutes, Nathan got up. "It's ready to go. After I'm in the transportation room and seated, I'll give you a signal and all you have to do is press this button. Then you wait for my return."

"But we need to get to G Block," I said.

"You wait." That sly smile crossed his face again. "It won't take long."

He left the control room, stood by the transportation chair and took off his clothes. They wouldn't be transported with him anyway. He didn't even fold them which didn't seem like Nathan at all. As soon as he sat down, he looked up and signaled.

I pressed the button. He disappeared.

"It worked," Ben said.

Seconds later, Nathan was back in the chair, his head hanging down. I blinked, not sure if we'd imagined his departure or if he was really there now. I'd never been on this side of the one-way glass and had no clue what to expect or what to make of this.

Ben grabbed my arm. "Come on."

By the time we were back in the transportation room, Nathan was standing, his head in his hands.

"You didn't tell me the pain would be this bad," he said.

Or maybe he hadn't been listening. "It'll pass."

Nathan reached for his pants and pulled them on. "I've disarmed the security door."

He rattled off the codes. I repeated them out loud to help the numbers sink in, one code to get into the general area, another to open the correct door within the storage room.

Straightening, he said, "That was truly a remarkable experience. I went forward in time to change a small part of our history that hasn't been created yet."

"Ben and I have to go," I said.

"Certainly. I'll start programming the timer and meet you two back here in exactly forty-five minutes. Actually, not here. Lucien's office. That's where I hid the remote devices I've been working on."

"You hid them?"

"Yes, my superior officers insisted on storing them elsewhere but I wanted to continue the project in my spare time."

Another thing came to me, another thing we'd nearly overlooked. "You'll need to program the time travel mechanism for our return to Altabena too."

"Of course."

I gave Nathan the date, time and exact coordinates for our landing.

Ben and I didn't have time to waste. My pulse was racing though I'd barely moved.

"How do we get to G Block?" Ben asked.

"We run."

CHAPTER THIRTY-TWO

Sometimes the most basic option was the best one. We were both young, fit and able, and there was nothing strange about two people running or jogging through the military compound. Pods only circulated on the edge of the complex so they weren't an option anyway.

I kept an eye out while we ran. We might not look odd now but we could hardly jog back holding a molecular bomb out in the open. I had to get hold of a bag or some way of covering the device.

We were nearly there and I was worried I'd have to knock someone out to grab their bag. Too much risk, too much attention. G Block was just around the corner when I saw a small group of soldiers gathered on a patch of grass for drills, their personal belongings in a pile by the path. As we ran past, I reached down, swept up a backpack and kept going. No looking back.

Ben stopped outside G Block, leaning over to catch his breath. I wiped as much of the sweat from my face and neck as I could, then swiped my hands against my pants. Ben didn't look too bad. If he still had his long hair, he'd have sweated right through it.

Still, I wanted his long hair back. I wanted my life back.

The air conditioning inside the building was truly magnificent as the two of us followed Nathan's directions and headed toward the bomb storage facility. Other than several military personnel in the entry foyer, we barely saw a soul. It put me even more on edge.

The entry door to the main area was marked only by key code access on the wall beside it, just as Nathan had pointed out on the map on his PR. I punched in the numbers, heard a reassuring click, then pushed the steel door open.

Next we had to get into the inner room. This door, I noticed, was plithium with a hand recognition device and security panel on the wall to the left. If Nathan had disarmed the device we could get in. If he hadn't, we'd have no chance.

I sucked in a deep breath, punched in the numbers and waited for a click or some signal. Nothing. My heart was racing. Placing my fingers on the door, I gave a gentle push. It didn't take much pressure. The door opened. Either it was a miracle or it was Nathan. The breath left my body. In the best way possible. Such a relief.

I walked in first. Then stopped and blinked. I could've sworn I'd seen a pale shadowy figure in front of me. Now there was nothing. Had that been Nathan getting here just ahead of us?

I reached for Ben's arm. "Did you see anything?"

"No."

But he'd been behind me.

No time to waste. From here, we had access to the

correct door. Nathan had said it was the second door from the right. Inside, the items on the shelves looked exactly the way Nathan had described them, the smallest device right at the front, exactly where he'd said it would be. A rectangular metal box, it didn't look deadly, didn't look like much at all.

I turned to Ben. "You can do the honors."

He reached for the bomb, picked it up with both hands. "It's not that heavy."

No, but it'd be effective. I held the backpack open while he slid the device inside. Placing the bag on the floor, I reached to the bottom for a towel, probably a training towel the owner had left inside, and used it to pad the backpack, then slung the whole thing across my shoulders.

"We've got to hurry." I took Ben's hand into mine, then let go when we reached the door and exited the building.

"This way," I said as soon as we were outside. I didn't want to backtrack past the soldiers we'd passed earlier in case one of them was looking for their backpack, so we went around the side of the building and jogged up an alternate path.

A soldier was coming our way. Something in the set of his jaw and the way his eyes narrowed told me he recognized me, though I didn't know how. Maybe it was the backpack. In fact, that had to be it. It gave me a moment to think. A moment was all I needed.

He was heading straight for me, staring, gesticulating. I clenched my fingers into a fist and sent it into his face. Not much of a punch but he walked straight into it. Crumpled to the ground. Too good to be true.

Meanwhile Ben and I upped our pace. He didn't question what I'd done, didn't say anything. He just kept going. Yet another reason for me to love him.

I couldn't have told you how much time had passed by the time we made it back to the main building or how relieved I felt when we got there. Still, time was running out.

"This way," I said.

"But Lucien's office is that way."

One more thing to do, one very important thing. I motioned in the other direction. "My parents are in the Rhodes Room."

"Nicola, no. We don't have time."

"I have to do this."

Ben grabbed my arm. I shook him off and he followed.

I stood in the doorway, surveying the room. By New Nation standards, this was a large comfortable waiting room, one used by visiting dignitaries. And my parents.

Sitting at a coffee table in corner of the room, the two of them stood as soon as they saw me.

"You've got to be quick," Ben said.

I nodded, left him to go to them. I couldn't hug my parents, not here with other people around. It wasn't the done thing in New Nation and the last thing I wanted was to attract attention. I shook my mother's hand first, then my father's.

"Do you trust me?" I asked.

"You're a fine solder, a credit to our country," Father said.

"Do you trust me?"

My mother stared at me. "Yes, of course."

"Then leave right now," I said. "Go straight to the transportation dock. Take the first pod out of here, go back to your barracks in the compound."

Father's brow furrowed. "We have a meeting with Supreme Ruler Bartley, a tour. We can't go."

"Trust me.

"But this is—"

"Just this once." I looked from him to Mother. "You have to go. Now."

Father opened his mouth to argue. My mother reached for his arm. Her eyes were still fixed to mine but she was speaking to him. "I'm leaving and you're coming with me."

"We'll be punished," he muttered.

She reached over to pick up her jacket. "We have to go. I've come down with a sudden illness."

I flicked my eyes toward the rear. "There's an exit back there. It'll be safer."

She gripped her jacket. "Nicola, we'll see you again."

I shook my head. "I'm…going on a mission."

Her lips parted. "You're a hero of New Nation."

Not any more. "I'll be safe. That's all I can tell you. I'll be far away and I'll be fine."

My mother put a hand to her chest, as if she knew she'd never see me again. I could see it in her eyes, and it was ripping me apart. And I couldn't even give her a hug.

Screw New Nation. Screw the rules. I drew her closer for a hug and whispered in her ear. "I love you both."

Her mouth fell open, her eyes wide with trepidation. My father looked at us blankly.

"Nicola…" was all she could say.

Maybe I didn't feel the same way about them as I did toward Jan and Phil Gray in Altabena, but I loved my birth parents nonetheless.

And I had to leave them.

I said in a loud voice, "Goodbye and thank you for everything."

Father took my mother's arm, his eyes on mine for a moment before he led her to the rear. Then I strode toward Ben. I didn't turn back. I couldn't.

Next stop, Lucien's office to meet Nathan. My heart was pounding. I had a heart and I had to do this.

We headed to the left, then saw them at the far end of the hall. Three bodyguards at the front, three at the rear. Lucien was beside them near the front. I couldn't see Bartley but he was there all right.

And they were heading our way.

CHAPTER THIRTY-THREE

Bartley hadn't spotted us or at least I hoped he hadn't. Meanwhile, the guards didn't notice anything unusual. Ben and I were just two soldiers as far as they were concerned.

In that split second, I thought about my family and friends in Altabena. I thought about the massacre of college students in Altabena Square by the first Bartley. I thought about the reign of terror brought on by generations of Bartley rule. I even thought about the poor waiter whose execution was ordered after he accidentally spilt wine at the celebratory dinner.

Lucien saw me, his eyes suddenly wide. He stopped and turned, gave some sort of oratory to hold the group up, or at least that was what it looked like.

I grabbed Ben's arm and we turned, headed the other way.

"That was close," he said.

Too close for my liking. Luckily I knew the layout of the compound so we took a more circuitous route to Lucien's office.

I knocked on the door. "It's us."

After some shuffling from inside, Nathan pulled the door open, then sat back down. I closed the door behind us.

"Did you get it?" he asked, engrossed in the small metal device on the desk.

"Yes." I deposited the backpack on the floor behind the desk.

"Excellent, I'm nearly done."

He unzipped the bag, reached for the bomb and placed it on the desk. In less than a minute, he opened up part of the bomb, soldered a chip to the inside wall and sealed the device again.

Grabbing something which looked like a miniature PR device, he pressed several buttons only for a red warning symbol to start flashing.

He jabbed another button, put the mechanism in his pocket and stood. "Excellent."

"That's the timer, I presume?" I asked.

"Yes, I prefer to be ahead of schedule wherever possible."

I pointed to a computer by the side of Lucien's desk. The screen was black, a series of symbols racing across the screen so fast I couldn't make out what was happening.

"What's going on?" I asked.

"I believe I mentioned the highly effective computer virus to you earlier. I'm deleting all research and records related to the time travel program. This is what's known as multi-tasking. I was creating the timer while erasing the records at the same time."

"You sure you know what you're doing?"

A sly smile crept to Nathan's lips. "I'd always wondered why anyone would defy authority. Now I know why. This is so challenging, so satisfying, so incredibly exciting."

"Ben and I are ready to go back," I said.

"So I can see."

"How much of the building will explode?" I asked.

"Enough. The transportation and control rooms along with their computers will be obliterated to dust. The procedure will be extremely effective. This is a small molecular bomb, remembering that 'small' is relative. The transportation and control rooms will bear the brunt and there should be minor damage to neighboring parts."

"And you?" I asked.

"I'll transport you and Ben, place the bomb in position in the control room, and then I'll wait. After Lucien arrives with Supreme Ruler Bartley and his entourage, I'll exit the room. I'm not supposed to be here anyway. I have the remote ignition device and can detonate the bomb as soon as I'm far enough away."

"Let's move," Ben said.

He hadn't been saying much because there wasn't much for him to say, but he was right about leaving.

I slung the backpack over my shoulder and the three of us walked out the door. Two female soldiers deep in conversation were ambling toward us.

"Nathan," one of them called.

"Good afternoon." He kept walking.

"Wait." She reached for his arm, giving him no choice but to stop. "Have you heard about the break-in at G Block?"

Nathan wore his best innocent expression. "Pardon?"

"I thought you'd want to know, given all the work you've done. They've closed off the whole block and

271

there's an investigation underway."

"As there should be." He looked from one woman to the next. "Please excuse me."

He turned and the three of us left.

I kept walking. "You have friends?"

"Colleagues." He corrected me.

"They'll know it was you from the handprint analysis. Won't be hard to work out."

"I've deleted those records too."

He made me smile. "Nathan, you're good."

"Indeed I am."

We turned the corner to see a soldier standing outside the transportation room, glancing up at us as he checked his PR device. I didn't want to think about what communications he might be receiving.

He stepped forward as we neared the door. "You can't go in there."

Nathan stopped. "I'm a science officer with legitimate access to this area."

"There's been a security breach. We're going in to–"

I punched him in the gut, watched him double over as the air left his body. Nathan was quick, I had to hand it to him, as he grabbed the soldier's laser from his belt, set it to 'stun' and squeezed the trigger. The man fell into a heap.

Ben grabbed the soldier before he made it to the ground, his hands under the guy's arms. "Now what?"

Nathan pushed open a door opposite us and helped Ben drag the man in there, closing the door as they left.

We made it to the transportation room and secured the door behind us. I wiped the sweat from my brow. Handed Nathan the backpack.

"I'll leave this in the control room," he said. "It's the

best place for the job."

This was it. The last time I would see New Nation. Hopefully. And Nathan? He'd grown on me, helped me, surprised me. I'd miss him.

If it was anyone else, I'd have hugged him. Instead I said, "Goodbye."

"Farewell, Nicola," he said. "You too, Ben. Good luck in Altabena."

That strange feeling of wistfulness crept up on me again. "We won't see you again."

"And that's as it should be."

Without another word, Nathan entered the control room. I took Ben's hand and he turned to the transportation chair, sitting down first. I settled on his lap, my arms around his neck.

Everything was in place. Nathan was sending us back, then he'd leave. The bomb was in the control room. Lucien would be approaching soon and he'd bring Bartley with him. The facility would explode, along with everyone in it, and the time travel programs were already being eradicated so time travel would be only a memory in the minds of scientists.

No one could come after us. We hoped.

I looked around the room, gripped Ben tightly. "We're leaving. We won't see what happens. How do we know...?"

"This place will blow, Nicola," he said, "regardless of whether we're here to see it or not."

He was right. Still, I wished I could see the result. Could I be sure this would work?

I held Ben closer. This would be the last time we time traveled together. It had to be.

Pain smashed through my face like being punched in the nose by an iron fist. More pain ricocheted around in my head, shooting around, bouncing back, sharp bursts that nearly knocked me out.

The last time...

CHAPTER THIRTY-FOUR

My head was in a vise. Pressure building on all sides, my skull felt as if it was about to be crushed. It hurt so much I couldn't scream, couldn't breathe, couldn't move.

Then the pain lifted. Just like that. There one minute, gone the next.

I opened my eyes. Ben's face was beside mine, his eyes squeezed shut, his hands on his ears.

"Are you okay?" I whispered.

His eyes sprung open. He was panting, his mouth open. "Yeah, I think so."

We were lying on something hard. My arms were around him, our legs intertwined. Naked again.

And if we were naked, that meant we'd made it.

Disoriented, I tried to take in my surroundings. My bedroom looked different when I was lying on the floor but that's where we were.

My room. My home. Such a relief.

Cupping Ben's face in my hand, I pressed my lips to his. I could kiss him whenever I wanted. I could be with him. I could stay in Altabena.

A stab of guilt shot through my chest as I remembered what I'd left behind. I sat up, tried to get my head together. Lucien had given up his life for me. *His decision*, Ben had said. *His gift to me*, Lucien had said. At least that's what I thought had happened but I could never be sure.

Then there were my biological parents and Nathan – were they alive somewhere in the future? Or were they being punished by a totalitarian regime that tolerated nothing less than complete obedience?

And the ultimate question – would the time travel program and apparatus be recreated one day? Because then someone might come after me.

I must have my head together if I could think these things through. It gave me some solace.

Ben sat up, leaning against the bed. "We made it, didn't we?"

"Sure did."

I opened my closet, grabbed some clothes and pulled on a tee shirt and jeans.

Ben raked a hand through his short hair, perhaps expecting more. I was getting used to seeing him with cropped hair but the look on his face told me he wanted his hair back now he was in Altabena again.

He pointed at my clothes. "Great, what am I going to do?"

I reached for the pink toweling gown hanging on the back of the door and tossed it onto his lap. The look of disgust on his face intensified.

"It's better than nothing," I said.

He raised his eyebrows. "You think?"

"Wait here."

I left the room, bounding down the stairs and racing

out of the front door. Ben's car was there, thank goodness, and that meant this had gone to plan. We'd each packed two small backpacks to take to the cabin with us and they were both there on the back seat.

I scooted back upstairs, opened my bedroom door to see Ben was sitting on the bed, my pink gown wrapped around him, a sheepish expression on his face. A nervous laugh escaped my lips.

"What?" he said.

I stopped giggling, tossed his backpack to him.

He unzipped it and rummaged around inside. "These are my things. How did you get them so quickly?"

I dropped down onto the bed while he stood and got dressed.

"Nathan was spot on with the coordinates," I said. "And I did pretty well too. I asked him to deliver us to my room the day after the student massacre at Altabena Square. "

Ben put a hand out. "So we've come back from the cabin?"

"Yep, we've come back for the next protest, the one that'll be bigger than yesterday's, though hopefully without the bloodshed. I got the timing just right. You've just dropped me off at home. Your car's outside and your stuff was in it."

Ben dropped his head into his hands. "We're back. I get that. It's what I wanted too. But we've just been in one world stealing bombs and blowing up time travel devices and now we're supposed to pretend everything is normal?"

"It's not normal though, that's the whole point. Yesterday, hundreds of young people died in Altabena Square, killed when soldiers opened fire. That's not normal. And today's protest will be bigger. More people. Power in numbers."

And Bartley would be there. He'd said he was coming to Altabena Square to reassure the community everything was all right, that all people who behaved reasonably would be safe, that any military presence was only there for state and national security.

The seed of an idea came to me. I grabbed a pair of gloves from my top drawer and shoved them into my back pocket. Ben was still recovering so while he wasn't looking, I grabbed something else and strapped it to my leg under my jeans. A hunting knife.

I turned to Ben. "I have to see my parents." He looked up at me strangely and I realized I'd already said goodbye to one set of parents, so I added, "Jan and Philip. They're my real parents, the ones who helped make me what I am, the ones I love."

He stood, taking my hands into his. "It feels like we've been gone a hundred years. I want to see my family too."

I smiled. "I know."

"I even want to see Josh."

Wow, we must've been gone a long time. He picked up his backpack and I led him downstairs, calling out for my parents who must be around somewhere.

Mom and Dad were at the kitchen table, drinking coffee with the newspapers spread out in front of them, looking like two ordinary people. But they weren't. Not to me. My heart felt ready to burst.

A hand on Dad's shoulder, I kissed him on the cheek over and over again, then threw my arms around Mom and hugged her.

"It's so good to see you," I said.

Mom held me at arms' length. "You're very perky, honey. I take it you had a good trip back from the cabin."

Reaching across, I put an arm around each of them. "I'm so glad I've got you guys."

Dad said, "It's really good you're so excited to see us. Also a little strange."

Mom gave him a gentle whack on the knee. "Phil, we should make the most of it while she's in such a good mood."

But nothing about this was normal and I couldn't forget it.

The newspaper lay open on the table, a spread with stories about families affected by yesterday's massacre in full view. Innocent people gunned down. Families who'd lost children. Such a tragedy.

There was a photo of a middle-aged woman with short sandy hair in combat fatigues, a pained expression on her face. In fact, the look in her eyes went beyond pain. I could feel her agony, her grief, her despair at the senseless loss of life. Her daughter's life.

I leaned over to read her story. She was a lieutenant in the army and her daughter had been shot dead during yesterday's protests. The woman had experienced loss during her time in the military and had been at the receiving end of gunshot wounds, but nothing compared to this orchestrated, unforgiveable loss of young lives including that of her twenty-year-old daughter Christine. They were her words and she was urging all of us to join in the protest today.

Hell, I was convinced.

"I don't even know how to express my disgust," I said. "We have to stop this happening ever again. We have to let the authorities know we're not putting up with this." I shook my head. "Not that it'll bring that woman's daughter back. Or any of the others who were killed."

Mom squeezed my hand. "You've matured so much, just in the last year. I can't tell you how glad I was that you weren't there yesterday. And I'll be proud to have you at my side today."

My mind was on something else as I reached for the tablet next to the newspaper, already open to the news sites, of course. Skimming through, I found the proposed path of Bartley's motorcade. There'd be security, of course, lots of it.

I knew what was going to happen because the most senior Bartley had told me the legend when I was back in New Nation. There would be an assassination attempt on Bartley during the parade – this Bartley, the first one. The shooter would be on top of the Bryson Building but the attempt would be foiled. An officer would see the shooter and prevent the assassination.

That's where I came in.

If this Bartley was shot, his son would never be born, nor his son after that. Bartley was a killer. He'd ordered the deaths of innocent people in the square.

I wasn't a killer, though, not like that. I had a plan. I didn't have to kill. My job was to stop the officer who was going to foil the assassination attempt and leave the rest in the hands of the shooter.

I had the tablet in my hands. "Can I take this?"

"Sure," Mom said. "Ben was just telling us you're going to the protest with your friends." Disappointment in her eyes. "I thought we were going together, the three of us."

"Sorry, Mom, I need to be with my friends, just this once."

She nodded. "That's okay, honey."

"After that, I'll be back on board one hundred percent. You won't be able to get rid of me, I promise."

Dad smiled. "I'm not sure if that's good or bad."

"I'm not going anywhere." I stepped closer to Ben. "Well, I am going somewhere now but that doesn't count. After that, I'm all yours."

"Honey, you don't have to hang around here." She looked up at Ben. "Take care of her."

"Always," he said.

Ben was stiff and quiet on the ride to his house, anxious to see his family. When we got there, I gave Celia a big hug and then she gave all her attention to Ben. I'd already greeted Ben's dad and brother. They were so involved with seeing Ben, so grateful he was okay, that it was easy to slip into the hallway and search the tablet for information.

Google Maps was a godsend. The Bryson Building and others beside it were four floors high, the buildings behind it smaller. An alley sat on one side of the building then veered off to the right. On the other sides, the building butted up against neighboring apartments and stores. A couple of nearby buildings had skylights in the roof.

The front of the Bryson had steel grilles, albeit attractive art deco ones, covering the windows. I had to hope there was access at the side of the building and that I'd be able to break in that way. Because I'd need to get in first in order to get to the top of the building.

Traffic was heavy on the trip into town and Ben was talking about how pleased he was to be back, how thrilled he was about seeing his family and soon his friends.

Meanwhile I was a soldier sitting on the front seat on the way to my final mission. And I was determined this would the last time. I visualized the scene, breaking into the Bryson Building, flying up the stairs, scanning my surroundings when I reached the top. I pictured the shooter being disarmed by an officer. That was what I had to prevent. I ran over it in my head again. This time I was taking the officer from behind, incapacitating him, doing whatever had to be done to allow the shooter to take aim.

We parked a fair way out of town and walked toward the center – us and about fifty thousand other people. Ben held my hand, led the way, made me feel secure. He would lead me closer, then he'd let me go.

Reece and Dominique were waiting for us at a corner not far from the town square. I hugged the two of them and forgot I was a soldier for about two minutes.

I held Dominique at arms' length. "It's so good to see you."

"Yeah, 'cause I haven't seen you since, like, this morning," she said.

I didn't even mind her sarcasm.

Reece was the only other person who'd understand but this wasn't the time to talk. Instead, I drew him in for another embrace and whispered, "I've got a lot to fill you in on."

He nodded. "Everything okay?"

Ben put his arm around me. "It's all good."

Suddenly, I was desperate to see Lauren again but she couldn't be here because it wasn't safe for her. At least she had Will.

People were passing by in huge waves, hundreds of

them, people who wouldn't put up with the slaughter of their young ones, people who'd had enough. The shuffle of footsteps and the hum of voices formed a wall of noise around us.

Reece said, "We should get going."

I gave Ben a hug, not the last hug I'd ever give him, just a hug, and pulled him aside. "I have to go. There's something I have to do. I'll tell you about it later but I don't have time now."

Fear in his eyes. "Nic, what are you going to do?"

"I'm going to finish this once and for all."

"It'll be dangerous," he said, though he could have no idea what I was talking about. "Nic, whatever it is, you don't have to do it on your own."

He was right. I didn't have to do everything on my own. I'd learnt that. And he was wrong. Because this was one thing I had to do on my own.

"This is different," I said. "I've got one chance to do this."

He grabbed my hand. "Nic, no…"

"I'll always come back, Ben."

I kissed him and he let me go. I had to backtrack to get to the Bryson Building, so I stuck close to stores that lined the street, a single person going against the flow of foot traffic. I kept going until I reached Ford Street where people with protest signs stood behind police barricades. And police. Plenty of police.

The center of the street had been left free for the motorcade. I had to get to the other side so I slipped between two metal barricades on one side, then jumped over the one on the other side. A police officer shouted at me so I gave him my best smile and kept going.

I ambled past the Bryson Building, its front windows covered in grilles, as I already knew. The store at the front of the next building sold antiques and bric-a-brac. Closed, like everything else today. Turning into the alley, I sped up as I strode toward a set of double doors at the side of the Bryson, then stopped. Steel doors with key code access. For an old art deco building, this was security overkill. No way I could get through that.

Glancing back the way I'd come, people were walking past and gathering for the motorcade.

I kept moving around the corner to the rear of the antiques store, figuring if I could get to the top of this building, I should be able to jump across to the Bryson. It was quiet here as I stared at the wooden door at the back of the building.

Someone had got here before me. They'd shot the door open. And no doubt made their way to the roof, thinking the same thing as me.

My heart beat faster. I had to proceed with care. I took the gloves from my back pocket and pulled them on.

As far as I could tell, the building was empty. The stairs wrapped around an ancient lift that didn't look trustworthy so I shot up the steps two at a time. I got to the top and looked for a way out onto the roof. It didn't take much searching before I found another set of stairs hidden behind a door. One more flight and I'd be on the roof.

At the top, I waited until I'd caught my breath, then pushed the door open. I stuck close by the stair housing and looked around. Nothing here, other than some air conditioning ducts and maintenance units.

Then I saw them.

Two figures on top of the Bryson Building.

CHAPTER THIRTY-FIVE

One guy was in police uniform, his back to me. Not far from me at all actually, except for the four-story drop between the two buildings. His arms stretched forward, he was no doubt gripping a gun while he waited, crouching behind a small water tower.

He was staring at another guy in khaki tee shirt positioned behind one of the art deco capitals that decorated the building. This guy was focused, looking out onto the street, a sniper rifle resting on his shoulder. The shooter.

I crept closer to the edge of the building. If the officer turned he'd see me, and given the circumstances, he'd probably shoot. I swallowed. There was no 'probably' about it.

I stopped a few feet from the edge. Didn't go closer. Couldn't bear to look down.

What would I do if I had a gun? Shoot him? I wasn't sure. Maybe I should've taken my father's gun before I left home. And maybe that would only have caused more problems.

The officer stood up, his gaze still fixed on the shooter. He was near the edge as he stepped to the side, ready to head off.

Now or never. One giant leap. My heart racing, I took a few steps back to give myself a run-up and leapt across the space between the two buildings. Landed on the officer's back. Knocked the wind out of him. His gun skittered across the concrete. Pain shot through my elbow and shoulder. Adrenaline took over.

I glanced up at the shooter. He'd turned his head to see what was happening but his rifle was still pointing to the street. The officer tried to get up from beneath me. *No way.* I slid one arm under his neck, securing my hand on my own shoulder. A rear naked choke. He struggled but he had no chance, not given the lousy position he was in.

Glancing up again, I saw the shooter was facing the street again, getting ready to do his job and shoot Bartley.

I had to make sure the police officer was incapacitated so I grabbed some cable ties hanging off his belt, strapped his hands together, then took the bandana from his back pocket and used it as a blindfold.

So far, this was easy. Too easy. I hadn't even needed the knife strapped to my leg.

'Easy' didn't mean good. 'Easy' made me nervous.

I kept my gaze on the shooter. A pair of binoculars sat on the concrete beside him. He was focused. Didn't take his eyes off the street below. Didn't seem perturbed by my presence, which was weird enough in itself. He reached for a handkerchief and mopped his brow with it.

Something wasn't right. I couldn't put my finger on what. My pulse racing, nerves ricocheted through my body.

I didn't leave. Couldn't leave. I had to trust my gut. As

I stepped closer, I got a better picture. The guy was sweating like crazy, huge circles of perspiration under his arms. He was panting, his chest heaving.

This was all wrong. For a start, this wasn't a man and this wasn't the way a sniper would work.

The woman glanced back at me. "Leave!"

Shock rocketed through me. I'd seen that short sandy hair and that face before. The face of the woman soldier from the paper, the one who'd lost her daughter. Out for revenge or justice.

The woman mopped her brow again, let out something part way between a sigh and a moan. She wasn't going to shoot me. She would've done that already if she wanted to.

And I wasn't going anywhere. My chest constricted.

I knew a lot about her already. She was a lieutenant, a trained soldier and she'd shot a gun before. She was motivated enough to steal a large-caliber, single-shot rifle. A large round for maximum precision and accuracy. Perfect for the job. The goal was to use just one shot. She'd be successful too, I was sure of it.

If she went through with it.

Problem was, she was nervous as hell. Her hands were shaking, her shoulders scrunched up, the tendons in her neck taut. This wasn't the way snipers worked. No way could she get an accurate shot in this state.

Despair sank deep into my bones. Because she had to do this. She had to succeed.

The tremors in her hands intensified, her whole body shaking now. She lowered the rifle. Shuffled back on her butt, horror in her eyes.

"I can't do it," she mumbled. "Not even for my

Chrissy."

I put my hands on her shoulders. "Yes, you can."

A lie. I wasn't even a good liar.

"My poor Chrissy…" A sob escaped her lips.

My world stood still. *No, no, no.* She had to finish the job. She had to.

I couldn't do this. Couldn't take that next step. I was a skilled soldier and an excellent shot.

But not a killer. Not a sniper. Not what I had to be.

I had one chance. One chance and only a few seconds to make a decision. Shit, shit, shit.

Could I live with myself if I did this?

Could I live with myself if I didn't?

I gritted my teeth. Picked up the rifle. Got into position, my heart thumping in my chest. Deep breaths. I had to regulate my breathing. This was all about control and precision.

"Pick up the binoculars," I said to the woman, hoping she wasn't a lost cause. "I need you to be my spotter."

She shuffled next to me and looked out onto the street, the binoculars in her hands. A few moments passed.

A deep breath in. A deep breath out. My heart rate slowed.

"Coming into view," she said. "The first vehicle of the motorcade is turning the corner from Stanton Street."

Not a lost cause, after all. There was still a soldier inside her. Or maybe a grieving mother.

"He'll be wearing a bullet-proof vest," she said, her voice shaking. "Aim for the head."

The woman was back on board. She wanted this done.

I thought about Lauren who'd be thrown into prison forever if the authorities could get their hands on her. I thought about Charlotte, the girl who'd lived up the street. Until she'd been shot yesterday. I thought about this woman's daughter, Chrissie, her picture in the paper. I thought about all the other people who'd been shot yesterday.

And I remembered Bartley on the television, saying the military had done what needed to be done.

"The target is in full view," the woman said.

A target. That's what this was. And it was so much more.

This was Altabena. I couldn't let it become New Nation. Couldn't let Bartley assume absolute power. Couldn't let a future Bartley send someone back to eliminate me.

I had to finish this once and for all. Or *they* would.

Bartley was in the back of an open-topped car at the far end of the street. He raised his arm to the crowd. *Stay calm, Nicola.*

All noise from the street ceased. There was only the slow beats of my heart, my finger on the trigger, and my target. Nothing else existed.

I took aim. Waited. My breathing was nice and slow now. *My heart beat.* I squeezed the trigger. *Another beat.*

It happened in slow motion. I saw the bullet spinning as it left the rifle, actually spinning. The shot left a vapor trail through the air. I could see through space. Could see the distortion. I'd heard about this happening and now I was experiencing it.

And for a moment, just a moment, I was locked in the confinement box again, being tortured. A flashback.

Beside me, the woman put the binoculars down. "You got him. A clean shot."

I lowered the rifle.

But the distortion didn't stop. It intensified, the air shimmering. The line of the bullet caused two planes to split so the atmosphere was rubbing against another part of itself. The air was splitting in front of me, being pulled apart, ready to shatter. What the hell was going on?

I was under a lot of stress. I got that. This could cause hormones that sped up the brain's internal processing, hence the slow-motion thing. I got that too.

But this was something else.

It was a time warp, a temporal shift, the fabric of time changing. This was bigger than Bartley, bigger than me, bigger than anything I'd heard of.

Then a tremor from below. A small quake. I felt the building sway. Shouting and yelling from below.

My eyes were on the crowd, then on Bartley lying still on the trunk of the car. Dead. My gaze was riveted to him. Something was going to happen.

Something…

His body exploded. Blown up, just like that, into dust so fine there would be nothing left but mere molecules.

I'd seen an explosion like this before and knew exactly what it was. A molecular bomb – except they hadn't been invented yet. So what was going on?

Noise from below hit my ears again. Shouting, yelling, sounds of confusion and commotion.

No time to think. I had to get out of here. I grabbed the woman's shoulder, trying to pull her back.

She shook her head. So calm, much calmer than before. "I'm staying."

I got to my feet, far enough from the edge that no one below would be able to see me.

The woman looked up, her eyes sparkling with tears. "Let me take the glory."

"What glory?"

"Let me take the blame. Please. I wanted this so badly. For my Chrissie." She reached for the rifle, not to take aim, but to hold it, cradle it. "Let this be mine."

"Good luck, lieutenant," I said.

She could have the glory or infamy or whatever you wanted to call it because God knows I didn't want it. Still, she'd never have the one thing she wanted the most. Her daughter back.

The police and the military would be looking for a shooter. For someone who'd planted a bomb too, not that they'd ever work out there'd been a molecular bomb, because I was certain that's what it was.

I strode to the edge where I'd jumped across before. The officer was coming to, shifting on the ground. I looked across. If I jumped I could make it back down through the next building, the same way I'd got in. But police would be searching that side of the street.

I headed to the building behind this one. The rooftop was one story lower down, quite a drop. I clambered over the edge, hanging by my fingers until I let myself fall – a controlled drop that meant my feet were closer to the ground.

There was a large skylight in the roof. I looked around for something to smash the glass with but there was nothing. I'd have to use my body. Not so good. The rooftop also held lots of exposed ductwork and a door that probably led to a set of stairs. I pushed the door and couldn't believe my luck when it opened.

Scooting down the stairs, I made it to the ground floor

in record time and searched for a door that led outside. I closed the door behind me and joined the crowd on the street. Looking one way, I saw police with shields, probably called to action. I headed the other way, wearing the best disguise of all. I looked like a girl.

And I was. I was just a girl and I was so much more.

Would there still be a killer virus? Probably, though I couldn't know for sure. Would some other totalitarian regime take control now that Bartley was out of the way? I didn't know that either.

Had I done the right thing?

Maybe I'd never know.

CHAPTER THIRTY-SIX

If someone could go back in time to 1939 and assassinate Hitler before he invaded Poland, before he built concentration camps, before he killed six million Jews, not to mention the fifty million other people killed during World War II – not me but someone else – would that be a good thing for them to do?

Would that person be a hero or a murderer?

Could you be both?

I didn't have the answers. My main problem was that the big question was too close to the bone. I didn't know if what I'd done was right or wrong.

It was what I'd done, that was all.

I dropped back down onto the bed, my head in my hands. A shower should have left me feeling refreshed but it didn't feel that way. Last night had been free of nightmares and it wasn't often that happened. Unfortunately it had also been free of actual sleep or that was how it felt.

The nightmares were always the same and they were different. Sometimes I imagined the transportation room blowing up, soldiers blowing up with it, the explosion expanding, more people being killed, more screaming. Sometimes I was back on the roof of the Bryson Building, unable to see Bartley, shooting innocent citizens on the street. Sometimes I was even back in the schoolroom in New Nation where I'd killed two crazed gunmen and saved a roomful of children.

Different things would happen in each nightmare but the feelings of dread and terror were always the same. You couldn't kill and be untouched by it. Things like that didn't just go away. That wasn't possible. Unless you were a psychopath.

And the Bartley I'd killed hadn't even been a person. I'd discussed this at length with Reece and Ben, the only two people who could understand, and they agreed Bartley must've been a drone. For one thing, drones were designed to explode not long after they'd been eliminated.

Reece's theory was that the creature had been sent here to control the government so future Bartleys could secure power. Drones were made from newly dead bodies, so presumably that thing could have gone on to father a child, another Bartley to lead the country. Or maybe future Bartleys were drones too.

I stood up. At least I wasn't a psychopath. It was some consolation.

And I was getting better, even if it was taking months. I was good at acting as if everything was fine, and had pretty much everyone fooled. My great hope was that if I acted like normal, I might actually end up being that way.

A regular person in my position would pack a towel and swimsuit so that was what I did, then headed downstairs.

Mom – or should I say Super-Mom – was baking cookies in the kitchen. I gave her a hug because that was what I did every time I had the chance. Dad was away for work, flying back later this afternoon.

"You know I'm working tonight?" I asked.

I was waitressing at a restaurant in town, partly because it was nice to have money of my own and partly because it gave me something practical to do since I was taking a year off before college. I wasn't ready for college, not yet, not after what I'd been through.

Mom nodded. "I take it you're off to Ben's now?"

"Sure am."

"Say hi to Lauren for me and give her one of these." She threw her arms around me.

I laughed. "Any excuse for a hug."

"Absolutely. Have fun, honey."

Slinging my backpack over my shoulder, I walked to Ben's because it gave me a few extra minutes to get my head together. Yep, there was plenty of fresh air in Altabena.

Lauren was studying communications and journalism at Berkeley, but she was back for the weekend because she'd been invited for a youth congress on politics and freedom of speech. She was making a name for herself now more and more of her articles were being published and attracting attention. In a good way. The congress was here in Altabena because this was the location of the student massacre and Lauren was making a special address.

I walked down the side path of Ben's house to the rear where barbecue smells were wafting through the air. My boyfriend looked very manly flipping burgers at the grill, so manly I had to give him a kiss.

Lauren gave me a big hug, babbling about how happy she was to see me and how excited she was about the congress.

I gave Reece a fist bump because he wasn't into hugs. Ben served the burgers and we sat at the table under the patio.

After telling us how much she loved it at Berkeley, Lauren turned to me. "Have you thought about where you'll go to college?"

I didn't want to give too much away. "Not yet."

"You can't keep waitressing for the rest of your life," she added.

"I believe Nicola is interested in Stilton College." Ben gave me a pointed stare. "Aren't you, Nic?"

I smiled. Ben and Reece had both chosen to go to Stilton in the next town. Reece wouldn't admit it was so he could be near Connie who he considered to be his mom, whereas Ben was open about the fact. He wanted to be close to Celia and his dad and, after that, he planned to live in New York for a few years. With me, of course. He was confident he'd eventually end up at the institute outside San Francisco and planned on broadening his horizons in the meantime.

He'd completely dropped the idea of an internship with his idol, Dr. Max Alonzo because he'd seen more than enough of the man while we'd been in the future.

One thing was for sure, I didn't miss the arguments we'd had about Ben moving away for an internship after we'd finished high school.

"Okay, Ben," I said. "I'll put you out of your misery. Stilton is the only college I'm interested in."

Ben raised a fist in victory. "Yes!"

"So what course are you looking at?" Lauren asked.

I threw my hands up. "What is this? Twenty questions?"

Lauren hunched her shoulders. "Sorry, I was just asking."

"Truth is I'm not sure about which course," I said. "I'm allowed to *not* know exactly what I want to do."

Reece raised his glass. "I second the motion. Most people don't know what they want to do but they end up doing something. Like me. I'm studying...something."

Ben laughed. "And getting straight A's."

Reece gave him a pointed look. "You can talk!"

"You know what we don't ever talk about?" Lauren said. "Our dreams. No one talks about what they truly dream of doing."

Reece leaned back in his chair. "Easy for you to say. You've always dreamed about writing. And that's what you're doing."

"I've got a secret dream too," I said.

Lauren leaned forward. "Do tell."

"You know what I really want to do? Open up my own martial arts dojo and teach people how to be more aware, more confident, how to defend themselves."

Ben grinned. "Go, Nicola!"

"Especially girls," I added. "I'd love to make other girls feel powerful, make them believe in themselves."

Lauren raised her eyebrows. "So what are you waiting for?"

"Give me a break," I said. "I've only just come clean about this. I need a chance to get used to the idea."

The others laughed. I did too. I'd had enough action for one lifetime and now all I wanted to do was enjoy a normal life, spend time with my friends, and maybe relax by the pool.

After lunch, Lauren and Reece went in for a dip.

"We'll join you in a sec." I slung one leg over Ben to straddle him while he relaxed on a banana lounge.

He grinned. "Looks like you've captured me in one of those fancy martial arts moves."

"Sure have." I smiled. "There's something I didn't mention before when I was talking about the things I want."

"What's that?"

"I want to be with you, Ben."

He cupped my chin in his hands and drew me in for a long kiss. This was right. This was what I wanted.

Now and in a hundred years.

INFILTRATION (BOOK 1)

2120: A world ravaged by a devastating virus. Those healthy enough to live in New Nation lead a sanitized, orderly life where everything is tightly guarded by a brutal government. Lives, thoughts, information and emotions are all strictly controlled.

Now: Seventeen-year-old elite soldier Nicola Gray is sent back in time for an important assignment. She alone will stop the virus before it takes over the world – her mission, to gather intelligence, find the cause and stop the threat, whatever it takes.

She is trained to kill.

But the past is not what Nicola is expecting. Overwhelmed by an alien world, she discovers feelings she can't handle and a world with immense personal freedom and people who care for each other. She wants to stay. She wants to live. She wants a lot of things she can't have...

REGENERATION (BOOK 2)

Nicola Gray is a typical, slightly awkward high school student. Or so she appears. In reality Nicola is a hyper-fit, elite soldier from the brutal New Nation of the future. Her superior officers have given soldier Gray strict orders to eliminate their greatest threat, Ben Tanner. Her boyfriend.

And New Nation will not give up.

Nicola fights as only she knows how to keep Ben and those around her safe. Pushed beyond limits, she grapples with questions of love and loyalty, right and wrong, life and death. Nicola has a line she will not cross. But that's exactly what she must do...

PARALLAX ERROR

Coming early 2018
Excerpt follows

One girl. Two lives. No way back...

Sasha Pierce is the school nerd – bullied, abused and alone.
Alienation takes on a whole new dimension when a global
glitch catapults her into an alternate universe. And into the
body of an elite military bodyguard.

Suddenly she's a ripped, ultra-honed, teenage fighting
machine. Except that inside she is still the same Sasha,
flung into a body and a world she can barely comprehend.
All she wants is to go home and she is ready to risk life
and limb to return. There will be no second chances. This
will be the biggest fight of her life.

PARALLAX ERROR – EXERPT

The Primary

Nothing stops.

It hasn't stopped now.

I open my eyes but everything stays blurry. My head sways on my shoulders and a face in front of me comes into focus slowly, the face of a boy I've never seen before. He's shaking me awake.

I should get up. I should do something but I can't. I'm listless. No energy. As if the blood has been drained from my body. Maybe it has.

And I remember everything. It all comes back to me, so shocking it takes my breath away but it's definitely my breath and my body and that's what matters. I'm in one piece and so grateful I can't believe it.

The guy leaves his hands on my shoulders and now that he's stopped rocking me there's something soothing about his presence. It must be the warmth in his pale eyes because it's certainly not his cropped sandy hair.

"Are you okay?" he asks.

"Much better now you've stopped shaking me," I say.

I sit slumped against a wall, my knees up in front of me, the ground hard below. No, it's not the ground. These are ceramic tiles and I'm indoors. The smell of lavender rises from the floor as if it has been recently cleaned.

Looking around, I see a desk, a bookshelf, a wall covered in plaques. Must be an office. I've been in the principal's office often enough recently and this room has the same air of importance.

Suddenly, it hits me that I'm still here. Except I'm not

here. I'm somewhere else and that's okay. I can do this. I can work it out. A wave of renewed energy surges through me.

The guy stays crouched in front of me as I peel his hands from my shoulders. Sure, he's good looking but he's also acting a bit too familiar for my liking.

"Where am I?" I ask.

"Mason's office," he says, as if that answers my question. "What are you doing in here?"

In here? As opposed to where? I've definitely never seen this guy before. I wouldn't forget a face like that in a hurry.

"Who are you?" I ask.

"It's me, Remy." He stares, puzzled. "Remy Christensen."

"Nice to meet you, Remy."

"Is that a joke?"

His stare is intense and concerned. He takes my hands into his, getting a lot more cozy with me than he should. It sends a shiver up my spine.

"I'm not laughing," I say.

"Sasha, that's not funny."

I jerk my hands away. Nerves settle in the pit of my stomach. "How do you know my name?"

"Don't be ridiculous. Of course I know your name."

My mouth drops open and I hold his gaze. Weird is being taken to a different level. The downy hairs on the back of my neck stand on end. Something is wrong, more wrong than usual.

Suddenly blood rushes through my body. Where I was listless before, now I feel ready though I'm not sure exactly what for.

I lift my hand to brush my hair back from my face, only to find it's already been pulled back into a ponytail. I look down at my arms resting on my knees and wonder why I'm wearing boots, khaki pants and a black tee shirt. These aren't my clothes.

I pinch the skin on my wrist. It hurts as I give it a little twist. I'm here. I can feel it.

Letting out a long sigh, I lean my head against the wall behind me and fold my arms. They feel strong and muscular, my bicep flexing beneath one hand. Looking down, I notice my breasts seem bigger and wonder how that could've happened. Must be some bra I'm wearing.

"Come on, Rodriguez," Remy says. "You've got to snap out of it."

"Who's Rodriguez?" I ask.

"You. You're Sasha Rodriguez."

Relief washes over me. He has me mixed up with someone else. We'll be able to sort this out and maybe then I can get out of here.

"You've made a mistake," I say. "My name is Sasha Pierce."

He looks bewildered. "No, it's not."

"I think I know my own name."

"Sasha, please tell me you're mucking around."

I hold his gaze. I'm getting good at that. Then I decide a staring competition might not be such a good idea.

My eyes flit around the room. "Do you want to tell me where we are?"

"I told you. Mason's office. You've been here loads of times."

I grit my teeth, hope my nerves don't show because this is getting harder to handle by the minute. "Let's start again and maybe you can tell me what's going on."

Remy jumps to his feet and stands back, one hand covering his chin before he lets it drop. "This can't be happening. This is bad."

I don't want to ask more questions. I just want this all to go away. I press my eyes shut, cover my ears and sit back on my haunches, curling myself into a ball. I must be dreaming, having a nightmare or some weird waking vision. This will go away. It has to.

I open my eyes. Remy is still there. The room is still there. I struggle to my feet and face him. Though I know it can't be the case, I feel stronger than ever before. Taller too.

"Slap me," I say.

He steps closer. "Are you sure?"

"Slap me and it'll shake me out of this. Just do it."

His hand lands. My cheek burns. Though he has done exactly as I asked, it still shocks me.

"Ow!" I cover my cheek.

His eyes glimmer with concern. "Sorry, Sasha, you know I'd never hurt you on purpose."

He seems genuine but I don't know this guy. I don't even know where I am. And I have to do something.

I walk to the other side of the desk on shaking legs and lean over, looking for clues. A computer and a document tray with some papers sit on the immaculate desktop along with a black diary, the current year embossed in gold on the front. I open it at the page marked with a burgundy ribbon, check the date and find it's correct.

I take a deep breath. "Let's try again. Where are we in geographical terms? This is California, isn't it?"

"Yes, it's Planalto," he says.

"Never heard of it. Is it near LA?"

His brow furrows. "No, LA's not there any more. This is Northern California. It's too hot in the south anyway."

That doesn't make sense. I stop my eyes from widening because I don't want to give too much away.

He ambles around the desk closer to me. "Sasha, I'm getting worried. Are you feeling all right?"

I step away from him and look at the plaques on the wall. I'm half-expecting school certificates and awards of academic achievement, only to find they appear to be military plaques.

One award catches my eye. Not the award exactly but the mirrored surface on which the writing is etched.

I look into the mirror.

And someone else stares back.

Panic rips through me. My heart is in my throat. No, I'm not going to have an anxiety attack. That's not going to help.

Deep breaths. In through my mouth. Out through my nose.

"You don't look so good," Remy says from behind me. "Are you okay?"

I don't answer.

Staring into the mirrored surface, I lift my fingers to my face and a hand appears in the mirror covering the strange girl's cheeks. I open my mouth. She opens hers. I lift my eyebrows. She lifts hers.

She's very exotic looking, I'll give her that. Her black hair is pulled back into a ponytail revealing striking blue eyes, olive skin, high cheekbones and a full mouth. There's an air of confidence about her and that's what gets to me. Confidence, the one thing I wish I had.

Stunned, I keep staring as if this is a science experiment and the answers will miraculously come to me. I lift the plaque and check the other side before replacing the item on the wall.

"Come closer, Remy," I say. "Put your face next to mine. Now poke your tongue out."

As he does this, I start pulling faces, then shifting out of the way of the glass surface. Each time, the girl in the reflection follows my every movement. As if that's me in the mirror.

"What are you doing?" he asks.

Fear slices through me like a knife, so deep it takes my breath away. I don't know what I'm doing, where I am or how this can possibly be happening. Except I have a horrible feeling I do know what's going on.

I'm in someone else's body.

ABOUT THE AUTHOR

Susanna Rogers is the author of kick butt books for young adults. She also writes romance and at one point moved to a life of crime – you might be seeing more of that. She loves writing young adult, partly because she's an overgrown teenager and partly because she can write the kick butt heroines she adores. She's also a kickboxer and dreams of empowering girls and guys around the globe to believe in themselves, to take care and follow their own dreams.

Susanna believes in love and kicking ass and a little bit of murder here and there.

She would love to hear from you – susannarogers.com.

If you like her books, please post a review on Amazon or Goodreads. She'd like that a lot!